DEL RYDER AND THE
RESCUE OF ELEANOR

Matthew David Brough

DEL RYDER AND THE RESCUE OF ELEANOR

Matthew David Brough

Background image from www.Shutterstock.com
Cover design by Roseanna White Designs, www.RoseannaWhiteDesigns.com

Edited by Elizabeth Buege, www.elizabethbuege.com

To the best storyteller I know:
My Dad

(And to Ruth and Joanne)

Blythe Thicket's Riddle that he gave to Del Ryder and Crimson

Old Blythe signed next to this one's name;
Trust her completely, despite her fame.
Over the sea where the new birth falls,
Choose the tunnel or scale the walls.
When you arrive at the desert's edge
And stand looking out from the highest ledge,
The sun will touch the place you must go,
And there will you see the ominous glow.
You'll find what you need by looking below.

CHAPTER ONE

Looking For Answers

Del's phone went off. Groggy, she turned over in her bed. A few seconds passed. The phone chimed again, and a third time. She checked the time—8:42. Who would get up that early on a Sunday morning?

The phone beeped again, and Del, awake enough now, recognized the tone as Sam texting her. She grabbed the device and looked at the screen through bleary eyes.

"wake up / we're going to church / together / today"

Del texted her reply. "?"

Sam replied. "My mom said if you were willing to go to church it was okay if I skipped ours and took you to the Lutheran one instead."

Del replied. "so?"

Sam's last message came through. "Clearly you're not awake yet. I'm coming over."

Del groaned, knowing that she would now have to get out of bed. She looked around for some clothes off her messy floor to throw on. Anything would do for Sam, she supposed.

She left her room and crept past her sister, Suzanne's,

bedroom and along to her mom's room. Her mother lay asleep in her bed, still with her makeup caked on and still wearing date clothes from the night before.

A lump formed in Del's throat. She felt as if she hadn't seen her mom in months, which for Del was true. She and her best friends had traveled to another world, a world called Azdia, and it had taken them forever to find their way home. When they finally did return, hardly any time on earth had passed at all. That was just yesterday.

While in Azdia, Del had longed to see her mom, to be held by her and loved by her. Sam's mom loved him, and it wasn't the sappy, embarrassing love that she sometimes saw kids have to go through—it was the good kind, the honest kind. Why didn't Del's mom love her like that? Del would have even taken the sappy, embarrassing kind.

Del wished her home was the way Blythe Thicket's home was back in Azdia, but she knew that could never be. Blythe Thicket's cottage was a place of magic and beauty, and her house would never be such things.

Del knelt by her mother's bed.

"I'm going to church with Sam, okay, Mom?" Del whispered.

Del knew her mom couldn't hear her, nor would she care where she went, but Del liked to sometimes pretend that her mom was different than she was. She wished she could tell her mom everything about what she had been through in Azdia, but she knew that even if her mom, by some miracle, believed her, she would never really understand. Sam was the only one she could really trust—he was her best friend.

Del scurried down the stairs and quickly wrote a note

to her mother. "Gone to the churchyard with Sam. Be home later."

Del thought this note was a little more believable than "gone to church with Sam." Why on earth would she go to church? But the churchyard—they went there all the time.

*****

Del waited for Sam on the front steps, her sweater wrapped around her.

When he arrived, Del said, "What's this all about?"

"We shouldn't wait until tomorrow," said Sam.

"You think we should go back to Azdia today?" Del asked.

"No, but there are things to do before we go back. The riddle you told me."

Del had learned a riddle in Blythe Thicket's cottage that was supposed to help them find a Crystal Seed once they were back in Azdia.

"What about it?" Del asked.

"I'm thinking we should ask the priest or his wife about it. The priest gave us the first riddle, after all. What if we just went to their church today, waited until everything was over, then cornered one of them and asked to talk to them?"

"Can you just show up at a church?"

"Of course. They won't mind, either. Kids coming to church! People there will be thrilled."

"You'd be the expert in that department."

"Not an expert. I just go to one, that's all—and not to an old one like this."

"Whatever—my mom says they're all the same."

"Basically, they are, I guess. Still—that's not why we're going today. Today we're going to get some real answers."

Sam looked Del up and down. "That's not what you're going to wear, is it?"

"Seriously, Sam! I'll wear whatever I want. If church people are going to be all judge-y and everything, too bad."

"Del, you still have your pajama pants on."

Del looked down. Sam was right. She had only put on a big sweater and completely forgotten anything else. Embarrassed, she ran back into the house and upstairs to her room.

She returned wearing black leggings.

"Better?" Del asked.

"Much," said Sam.

*****

Sam and Del arrived at the church and noticed a few people going in through the main doors. Del glanced over at the hedge. A big part of her just wanted to run over there, activate the Crystal Seed, and leap into Azdia. Mostly, she wanted to see Blythe Thicket and Crimson. It had been less than twenty-four hours, and she missed them already. She really wanted to go back.

A sign in front of the church indicated that they had two service times, one at nine-thirty and another at eleven o'clock. Clearly, they were there for the nine-thirty. They walked together up to the front door and went in.

A friendly older lady welcomed them. "Good morning," she said, extending her hand.

Sam shook the lady's hand. "Good morning," he said.

Del walked a little behind Sam, trying to hide behind his smaller frame. She whispered to him, "Do you know her?"

"No. That's just what you do in church," Sam whispered back. "Let's go find a seat."

Sam led the way. There were a lot of old people, many of whom looked at Del and Sam and smiled. Del didn't see any other kids—it was a little eerie.

Maybe all the kids come at eleven o'clock, she thought.

Another older lady slid into the seat next to Del. Del tried not to look at her likely smiling face or to have to say "Good morning" to another old stranger. The woman put her hand on Del's knee. What was this? Was this some other church thing? No—this was weird.

"Nice to see you here, Delaney. And you too, Samuel." It was the priest's wife, Mrs. Manters.

Del relaxed and instinctively hugged her. Then she pulled back. "I'm sorry," Del said.

"No need to apologize," said Mrs. Manters. "You can hug me anytime. It's too bad you're here for the nine-thirty. Eleven is much more contemporary. You would probably like that more. Anyhow, I'm thinking you're not here for the service or my husband's preaching. How about after the opening songs and prayers, the three of us slip out, and we can talk?"

That sounded great to Del. She nodded.

The service began. Prior to ever being there, Del had been told church was boring, so she was ready to slip into tune-out mode. To her surprise, the opening of the service was loud. An organ blasted big sounds unlike anything Del had heard before. Did they do this every week? She looked around, and people seemed unfazed by it. Many of them seemed, in fact, bored. Many of the smiling faces from before the service had become expressionless. This was all very strange to Del.

Rev. Manters walked in wearing flowing black robes. He looked like he was about to teach a class at Hogwarts. He said, "The Lord be with you," and everyone replied, "And also with you." Del thought that was kind of nice. If there was a God, she figured it was pretty nice to be told by Reverend Manters that he was with you, and it was nice of the people to say it back to him. The proceedings continued in this nice way. The organ blasted again, and everyone stood up and sang along. There were books full of music for everyone. It was like being in choir at school. Del listened to the old voices around her. They weren't very good, but the singing was mostly drowned out by the organ. Del liked that.

After the song, Mrs. Manters tapped Del. "Come with me," she said.

Del and Sam slipped out of their seats and followed Mrs. Manters to the back of the church and along the main hall, past the pictures of the old ministers that had served the church.

"This way, children," Mrs. Manters said as she opened the door to a bathroom.

Sam gave Del a puzzled look. Del shrugged—she had no idea why Mrs. Manters was leading them into a bathroom. All the same, they followed her in.

It was a large, wheelchair-accessible bathroom. Next to the sink was a large floor-to-ceiling mirror. Mrs. Manters reached her hand around the back of the mirror. Del heard a click, and the mirror slid along the wall, revealing an old wooden door with an ornate doorknob and keyhole. Mrs. Manters pulled a brass key out of her purse and unlocked the door.

"When this bathroom was built, this was the only way to preserve the way into the cellar of the old church," said Mrs. Manters. "Most church members have no reason to come down here anymore—it's just some dusty old books and records."

Sam and Del had both been in the church basement before, and they remembered it being bright and fun, designed for children at play. They passed through the doorway and began descending the stairs. Del realized that there must be a new basement and an old basement. Mrs. Manters slid the mirror back into place and closed the door carefully behind them. She pulled a flashlight from her pocket to light their way.

*****

The cellar was dark and dingy. There were cobwebs and dust everywhere. At the bottom of the stairs, Mrs. Manters pulled a chain attached to a bare lightbulb, giving them some dim light to partially fill the room. The cellar had a dirt floor, and the walls were made of what looked like very old stone. There wasn't enough light to shine into the corners of the room, and there was one wall that they couldn't see at all. The room just faded into black.

Several small wooden crates were stacked up against the nearest wall. Mrs. Manters picked one up, placed it on the ground, and sat on it. Sam and Del did the same.

"We never did ask you yesterday," Mrs. Manters began. "I didn't want to ask anything because I could tell something was not quite right between you two and your other friends. We thought perhaps we were mistaken to send all of you the way Phillip was talking when he first returned. Something was off in the way he spoke of Mr. Thicket."

Del and Sam looked at her blankly, unsure of what to say.

"Did you really meet Mr. Thicket?" Mrs. Manters asked.

"Del did," said Sam. "No one else. The one we thought was Mr. Thicket was an imposter."

"I see," said Mrs. Manters. "Things have perhaps gotten worse in Azdia than any of us had expected."

"The darkness has returned," Del said. "The imposter was the Heir of Mordlum. He lied to us and told us that he was Mr. Thicket. We all believed him at first, but then I met the real Mr. Thicket. Phil and Guy still believe in the wrong one."

Mrs. Manters' face went pale. "Are you sure you met the Heir of Mordlum?"

"Yes," said Sam.

"What did he look like?"

"He had long blond hair and blue eyes," Del explained. "He was thin but strong looking."

"That's him," she said. "I can't believe it, but it's him."

Mrs. Manters quickly opened her purse, and Del saw a glint of green coming from inside.

"We've been too complacent," said Mrs. Manters. "We have to go together—now."

She pulled the Crystal Seed out of her purse. The glow within it swirled green.

Del was taken aback. She looked at Sam, and he

wore a look of shock as well. Just like that, they were going back to Azdia—this time with the priest's wife.

"Every second we delay means hours wasted in training that you will need," Mrs. Manters said.

"Training?" asked Del.

"You must learn to use the Crystal Seeds," she replied. "And there is too much more to explain about Azdia than we have time for. We must go through now."

"But why right now?" asked Del.

"Because darkness, when driven by the Heir, will grow faster than anything in Azdia."

"Then why did you send us on our own before?" Sam asked.

"Because we didn't think there was this kind of danger," said Mrs. Manters. "We thought he was dead."

"So why go back at all?" asked Sam. "Let's just stay here and be safe."

"Because an entire world depends on us," said Mrs. Manters. "I can't explain everything now. That is why we need to go. I can explain much more when we're there. Surely you understand that everything is slower in Azdia. If we go now, we will have several days to talk, and we can be back before the service upstairs is over."

"Do you have a way to get back home?" asked Del.

"Mr. Manters and I know a place of safety in Azdia where there is a Crystal Seed nearby that can bring us home," Mrs. Manters explained. "Now, trust me. We must go. There is so little time."

Del looked at Sam. He nodded. Mrs. Manters placed the Crystal Seed on the floor in front of them.

Del looked at the seed. The swirling green light within it seemed to match her own thoughts. So much had happened to them in Azdia that she wanted to know about. Was she really the chief of the Malak? Was she supposed to bring light back to Azdia, and how? And what about Eleanor and Mordlum? Who were they? Was the Heir of Mordlum their son? She thought as well about the riddle that Blythe Thicket had given her. They were going to need Mrs. Manters' help, or *someone's* help, in solving it.

The swirling inside the seed began to move more rapidly, and the green got darker and darker, bordering on black.

"What is the seed doing?" asked Del.

Mrs. Manters looked down. "I don't know," she said. "I've never seen it do that before."

Suddenly, a beam of dark green light shot from the seed and created an oval in midair. They had all seen the seed produce an oval of light, but this couldn't really be described as light. It was more like an oval of darkness.

Before Mrs. Manters or the children could respond, two plumes of black smoke came out of the oval and wrapped themselves around Mrs. Manters like two powerful arms.

A terrifying voice came from the oval. "Where is the other seed? You know where it is. Tell me."

The smoke coming from the Crystal Seed seemed to have Mrs. Manters immobilized. She struggled to get free as the voice repeated, "Tell me where the other seed is. Tell me!"

Sam backed away from the sight before him, but as he did, his crate flipped over and he stumbled to the ground. The noise of the crate and Sam's fall echoed throughout the cellar.

"No!" Mrs. Manters cried.

A third plume of smoke shot from the dark oval and toward Sam. Del leapt off her crate to help Sam to his feet, but it was too late. The smoke wrapped around one of his legs.

"Run, Del!" yelled Mrs. Manters. "Run upstairs. Get my husband!"

CHAPTER TWO

The Company of Light

No more than fifty lumens gathered at the Old Oak —a much smaller group than Kita had expected. In times past, the Festival of Light had drawn thousands of lumens from all across Azdia for several days of great celebration. This was not a festival atmosphere at all. Kita looked around at the grim faces and wondered if there was any hope for Azdia now that the darkness had returned.

Kita had traveled all the way from the thirteenth province, far away in the north. She was the only lumen from her distant town. She was young, yet to learn her abilities, but she considered herself brave. She settled in beside a leafy tree as Panak, the elder statesman of the gathering, climbed the ancient stairs.

Never having been to the festival before, Kita imagined what it must have been like to hear Eleanor speak from that very platform under the shade of the Old Oak. Closing her eyes, she pictured the great leader of the Malak speaking of how light would overcome the darkness. She thought of the forging of the Company of Light and the firm establishment of Azdia's highest value—forgiveness. It was under this very tree that a few brave souls, against the will of the majority, had decided to have mercy on their enemy, Mordlum. It was also under this tree that their leader and their reformed enemy were married. Eleanor must have been so inspirational. They needed that kind of inspiration again.

She looked at Panak, a wise old lumen, hunched over and barely able to climb the stairs. She wondered whether he could inspire the way Eleanor had. After the first sentence of his speech, Kita had her answer. He couldn't.

"We all need to remind our towns and provinces to wait out this temporary darkness," Panak croaked. "It will blow over—we simply must be patient."

"What about the rumors concerning the Heir of Mordlum?" A green-glowing lumen spoke out.

"They are rumors," Panak replied, "and nothing more. Azdia naturally undergoes cycles of light and dark. The dark times are difficult, but the light will come again eventually."

"But the legends of old tell us differently!" the green one protested. "The Malak will come again to rescue us from the darkness the same way Eleanor saved us back then."

"We all know that the legends are simply stories passed on by our ancestors to teach us lessons," Panak said. "The legend of Eleanor is there only to teach us to be forgiving even in the darkest times. It is an important fable, and it illustrates our highest value—but we all know it never actually happened."

Kita couldn't believe what she was hearing. She had thought she was coming to a gathering of the faithful.

Instead, their leader didn't even believe in the legend of Eleanor! She looked around when Panak spoke, and it seemed that most of the lumens were nodding their heads in agreement. Kita was shocked.

The green-glowing lumen persisted, however. "Surely some of you have heard that there have already been Malak present in Azdia again—even in this very forest! Surely some of you have heard of the lumen known as Crimson, who traveled with them and fought against the Heir of Mordlum with the help of Mr. Thicket. Surely some of you believe in the old legends and will stand against the darkness that has come upon our land once again!"

"I think we've heard enough," said Panak, waving his hand dismissively. "This gathering is not about bedtime stories for young lumens. We are not going to indulge in false hope. Our task is to ensure that the lumens of our towns do not worry and stay put in their homes. It is a hard time, but the light will eventually come back."

"That's ludicrous!" the green one yelled. "There is not a single lumen here from the eighteenth province. Do you know why? Because almost all of them went dark. How can you all stand here and not see it?"

"It's just the natural way of things," Panak said coolly.

"No it's not," said a new voice.

Three new lumens emerged from the trees. The one who spoke was thin, and she glowed blue. One looked a little rough around the edges, and he glowed with a kind of gray color. The third lumen glowed with a deep red.

"I'm from eighteen," the blue one continued. "It is now completely dark. Some lumens got out, but most now serve the Heir of Mordlum. My sister is among them." Her voice cracked as she mentioned her sister.

"This is all lies," Panak said. "Things will never get that bad in Azdia. They are just trying to scare you into battling against their enemies. These lumens are deluded!"

"Don't listen to a word this lumen says," said the red-glowing lumen. "The Heir of Mordlum is real, and he is bent on gaining more and more power, stealing light from every lumen he can get his hands on. We cannot sit back and let him change our land. But there is hope. The Malak have returned. I first met them here in this very forest. Ask the trees; they will tell you. Ask the Old Oak—she knows."

The green-glowing lumen spoke up again. "Everyone, may I introduce Crimson?" Then, turning toward the group of three newcomers, he said, "It is you, right?"

Crimson nodded.

Panak sneered. "I have spoken to the Old Oak, and she knows nothing of the return of any Malak."

"That's because you're asking the wrong question," said Crimson. "The Old Oak doesn't know the Malak by that name. To her, they were just children, but to us, they are the hope of Azdia."

"You hear that?" said Panak. "The mighty Crimson believes that Azdia will be rescued from the darkness by children! That's priceless! Now let's put an end to this nonesense."

Panak straightened up and raised his voice. "Those who wish to go on some foolish quest may go with this band of three lumens. But those who wish to actually help our towns and provinces, who wish to address our common concerns of survival while we wait for the light to return, can stay and listen to me."

No one moved.

Crimson made his way to the front and stood below the dais on which Panak stood to make a final plea to the crowd. "The Malak have returned, and the chief among them is named Del Ryder. She will be coming to Azdia again, and we must find her. She will need our help to restore the light. Fortunately, I have an idea where she will be appearing again. Her destination is across the sea in Old Azdia. We will make for the coast, find a worthy vessel, and cross the Great Sea to find her. She will lead us to victory over the Heir of Mordlum. I will take anyone who wishes to come with me. Who will come?"

The crowd remained silent, each of them looking down. Kita felt a stir within her. She could tell that her glow was increasing. She looked at her arms and hands. They shook and glowed pink—something that happened when she got nervous. Her heart told her that everything Crimson had said was true, but she was afraid to stand out from the crowd.

The green-glowing lumen stepped forward and spoke up. "I am with you, Crimson."

"Who else?" Crimson shouted.

Silence again. Kita knew that if she did not step forward, she would always regret it.

"I wish to come with you," she said.

"Good, you are welcome," said Crimson.

He stood for a good long time after Kita volunteered, but no one else came forward. Kita couldn't believe that no other lumens there were stirred by Crimson's speech.

Together, the five lumens walked away from the Old Oak. Kita had thought that the Festival of Light would be exactly for this purpose—she just never imagined that there would only be five lumens committed to working against the darkness.

*****

Crimson led them away from the Old Oak to a smaller clearing where they could talk.

"Proper introductions are in order," Crimson said. "You obviously know who I am, but I don't know who you are."

"My name is Yah-yah," the green one said. "But I must tell you now that I have a brother who is going dark in province fourteen. I want to help, but I can't go across the sea when my brother needs me. I had hoped to find help here, but now all I have is the hope that the Malak will return in time to save him."

"We understand," said Crimson. "Although what would likely help your brother most is if you came with us."

"I just can't," said Yah-yah. "I need to be with him. I already took a big risk coming here. I'm sorry."

"We do understand," said Crimson. "What town are you in should we ever need to find an ally in fourteen?"

"We're in town three—it's small, and we've removed all of our addresses from our homes for safety. You'll find us at the house with the green door."

Crimson turned to Kita. "And what about you?"

"My name is Kita, and I will go with you to the other side of Azdia and back—anything you need."

"Well then, I guess you've settled any loyalty questions," said Crimson. "I'm sorry to ask this, but you seem young. Have you learned your abilities yet?"

Kita felt a pressure building in her chest and doubts

rising in her mind. "You can't stop me from coming with you—I'll just follow you!" she blurted.

"I'm not going to stop you; we just need to know," Crimson replied calmly. "I take it you haven't learned them, then."

Kita shook her head.

"Where are you from?" Crimson asked.

"The thirteenth province, fifth town," Kita said.

"That is a long way," Crimson declared. "Anyone who can travel from 1305 to the Old Oak without the use of their abilities must be tenacious."

Kita wasn't quite sure what Crimson meant by this, but she liked the sound of it.

"Now, let me introduce the other members of our group," Crimson continued. "This is Verdi. He's a little gruff, but you'll get used to him. And this is Cinder. She can get a little intense sometimes, but you'll get used to her too. And… show her, Verdi."

Verdi opened his satchel. Inside was small creature with soft purple fur, though Kita knew right away that the fur wasn't always that color. Verdi was carrying a winx.

"This is Tabby," Crimson said. "She rounds out our group.

"Yah-yah, I wish you would come with us—we could use the extra hands, but we understand. Before we part ways, however, I must say that the two of you encouraged me today. We haven't met many lumens in our travels who have dared to believe that the Malak are returning. Many aren't even sure about Mr. Thicket anymore. But we will change all that. We will find Del Ryder and show Azdia that darkness can never win!"

"But there are so few of us," Kita said.

"May I remind you that the Company of Light was very small in a time of darkness and confusion. We are in such a time again, and a new company is needed. For now, we are it, but we will add to our number. Yah-yah, do you commit to our company, though you cannot go with us?"

"I do, and I will do all I can to bring lumens to our cause," said Yah-yah. "I will wait for you and for the return of the Malak."

"Then it is settled!" said Crimson. "Today, we remake the old bonds. I declare that the Company of Light is reborn in us."

CHAPTER THREE

The Smoke and The Priest

Del scrambled up the stairs as smoke shot past her and around her. None managed to touch her, however. She flew through the bathroom and down the hall. She opened the door to the sanctuary and yelled, "Help!"

The entire congregation turned, looks of shock on their faces. Reverend Manters was calm, however. He smiled slightly.

"Don't worry, everyone," he said. "I know what this is about, and I'm sorry, but I will need to go attend to it. Mr. Jacobson will continue with the rest of the service."

A man stood up and walked to the front. Reverend Manters whispered to him, and with the congregation watching, he marched to the back of the church to meet Del.

"Let's sing together the next hymn, 'O God Our Help in Ages Past,'" Mr. Jacobson announced. The people seemed to relax and settle in with their new leader.

Reverend Manters reached Del and quietly escorted her through the sanctuary doors.

"Your wife," Del whispered.

"Where?" he cut her off.

"This way," she said, starting to run along the hallway toward the bathroom.

Once inside, Reverend Manters opened the door behind the mirror and flew part-way down the stairs with Del following. From under his robes he pulled a scepter, held it high over his head, and shouted, "Delaney, stay behind me."

Del stopped on the staircase and watched. The cellar was filled with smoke shooting in all directions. The voice from the dark oval continued to ask Mrs. Manters about "the other seed." She did not respond. Sam lay on the ground close to the foot of the stairs, exactly where Del had left him. Maybe Reverend Manters could still save them.

With the sceptre in hand, the priest straightened his back to his full height and shouted, "Be gone!"

The smoke stopped for a moment before slowly beginning to move about the cellar again. The priest swung the scepter at a nearby plume of smoke that was wafting towards Del at the top of the staircase. He struck it and shouted again, "Be gone!"

The smoke that he had hit retreated into the oval. The smoke holding Mrs. Manters and Sam, however, did not let them go. It began dragging them toward the oval.

"Stop," the priest yelled.

The smoke did not obey. If anything, everything began to move faster. Reverend Manters jumped down the remaining stairs and swung at the smoke that had Sam. A direct hit. The smoke dissipated, recoiling quickly into the dark oval that hovered above the Crystal Seed.

Sam got to his feet and scrambled up the staircase to Del.

"You okay?" Del asked.

Sam nodded, though it looked as if he were about to burst into tears. He turned with Del to see what would happen next.

The priest was now singular in his focus to rescue his wife. He ran through the smoke, which now swirled all around him. He flailed at it with the scepter, driving as much of it as he could back from where it had come.

Mrs. Manters called out, "Del, you still must come to Azdia. The fate of every lumen depends on you!"

The priest was getting close to his wife. He swung the scepter and struck the smoke that was holding her. It released one of her arms and recoiled into the oval. Smoke still held her other arm, and she was getting close to the oval. With her free hand, she reached out for her husband but their hands missed each other just as the smoke pulled her into the oval, where she vanished.

"No!" Reverend Manters cried.

He instinctively tried to reach for his wife and plunged his arm into the oval. "What have I done?" he said. The oval pulled him in quickly, and all the remaining smoke began flying into the oval.

The priest's voice, panicked, rang out from the darkness: "If I am not back tomorrow, you must find her. Eleanor must remain safe…"

The smoke disappeared, the dark oval closed, and the Crystal Seed remained still on the floor. All had gone quiet. Del and Sam descended the staircase and walked over to the seed. It had returned to its normal state with the lighter color of green swirling within it.

"She's Eleanor," said Del. "I mean—I thought it was possible that she was Eleanor, but—"

"It's crazy," said Sam. "That means all that stuff that happened in Azdia that they said happened long ago must of happened when she was young!"

"She was the one who did is all," Del continued. "She planted the Old Oak. She rescued Azdia from the ancient darkness."

"And she was the one who forgave—" Sam started.

"Mordlum," Del finished his thought. "Sam! The priest—he's Mordlum. And that means the Heir of Mordlum must be…"

"Their son?" said Sam with his usual hint of uncertainty. "What do we do now?"

Sam looked completely defeated.

Del didn't feel defeated, though. She was immediately taken back to Blythe Thicket's cottage, when he had told her that she was the chief of the Malak. At the time, she had not quite believed it. He had told her to look deeper, and at the time, she hadn't been able to see what Blythe Thicket could see in her.

But in the cellar of the old church, among the crates, dust, and cobwebs, Del felt different. Seeing the darkness creep from Azdia into her own world made her look into that place within herself that only Blythe Thicket had been able to look. For the first time, Del Ryder knew who she was.

Del bent down and picked the seed up from the cellar floor. She looked at Sam and said with determination, "You want to know what we do now? If the priest isn't here when we come back tomorrow, we go back and we rescue Eleanor. Then, we rescue all of Azdia. That's what we do."

*****

Del, though determined, was also very thankful for her best friend, who kept his practical nature intact despite his obvious fear.

"Del," said Sam, "what about the riddle?"

"And the book," said Del, picking up the Crystal Seed and pushing it into her pocket.

"What book?" asked Sam.

"Mr. Thicket told me to come to the church and look in a book that deals with birth, death, and marriage," said Del.

"You never told me that!" said Sam.

"Sorry, I kind of forgot until just now," said Del.

"Kind of an important thing to forget," said Sam.

"Sorry," said Del again. "Without the priest and his wife, we're not going to be able to find what we need anyway."

"Except Mrs. Manters did say that the only thing in this cellar was dusty old books," said Sam. "Maybe the book we need is down here somewhere?"

There were several shelves of boxes under the stairs. Del and Sam started pulling them down to examine the contents. Most of the boxes contained papers and books —old files and records.

They could still hear the service continuing without Reverend Manters upstairs. The congregation was singing again.

They really like to sing, Del thought.

"I think I might have found something," said Sam.

He had opened a box that was full of large black books. He pulled one out. On the front, it said,

"Register of baptisms, burials, and marriages."

"This is about birth, death, and marriage," said Sam.

"That might be the book," said Del.

"Except there's like ten of them in this box."

"So we look through all of them really fast," said Del. "Except we have no idea what we're looking for."

"What was the first line of the riddle again?" asked Sam.

"Old Blythe signed next to this one's name."

Sam opened the book. "Look at this," he said. "Signatures on every page. It's a list." Sam pointed at the page. "I think this is someone who died, there's the date they died, and there is a signature—Reverend Manters', I think. Maybe Old Blythe signed his name in one of these books."

"The second line is 'Trust her completely despite her fame,'" said Del. "We need to the find someone we can trust. So it won't be someone who's dead—that cuts out a whole bunch of looking."

They leafed through the books as quickly as they could, looking at all the entries for weddings and baptisms.

"I think the service is over upstairs," said Sam.

Shuffling footsteps could be heard above their heads. The toilet flushed, and the water of the sink started running.

"We've looked through all the books and found nothing," said Del. "Maybe there's another book somewhere else."

"The most current years are missing," said Sam. "These are all old books. If they still keep track of this stuff, we probably should be looking in the book they use today. Maybe it's someone who got married recently that is supposed to help us."

"Someone famous, you think?" said Del. She laughed quietly.

She thought to herself about how grim the situation was. They were in the cellar of an old church, the only people who could help them had been taken from them, and somehow, by tomorrow, they might have to go into the dangerous realm of Azdia to rescue them.

"Should we just leave and come back tomorrow?" asked Del.

"We should probably check the lists of dead people, just to be sure," said Sam. "Besides, the second service will be starting soon, and it'll be easier to sneak out once it starts."

"This is already too creepy," said Del. "I don't want to think about a dead person helping us."

"Blythe's name was on a gravestone—that was creepy."

The voices and shuffling upstairs died down a bit as the pair checked the books thoroughly. Then, just as the traffic above them picked up again with people coming in for the second service, Del saw it—a burial record from 1978, and next to it, a bold signature of just one word—*Blythe*.

"Sam, I've got it," Del said.

She held the book so he could see it.

"And look at the name," Del said.

"But she's not dead," said Sam. "She wasn't even alive in 1978."

Del read the name over again to make sure she wasn't seeing things. The name was Emma Coons.

"Phil's sister is one of the most popular girls in school," Sam said.

"So?" asked Del.

"The riddle—trust her completely despite her fame," said Sam. "She's famous, kind of—in our school, anyway."

"But why does it say she died in 1978?" asked Del.

"How should I know?" asked Sam. "What was Old Blythe doing here signing books?"

"Do you think its really talking about Emma, like Phil's sister Emma?" asked Del.

"Why else would Blythe Thicket send you here?" said Sam.

"So we need to trust her. But trust her with what?" asked Del.

Sam shrugged.

Del thought for a moment and then blurted out, "We should bring her with us."

"Are you serious?" said Sam.

"Yeah," said Del, hesitating, and then saying more confidently, "Something's telling me that we need to trust her… with Azdia… in Azdia."

"Was it something Mr. Thicket said?" asked Sam.

"No," said Del. "I just have this feeling. If we're supposed to trust her, we will need her here with us tomorrow."

"A feeling?" said Sam suspiciously.

"Yeah, a feeling. I'm the chief of the Malak, remember. We should listen to my feelings." Del laughed again.

"I'm glad you can laugh about all this," said Sam.

"I'm serious," said Del. "We need a plan to get Emma to come with us tomorrow."

*****

The second service had started, and it sounded very different from the first: there were drums and guitars, and Del strained to hear anyone singing along.

"We're going," Del said to Sam.

She led the way up the cellar stairs, opened the door, and slid the mirror across. Fortunately, no one was using the bathroom. As they entered the hallway, the music stopped. A man's voice was coming from the sanctuary, talking to the congregation.

"Due to an emergency, Reverend Manters is unable to lead us this morning. I will be stepping in today, but be patient with me—it was all very last minute."

Del and Sam left the church. Once outside, they crossed over to the large hedge and walked straight toward the concealed opening that led under the thicket. Del passed through the hole first, then Sam, and they found themselves where they had been a day earlier—where everything had begun. Del glanced down at the gravestone and read the inscription to herself: "BLYTHE 1875—1889."

"I say we leave the Crystal Seed here," Del said. "I don't think we should be carrying it around with us."

"I guess," said Sam, looking away. Then, turning back to Del, he said, "Seriously, Del, what are we going to do? Something terrible is going on! Why did that have to happen? Why did that horrible smoke take them? We can't do this."

"Calm down," said Del. "It's Azdia we are talking about. We have Mr. Thicket on our side, we have a riddle, and we think we need Emma Coons. We just need to stay calm and keep our heads, okay? Are you still in?"

"I'm in."

"Good. Now, how are we going to get Emma here?" Del asked.

"That might be our most difficult challenge," said Sam. "But if we could get Guy on board, we might have a chance."

"Guy?"

"Yeah. Don't you know? Guy has the biggest crush on Emma."

"Really? Phil's sister and Guy. I'm guessing Phil doesn't like that too much."

"Phil doesn't know."

"How have I missed all this?"

"You're sometimes in your own world, Del." Sam had calmed down a little bit and was getting that look on his face that he got when he was beginning to figure something out. "You and I have no chance of even talking to Emma. She's older, and she wouldn't be caught dead talking to us. But Guy—maybe. Guy and Phil don't want to go back to Azdia, but Guy will do anything to impress Emma. We don't have to convince Guy to come to Azdia; we just need to convince him that Emma will think the Crystal Seed is cool. We get Guy to bring Emma here tomorrow after school, we show her the seed, and we activate it and take her through."

"What if Phil figures out what we're doing?" Del asked.

"I don't know; I guess we take that chance."

"Okay—that's the plan. First thing tomorrow, at school, we find Guy."

Del got down on her knees and placed the Crystal Seed back in the hole in the ground. She packed dirt over and around it. The two friends got out from under the thicket and headed home.

CHAPTER FOUR

Emma Coons

Del got an earful of shouting from her mother when she arrived home.

"Where have you been all weekend?" her mother asked as soon as she walked through the door.

Del wanted to answer "at church," which would be true, but she knew that wouldn't go over particularly well. Instead, Del just looked at the ground and said, "I'm sorry."

"You better be," her mother said. "You're only eleven years old, Delaney. You can't just disappear for a weekend like that. Suzanne had no idea where you were, and the two of us were worried sick about you."

Del's sister was sprawled on the living room couch. As soon as their mom's back was turned, Suzanne glared at Del, held up the note that Del had left for her mom, and quickly crumpled it. Del was sure her sister was probably behind her mother's outburst of "concern."

"Do you have anything to say for yourself?" Del's mother continued.

"More than I'm sorry?" Del asked.

"Don't get lippy with me," said her mother. "Just go.

Go to your room and don't come out until tomorrow. I'm sick of seeing you."

From her mother's perspective, she and Del had spent a weekend without seeing each other too much, but from Del's perspective, this was the first conversation she had had with her mom after spending what felt like months in Azdia. It had not gone well. Tears began to well up as Del trudged up the stairs.

As she went, Del heard her mother mumble, "So glad summer is over. Back to school tomorrow." Then she called up to Del, "And no devices! Leave your phone outside your door."

Del hated that one. She couldn't even text her friends.

She settled into her room and tried not to think about her family. Instead, she thought about Emma and Phil Coons. Would they be able to get Emma to Azdia without her brother knowing or interfering? Tomorrow, they would find out.

*****

Del stayed in her room getting ready for school for as long as possible. She didn't want to spend any more time with Suzanne than she had to. When there were only a few minutes left before they would have to leave, Del ambled into the kitchen for what would hopefully be a very quick bite to eat. Her mother and Suzanne were finishing up their breakfasts.

"Look who came to join us from dreamland," her mother half sung. "You have just enough time for some cereal. Breakfast is the most important meal of the day, especially on the first day of school—always exciting!"

What has gotten into her? Del wondered.

As Del sat down and grabbed the box of Cheerios, her mom stood up and then bent over to kiss Del on the cheek. "Let's have a good day today, okay, sweetie?"

"Okay," Del said, almost bursting into tears again. This felt close to true affection.

"I'll drive you both to school," Del's mom announced. "Tonight I want to hear all about it. After all, it's your last year of middle school, Suzanne."

Suzanne was going into grade nine at their grade five to nine middle school. She was in the same grade as Emma Coons, but Emma, whose birthday was in December, was almost an entire year younger that Suzanne. Del was going into grade six, and she was glad to no longer be one of the youngest in the school. This was Sam's first year, and Del was sure he would be nervous this morning. Phil and Guy were both in grade seven, both turning thirteen before the end of September.

As she finished her cereal, Del thought about her mom. Maybe she had decided that with the first day of school, she too needed a fresh start. Maybe she was finally going to try a little bit harder. Maybe she was going to be a regular mom.

*****

After getting dropped off at school, Suzanne was gone in a flash, most likely to meet her boyfriend at some prearranged place. There were kids everywhere in the schoolyard—first day of school chaos. Del's mission for the morning was to find Guy and convince him to impress Emma by showing her the Crystal Seed. Del scanned the yard. Most kids seemed to be meeting up with friends. Many were making their way to the main doors of the school.

Del remembered what it had been like the previous year as a grade-fiver just starting in the big school. She had been apprehensive. Sam would be terrified. She should have made a plan to meet him. She didn't care about any other friends since she barely had any other friends, and certainly not any as good as Sam.

Del had actually been looking forward to Sam being in the same school as her again. Phil and Guy did stuff with her, but they would be in grade seven now, and there was this kind of unspoken rule about grade sevens not associating with grade fives and sixes.

Del pulled out her phone and texted Sam.

"Where are you?"

Sam's reply came back.

"Near B-ball. Guy's here. No Phil."

Del ran to the outdoor basketball court and looked around. Sam was on the sidelines of the court watching. Del raced over to him.

"Where's Guy?" she said.

"Playing," said Sam.

Guy was on the court with mostly grade eight and nine boys.

"He's actually holding his own," said Sam. "And look." Sam pointed to the other side of the court to a group of grade nine girls. In the middle of them Emma Coons. She was dressed in black jeans and a pink shirt, her blond hair cascading over her shoulders perfectly. Even from across the court, Del could tell that Emma was the center of the conversation with her friends. Del could also tell by the glances from the boys on the court that many of them were hoping to gain some attention from her or one of her friends.

"That's perfect," said Del. "Emma is seeing Guy play, and he's doing well. As soon as he's off the court, I'm going to talk to him."

Even though it was still two weeks until his thirteenth birthday, Guy was tall for his age, which is probably why the older boys let him play. He was bigger than most of the grade eights, and more skilled as well. Guy was strong and, fortunately for Del and Sam, easily led.

The five-minute warning bell went off. The players finished their game, and Del heard them making plans to meet back at the court during lunch. A couple of them made a point of asking Guy to be there. This was a big compliment to a grade seven boy. Maybe they didn't know he was younger.

"Guy!" Del yelled.

Guy looked up and smiled. He walked over to Del and Sam.

"Great game," said Del. She wanted to butter him up before she tried to ask him about Emma and the seed.

"Thanks," Guy answered.

"You seen Phil?" asked Sam.

"He was here earlier," said Guy. "When I got picked for b-ball, he said he'd see me in class."

"Y'know, I think I saw Emma cheering you on," said Del.

Guy's face turned a shade of pink. "Nah," was his only reply.

"Seriously," said Del. "Did you see her when you hit that last jump shot? She loved it."

"That's just because I was on the same team as Kyle Rivers," said Guy.

"I don't think so," said Del. "You're in grade seven

now. You got invited to the grade eight and nine game. You're totally in."

Guy was shaking his head, but Del could tell that Guy at least partly believed or wanted to believe what she was saying.

"You should find out what Emma's doing after school," Del suggested. "You guys could maybe do something together."

"You're crazy," Guy replied.

"No, I'm serious," said Del. "I could tell just by looking at her that she likes you."

Guy's face was bordering on red. It made Del think of Tabby, the winx that she had met in Azdia, except that winxes changed color based on the moods of the people around them. Guy's change in color was all him.

"Maybe," Guy started. "But I don't like her or anything."

"You don't like Emma Coons?" said Del. "What's not to like? I thought every guy in school liked Emma Coons. Listen, Guy, you've got to take your chance now before anyone else does."

"I, I don't think so," said Guy.

Del knew she was getting to him. "You know what would really impress her?"

"What?" Guy asked.

Del had him and she knew it. He genuinely wanted to know what he could do to impress Emma.

"You could show her the Blythe gravestone and the Crystal Seed," said Del.

"Okay, you're really crazy," said Guy.

"I'm serious," said Del.

"She wouldn't be impressed by that," said Guy. "She's in grade nine."

"Sam and I would meet you there to open up the oval of light for you," said Del. "That would impress anyone. You just have to get her there—that's all."

"I don't know," said Guy.

"Just think about it," said Del. "Sam and I are going back to Azdia today. You could come and send us off. The beauty of it would be that you and Emma would be all alone after we go through. Then, you could just wait for us to come back."

The second bell went off.

"We're supposed to be inside," said Sam. "Classes start in a minute."

They walked into the school, and Guy headed off along one hallway. Del and Sam stayed at the entryway.

Del called after Guy, "Just think about it."

Guy spun around. "You're crazy, Del Ryder. Just crazy."

"You got him," said Sam.

"I know," said Del. "Now let me show you how to get to your class."

*****

School had been boring for Del. She had spent most of her day not paying any attention to her teachers or any kids. She daydreamed most of the day about Azdia, but her fond memories were overshadowed by her fear. She had a bad feeling that the priest would not be there later when they got to the church. Whether he was there or not, she figured that she would probably be going back to Azdia. Del was also more convinced than ever that Emma was the one in Blythe Thicket's riddle. They had to get her to Azdia.

By lunch time, Del and Sam were both hearing rumors about how Emma liked Guy and how shocking it was that a grade nine girl, and the most popular one at that, liked a grade seven boy. They also heard a few rumors floating around that Guy had failed two grades and was actually fifteen years old.

"No grade sevener looks like that," everyone was saying. Del was pretty sure those rumors had been started by the losers of the morning basketball game. Del and Sam even heard people talking about how Guy and Emma had plans after school. All of this was enough for Del to believe that their plan was working.

Del met Sam after school by the flagpole out front. There was no point waiting around to see if Guy and Emma would really go to the graveyard. They needed to get there before them to see if the priest had made it back. If he had, there would be some explaining to do about Emma.

The two best friends jogged along the streets to the church. When they got there, the main doors were locked, and there were no lights on.

"Let's make sure we try all the doors," Del said as they walked along the side of the building. "We have to be sure. We have to know if he's here or not."

"I hope he is," said Sam. "I'm not loving the idea of going back to Azdia after what we saw yesterday."

"Try not to think about it, Sam," said Del. She was pretty sure that they were not going to find the priest. "If we have to go to Azdia, we'll find help—hopefully Mr. Thicket or Crimson."

They had arrived at one of the back doors to the church. Del pulled on the handle. The door didn't budge.

"We should probably try the basement door too," Del said. "Just to be sure."

I guess so," said Sam.

They rounded the corner of the church and were stopped in their tracks.

"I can't let you go back." Phil stood in front of them, blocking their way.

"What are you doing here?" said Del.

"I figured since neither of you talked to me all day that you'd be planning something," said Phil. "I don't want to fight. You guys are my friends, and that's why I can't let you go."

"Phil, you don't understand," Del started.

Phil, however, was looking past Del and Sam, towards the hedge under which was hidden the Crystal Seed.

"What?" he said as he pushed Del and Sam out of the way and began running.

Del and Sam turned to see Guy and Emma ducking into the small opening in the hedge. Their plan had worked. There was just one problem—Phil.

*****

Del and Sam ran as fast as they could toward the hedge. Phil got there before them and dove under it. A few seconds later, Del and Sam joined everyone else under the thicket.

To Del's surprise, the oval of light was already hovering over the Crystal Seed. Guy must have figured out how to activate it.

Phil, catching his breath, said, "What are you doing here with my sister?"

Guy looked at Del, then at Emma, searching for the

right answer.

Emma didn't seem to pay any attention to Phil, however. She simply stood in front of the oval, staring at it with her big blue eyes. "How? What?" she said.

"It's a bridge to another world," Del said.

"I know," said Emma.

"What do you mean, you know?" Phil asked.

"I just know," said Emma. "We're supposed to go through it."

"No way," Phil and Del said at the same time, although they both meant completely different things.

"Emma, what are you talking about?" Phil asked.

"I've seen this before, and I know I'm supposed to go through," said Emma.

"We've been through before," said Del. "But your brother doesn't want to go back."

"It's too dangerous," Phil said. "Nobody's going. Especially you." He grabbed for Emma's arm. As he did, she turned away, and the elbow of her other arm touched the oval of light.

"She's going through!" Del cried, reacting faster than anyone. She lunged forward and caught hold of Emma's hand as she was sucked through the portal.

"Sam, everyone, grab hold," Del called. She felt Sam's hand grab hers just as everything went dark.

*****

Del gripped the hands of Emma and Sam tightly in the nothingness of the bridge to Azdia. She had a feeling as though she could choose where she wanted to go. It was an inexplicable kind of feeling, as though she somehow had control of the bridge. But how could that be?

The first thought that popped into her mind was Blythe Thicket's cottage, but she remembered that Blythe Thicket had told her that by the time she returned he would no longer be there. She thought of Mrs. Manters and figured she was being held by the Heir of Mordlum under the mountain on the edge of the Violet Wood. This thought scared her, even though she was determined to rescue her. "We're not ready," she thought to herself.

She thought of Blythe Thicket and Crimson. If only they could find Crimson. Del was confused, so many thoughts rushed through her mind at once. She felt as if she were about to faint in the darkness. Then, suddenly, she was blinded by light.

Del squinted and slowly tried to force her eyes open. She still held tight to Sam's and Emma's hands.

"Are we there?" she heard Sam's voice say. "It's so bright."

"Are we all here?" asked Del. "Emma? Sam? Did we all make it?"

"I don't have anyone else," said Sam.

"Phil? Guy?" said Del, still unable to see fully in the brilliance.

"They're not here, Del," said Sam. "It's just us."

CHAPTER FIVE

Tolstoy

Phil was in the darkness of the bridge to Azdia, holding tight to Guy's hand. The last thing he had wanted was to go through the oval of light, but deep down, he did not want to abandon his friends, and even deeper down, he wanted to protect his sister. Phil had reached for Sam's hand and had just touched his fingertips; then, Sam was lost. Phil knew they would be separated when they arrived.

In the blackness, all Phil could think about was finding Mr. Thicket. He was the one person he trusted in Azdia. Mr. Thicket was their best chance for finding each other. No matter where they landed, whether it was near the Old Oak, in a purple forest, or somewhere equally dangerous, he was going to find the one who had rescued them from black winged creatures and had ultimately helped them all get home.

Phil repeated in his mind: W*hen we get there, find Mr. Thicket. When we get there, find Mr. Thicket.* Phil was sure that the blackness was continuing longer that it had the last time they had gone to Azdia. He began to feel faint, but he stayed focused on what he would have to do: *Find*

Mr. Thicket. Find Mr. Thicket.

Then, the darkness faded into a dim gray.

Phil let go of Guy's hand.

"Where are we?" Guy asked.

Mountains reached into the sky, which was covered by hazy clouds that hung there like a great gray sheet. They were surrounded by gray. Every tree they could see appeared dead, with no leaves and certainly no glow.

"The only other mountains we saw before were where Mr. Thicket lives—on the edge of the Violet Wood," Phil said. "Do you think we're close?"

"I hope so, because we don't have anything with us," Guy complained. "No food, no water, nothing."

As they continued to look around, Phil realized that they didn't have much choice for a direction. They weren't about to start climbing mountains, and the only path available ran through the valley in which they stood.

Phil took the lead as usual. "C'mon," he said. "We're going this way."

Guy followed.

*****

They walked for a very long time. The path climbed a little bit here and there, but always descended back into the valley. The valley sometimes narrowed, and one time, it became a very narrow path through a gorge, but then it widened out again. Phil's throat was dry, and he knew Guy would be starving. There had been no sign of water.

"I don't know how much longer I can…" Guy trailed

off.

"We've got to keep going until we find either Mr. Thicket or some water," Phil replied. "Just keep moving."

They pressed on along the mountain trail until eventually, they saw a sign of hope. A small path led away from the main trail, descending down a bit of a slope. Phil walked along the smaller path a little way.

"Look," Phil said, bending and looking at the dirt path. "There are footprints on this path."

Guy bent lower as well. "Doesn't look like any foot I've ever seen."

"We're in Azdia, Guy," said Phil. "I think it's a lumen footprint. Maybe we can find someone who can help us. We should follow this path."

The narrow path led them down for a long time until they reached a staircase that had been hewn into the rock. The stairs were steep and uneven. They went down between two massive rocks. Phil looked up a couple of times and could still see the gray clouds above them. It was getting dark, however, with no real daylight to speak of, and the rock walls on either side of the staircase made it even darker. Still, they descended.

At the bottom of the staircase, they found a hole in the ground that would be just big enough for them to fit through if they went one at a time. Phil knelt at the hole and looked in. It was dark in there—completely black. He looked at Guy.

"We're not going in there, are we?" Guy asked.

Phil looked around. It seemed like going into the hole was the only way. They were at the bottom of the stairs and completely surrounded by rock. There was nowhere else to go unless they went back the way they came.

Phil reached into the hole and felt around. His hand touched something. It felt like rope. He groped around some more and then pulled his hand back.

"I think it might be…" he said, as he swung his legs around and put one foot in the hole, then the other. "Yes! It's a rope ladder."

"And we're going down it?" asked Guy.

"You got a better idea?" Phil replied.

"How about not going down it?"

"We need water," said Phil. "We saw lumen footprints up there, and this is the only path. The stairs had to be made by someone, and a rope ladder had to be put here by someone, to be used by someone."

"Yeah, but what if it's the wrong someone?" said Guy.

"Then we die of something else instead of thirst," said Phil. "We've got to find food and water, and this is our best chance. We just have to do it."

"Okay," Guy conceded. "You first."

"Fine," said Phil.

Phil went into the hole and down the rope ladder. He counted the rungs as he went. When he got to thirty-five, he whispered, "Guy, you with me?"

There was no response from Guy. Phil scrambled back up the ladder and popped his head out of the hole. There was Guy sitting by the side of the hole.

"What's at the bottom?" Guy asked.

"I didn't get there," said Phil. "I got thirty-five rungs down and realized you weren't there."

"I figured you'd call when you got to the bottom," said Guy.

"Get on the ladder behind me," said Phil. "We're

doing this together."

Phil counted the rungs again as he and Guy descended the rope ladder together this time. He had gotten to fifty-five when the dim light from the hole way above them completely faded.

"Phil?" Guy checked in.

"Yeah," said Phil.

"It's really dark," said Guy.

"I know," said Phil.

They kept moving, and Phil kept counting rungs. *Seventy-six, seventy-seven.*

"Phil, you still there?" asked Guy.

"Yeah," said Phil.

They continued descending.

"How many rungs is it now?" asked Guy.

"Eighty-three," said Phil.

"Should we keep going?"

"Yeah."

Phil's count had gotten to ninety-one when he noticed that below them, it seemed less dark. "We're coming to the bottom, I think," he said to Guy.

"I still don't see anything," said Guy.

"Just keep coming down," said Phil. "The darkness is definitely fading."

Phil was right. As they moved farther down the rope ladder, they started to be able to see. They had been in a kind of vertical tunnel before. It had now widened into a small cavern. The walls were solid rock. There wasn't much to see, but they could see. Phil reached exactly one hundred rungs and was at the end. There was a floor of rock below them. He and Guy both got off the rope ladder and stood trying to catch their breath. Phil's arm muscles were tight, and his hands were raw from gripping the ropes for so long.

Together, the two boys surveyed the cavern. There were five large holes on the cavern wall that perhaps became caves or tunnels. It was clear that the source of the light was coming from one of the holes.

"That's where we're going," said Phil.

They went into the hole. The light was not bright by any means, but it was enough. It wasn't long after starting along the tunnel that they began to hear a noise.

"Is that what I think it is?" asked Guy.

"I think so," said Phil. "Running water."

Several more steps and the tunnel opened out to reveal an incredible sight. They must have been hundreds of feet underground, but there before them was a river, flowing swiftly through a massive tunnel. On either side of the river were banks of solid rock.

Phil and Guy knelt down on one of the banks to get something to drink. Before they could, however, Phil felt a hand on his shoulder.

"I wouldn't drink that if I were you," said a voice behind them.

Phil and Guy whipped around quickly. Before them was a lumen glowing with a beautiful golden glow. He had clearly been the source of their light.

"Now tell me," the lumen said, "what are the likes of you doing way down here in a place like this?"

"We're looking for something to drink and eat, and we're looking for help," said Phil.

"You've found help," said the lumen. "And just in time, it would seem." He waved at the river next to them. "You don't want to drink that."

As had happened in their previous trip to Azdia, the

boys were faced with a choice. Would they trust this lumen, or would they go it alone? Last time, they had always taken help when it was offered, and this time would be no different. Phil wondered, though, how long it would be before their luck in trusting strangers would run out.

"My name is Phil, and this is Guy," said Phil.

"I'm Tolstoy," said the lumen. "Come with me, and we'll get something better to drink—and some food too."

The boys followed Tolstoy, sometimes passing through rough tunnels hewn into the rock but always returning to the riverbank. Without the glow coming from their lumen guide, it would have been impossibly dark. Tolstoy led them through a short series of tunnels until they reached another larger opening.

Phil immediately saw a familiar sight. Before them, he could see a lake of beautiful glowing water, shimmering in a million colors. The lake's multicolored glow lit up the room around them. Phil had almost forgotten what glow-water looked like, but he did remember that the glow itself was actually the tiniest of glow bugs. He also remembered how incredible he would feel after drinking it.

"Go on," said Tolstoy. "You can drink this."

Phil and Guy knelt by the shore of the lake and scooped handfuls of the glow-water into their mouths. Phil had always thought it tasted a bit like Cream Soda, sweet and soft, but with the power of an energy drink, with more kick than anything he could get at the convenience store back home. He looked over at Guy who had given up on scooping and had simply put his face in the water to drink more quickly.

Once Phil had had enough, he glanced over his shoulder to see Tolstoy smiling at them. "That must be better," he said.

"It is, thank you," said Guy, who had taken his face out of the water and was getting to his feet.

"Now for some food and perhaps a bit of rest," said Tolstoy.

"Do you live down here?" Guy asked.

"Not just me," said Tolstoy. He pointed across the lake. In his excitement to drink the glow-water, Phil hadn't noticed the houses on the other side. Guy stood gaping at the sight—clearly, he had not noticed either. It wasn't just a few houses, either. There were a lot of them. Across the lake of glowing water, there was an entire town. What on earth was a town doing underground?

"Welcome to 1300," said Tolstoy. "The secret village of the thirteenth province."

CHAPTER SIX

On the Beach

Before Del's eyes could adjust to the brightness, her other senses were heightened. She could hear the lapping of waves against a rocky shore and the distant crying of birds from high above. She smelled fish and freshness and salt. A light breeze hit her cheeks, though it did little to lessen the heat from the sun. She took her sweater off and tied it around her waist.

Her eyes opened more, letting the light in. Things started to come into focus. They were standing on a long beach of white sand. The sand was broken up only by a few large rocks. Small waves lapped up gently on the shore.

"The sea," said Sam.

Del tried to get her head straight. She was in Azdia with Sam and Emma. She had been thinking about Crimson. Was he here somewhere? She looked around quickly, but no lumens were in sight. That didn't mean they weren't here, though, in some other form, perhaps.

As she looked around, she was very thankful that she and Sam had each brought some food and a couple of bottles of water in their backpacks. She wasn't sure if they would be able to drink the sea water.

Sam walked over to the surf, bent down, and touched the foamy water with his hand, bringing some of it to his lips. He turned back toward Del and Emma.

"It's salty," Sam said. "We can't drink it."

"This is all really weird," said Emma. She was breathing heavily.

The three children were sweating from the heat, but this was already a better welcome than the first time Del and Sam had come to Azdia, when they had been attacked by some very scared and startled trees. There did not appear to be any immediate threat to them, but Emma was panicking. She couldn't seem to catch her breath.

"Are you okay, Emma?" Del asked.

"No," Emma replied. "I feel like this should be a dream, but it's not, and I'm going to…" She collapsed.

"Sam," Del cried. "Get over here."

Sam ran to them from the surf. He and Del knelt down next to Emma.

"I think she fainted," said Del.

"Give her some water," said Sam.

Del took a bottle from her backpack and removed the cap. She held the bottle to Emma's lips and attempted to pour some water into her mouth. It seemed like some went in.

"We need to get her into some shade," said Del, looking around. Del couldn't see much of anything that could act as shelter on the beach itself. Away from the water there were large sand dunes with some plants growing on them. Maybe there, although Del hesitated when it came to plant life. What if the plants came alive like in the forest of the Old Oak? They would have to risk it. They could all use some shade—the sun was scorching.

"Let's get her over into those dunes," Del said.

Del and Sam lifted Emma and carried her across the sand. This was really hard work for the two smaller children, and by the end of it, Del was ready to collapse. She was sure Sam was too. They found a spot under a scraggly-looking bush. Unfortunately, the dunes blocked any breeze that might be coming off the sea, so even the shade was as hot as anything.

Del gave Emma some more water and poured a little bit on her forehead and face to see if it would revive her. It did, but she was groggy.

"Am I home?" Emma asked. "Is the dream over?"

"You're not dreaming," Del said, trying to sound reassuring. "You're with Sam Long and Del Ryder. We went through an oval of light to... somewhere else—remember?"

Emma's eyes rolled back into her head. "Wake me up when I'm not dreaming anymore," she mumbled.

"What are we going to do?" asked Sam.

"Emma! Wake up!" Del yelled.

"What?" Emma said, eyes opening slowly.

"This is not a dream," Del continued sternly. "You've got to snap out of it. We're here for you, but you can't faint or go to sleep!"

Del took a whole handful of water and threw it on Emma's face.

"Hey!" Emma cried, finally coming around.

"You fainted," said Del. "I had to do something."

"Here, eat something," said Sam, holding a granola bar out to Emma.

She took the bar and wolfed it down.

"I can't believe I'm not dreaming," said Emma. "I can't believe this is really real."

"What on earth are you talking about?" said Sam.

"I've dreamed of this place ever since I was a little girl," Emma replied. "I've seen this all before. How did you manage to make my dream real?"

"Sam and I have been here before," Del replied. "Not to this beach, but to this world—to Azdia. Your brother and Guy have been too. We were here on Saturday, but time works differently here. You can be here for weeks, and you're only gone for a few minutes at home."

"This doesn't make any sense," said Emma. "When I saw the oval with the energy light stuff, I thought it was all for me. That my dream had become reality."

"You really think you've dreamt all this before, don't you?" said Del.

"Yes," said Emma. "But you know how dreams are. I would walk into the oval, then everything would go dark. That happened this time, so I thought I must be dreaming. Every time, in my dream, I would end up on this beach, then it would flash to something else, then something else. I've had the same basic dream since I was young, but I can't remember it all. I wouldn't dream everything every time I was sleeping, and as I got older there seemed to be less of it—the dreams got less real, y'know?"

"I guess so," said Del. "You mean, like you used to remember more of the dream when you were younger."

"Kind of," said Emma. "It all feels like a memory, as though it all happened to me when I was younger. You know how you can kind of remember stuff that happened to you when you were really young? You know it happened, but it usually takes looking at a picture or something to remind you of exactly what it was like? It's like that. It's as though I dreamed the whole thing once when I was really young, but as I got older, I just dreamed certain pieces. But when I saw the oval and saw this beach, I knew it was my dream."

"Can you remember anything else about your dream?" Sam asked.

"Snow, I think," Emma replied.

"Snow? On a beach?" asked Del.

"No, not here. Somewhere else—and after the snow, I remember something really bright. Someone was there with me, but I don't know who. It's hard to remember, I'm sorry."

"Anything else?" asked Del.

"I don't think so," said Emma. "No, wait. There was a door. A door covered in vines, and all around were trees that had fallen. There's more, but it's hard to remember."

"We should probably tell Emma why we're here," said Sam.

Del nodded, and then Sam and Del set about telling the whole tale of their previous adventures in Azdia from start to finish. They told her about the ancient stories of the Old Oak, Eleanor, Mordlum, and the Company of Light and how they now knew that the priest and his wife were Eleanor and Mordlum. Most importantly, they told her about the Heir of Mordlum, who had posed as Mr. Thicket and was bent on turning the lumens and everything in Azdia dark. Del spent a lot of time explaining about the real Mr. Thicket. Emma was most interested, however, in her name being in the book at the old church.

They told her about the priest's wife being captured by the smoke and about the priest going through after her and calling her Eleanor.

"It was definitely the Heir that captured her," said Del. "We have to rescue her."

"But the Heir of Mordlum," Emma started. "Wouldn't he be their son?"

"We think so," said Sam.

"Why would he be so evil?" said Emma. "And why would he capture his own mom?"

"We don't know," said Del. "But maybe that's why they need us. Maybe Mordlum can't stop his own son, and they need us to stop him."

"What about Phil and Guy?" asked Sam. "I'm sure I felt Phil's hand when I was in the darkness of the bridge. I think they came through as well."

"But they're not here," said Emma.

"They might have been dropped somewhere else in Azdia," said Del. "That's what happened to us before."

"We're going to need help if we're going to find them," said Sam.

"We don't need to find them," Del said. "I know Phil, and he is going to do everything he can to find us, and we know exactly who they'll go to for help."

"We'll all be trying to go to the same place," said Sam. "They still believe the Heir is Mr. Thicket—they think he'll be their best chance to find us."

"So we need to get to the Heir first," said Del. "That way, we can free the priest's wife and protect Phil and Guy."

"The problem is," said Sam, "we don't even know where we are, let alone how to get to the heir from here."

"Staying here isn't going help us," said Del. "Emma, you're not going to faint again if we start moving, are you?"

Emma scowled at her.

The three children got to their feet. The heat had not let up.

"I say we stay close to the water for now," said Sam. "Our best chance of finding help is to find a town, and we're most likely to find a town somewhere on the water."

Del led them out of the dunes back toward the water. "I guess we just pick a direction. That way?" Del pointed along the beach.

"I guess so," said Sam.

The three of them set off along the beach with the sea to their left and the dunes to their right. They had only taken about fifteen steps when Emma stopped. "Wait," she said. "This doesn't feel right."

"What do you mean?" Del asked.

"The water should be on my right," said Emma.

"What?" said Sam.

"In my dream, when I walked, the water was always on my right," said Emma.

Sam pulled Del away from Emma and whispered to her. "Seriously? We're going to follow a dream?"

"I think we should, Sam," Del whispered back. "We have nothing else to go on, and remember the riddle —'trust her completely.' Maybe this is why we need Emma. Maybe Emma's dream is our guide."

*****

The children turned around and began walking in

the other direction, this time with the sea on their right. Del looked at Emma, who seemed to relax as she walked. It was tough walking through the sand, so they took off their shoes and walked closer to the surf, where the sand was cooler and firmer. Every now and again, a wave would wash up to where they were.

They walked for a very long time. This was something Del and Sam had grown accustomed to in Azdia. They walked everywhere, often with very little change in whatever landscape they were in. They didn't encounter anyone on the beach and only saw a few birds that occasionally swooped down to the water, presumably in search of food. The birds looked like ordinary white birds, seagulls perhaps. Del imagined that they might be glowing, but the sun was so bright it was difficult to tell.

They had used up about half of their water on their walk along the hot beach. They hadn't eaten too much, but Del wondered about where they might find provisions. She had hoped if they followed the shoreline that eventually they would find a river where they could refill their water bottles. She figured that they still had some time before the situation became critical.

The sand beach gave way to large, round rocks that formed a point jutting out into the sea. They were able to climb along the rocks, and the further they got along the point, the more coastline they were able to see. The beach didn't continue past the point. Instead, the coast was dominated by a thick forest leading to distant cliffs that stretched into the sea, cutting off any further view of the land beyond.

"Anything look familiar?" Del said to Emma.

Emma shook her head. "I don't think so."

"If that's where we're heading," Sam began, pointing at the cliffs, "I don't think we'll make it there before the sun sets."

"You're thinking we should look for a place to sleep?" asked Del.

"Yeah," said Sam.

"Who are you guys?" said Emma. "Some kind of crazy survival team? I've never even been camping."

"We've just been through a lot," said Del. "This is nothing."

After having a good look at the coastline from the point, they made their way back to where the rocks joined the beach and the forest began.

"This looks like a good spot," said Sam. He had found a sandy patch nestled between three large rocks.

"Why not get under the cover of those trees?" asked Emma.

"No trees if we can help it," said Del.

"What's wrong with the trees?" Emma asked.

"Did you not hear anything we told you?" Sam said. "About the trees that attacked us?"

"It was kind of a lot to take in," said Emma. "It's all a lot to take in."

CHAPTER SEVEN

The Secret Village

Phil and Guy followed Tolstoy around the underground lake and into the secret village. There were many lumens walking through the streets, all glowing and smiling at the two boys. Phil noticed a lot of them whispering to one another as they passed by, and the youngest ones were wide-eyed, as though they were seeing two celebrities. Tolstoy was beaming, a broad smile across his face.

Other than being underground, the town seemed fairly normal. Phil and Guy had only ever been in one lumen town before, and that one had been riddled with lumens who were in the process of going dark. There, the buildings had been run down or burnt out. Town 1875 had not been a pleasant place—a town divided between the dark lumens and the fearful lumens who labelled the dark ones as "sick." This underground village was in good repair with no dark lumens as far as Phil could tell. Not that lumens going dark was a bad thing, of course. Mr. Thicket had told them plainly that lumens simply didn't understand that their inner light was what killed them—dark lumens could live forever.

Tolstoy led them to an impressive building that had stone pillars lining its exterior. Two lumens stood next to the large double doors of the building. One of the lumens chirped at Tolstoy. Tolstoy chirped back. The lumen chirped something else, glanced at Phil and Guy, and stepped in front of the door as if to block it.

Tolstoy chirped again and then turned to Phil and Guy. "Follow me," he said as he pushed the two lumens out of the way, grabbed both door handles, and flung them open.

Inside, there were many lumens standing along the walls observing a group of seven lumens in the middle. The seven were seated at a round table, and they were chirping away to each other. The table had one empty chair. As soon as Tolstoy, Phil, and Guy came into view, the room went silent.

Tolstoy walked toward the table and, one by one, the lumens seated around it got to their feet. Most of them had looks of shock or worry on their faces. One elderly lumen had tears in her eyes.

Phil and Guy followed Tolstoy to the table. He went to the empty chair, pulled it out, and stood in front of it. Phil was sure one of the lumens next to him was about to jump on Tolstoy and attack him—he had that look about him, but it never happened.

Tolstoy began speaking in the lumen language. As he spoke, he motioned to Phil and Guy several times. Although Phil couldn't understand a word of the speech, he could tell it was impassioned. Tolstoy raised his voice one moment and then whispered at another. His fists waved in the air, he pointed up toward the ceiling, and a couple of times, he pounded on the table.

Guy leaned toward Phil's ear and whispered, "What

do you think is going on?"

"I don't know," said Phil. "But whatever it is, he's really excited about it."

Tolstoy turned and glared at Phil and Guy, who were standing just behind his chair. Obviously, he didn't care for their whispering behind him. They remained silent for the rest of Tolstoy's speech.

When he was done speaking, there was a short silence. The elderly lumen who had looked as if she was going to cry chirped a little bit; then, each lumen around the table took their turn, each chirping one or two times. When they were finished, the elderly one had gone from having wet eyes to full-on tears streaming down her face. She walked over to Tolstoy, who also looked dejected, gave him a hug, and then slumped back into her chair.

Tolstoy turned toward Phil and Guy. "We're going," he said.

The three of them walked toward the doors and left the building.

*****

"Fools!" Tolstoy declared in English once they were a few paces away from the building. "They don't understand. They don't believe."

"Don't understand what?" Phil asked.

"That you're here to help us resist," Tolstoy said. "That you're the Malak. I know you are. I didn't need to ask. Sirah knew as well."

"I'm sorry, but you're wrong," Phil said, deciding that on this visit to Azdia he would not play any games or tell any lies. "We're not the Malak. I don't know if they're real or not, but we're just two guys."

"Sirah suspected you may not even know," Tolstoy replied. "In any case, it doesn't matter right now."

"What's with lumens not believing us when we tell them we're not the Malak?" said Guy.

"So you've met other lumens?" asked Tolstoy.

"We've, um, been here before," said Phil. "To Azdia, I mean."

"Yet you don't believe you are the Malak!" Tolstoy cried. "Remarkable! Who else could you be?"

Before Phil or Guy could respond, Tolstoy was already moving on. "We really need to get off the streets. This conversation would be better off indoors."

Tolstoy led them around a corner and down a lane to a small building. He opened the door and led them inside. "It's small," he said. "But we should all fit for the night. You can stay here with me and get some food and rest."

Tolstoy motioned for Phil and Guy to sit on two couches that sat corner to corner in what Phil supposed was the living room. There was a table near the couches strewn with books and papers. Tolstoy scurried over and brushed some of them aside to make room for the large frames of the two boys. They sat down, and their host disappeared into another room.

"What is going on?" Guy said.

"Who knows?" said Phil.

*****

A knock came at the door. Tolstoy reappeared, nodded to the boys, and said, "That will be Sirah."

Tolstoy opened the door, and before him was the

frail, old lumen who had cried and hugged him. As she came in, the two lumens chirped to one another quickly.

Sirah looked over at Phil and Guy and bowed low to them. She chirped. Phil and Guy looked at each other and shrugged. Phil stood up from his spot on the couch and bowed back to Sirah. He was trying to be polite. Guy followed suit, doing the same as Phil.

Tolstoy chirped something again, and the two lumens walked out of the living room, leaving the boys again. It wasn't long before delicious smells were wafting into the living room. Guy's stomach grumbled loudly. Phil's stomach answered back.

"I guess we're both pretty hungry," Guy said.

"The last time we were in Azdia, the food was terrific," said Phil. "That's one good thing about being here, I guess."

"Do you think we should tell them about Del, Sam, and Emma?" Guy asked. "Maybe these lumens can help us find them."

"I don't think so," said Phil. "I think we focus on finding Mr. Thicket. We know him, and he knows Del and Sam. I think we just tell these two we're looking for Mr. Thicket."

Guy nodded.

Tolstoy reappeared, carrying a very large black pot. Sirah followed with a plate full of scones and four bowls stacked inside each other with four spoons balanced on top. They marched over to the table.

"Would you mind, terribly," said Tolstoy to Phil and Guy as he nodded toward the table.

Phil jumped up, then Guy. They cleared some space on the table for the pot. Tolstoy set it down and then helped the boys clear the rest of the papers and books away. Sirah laid out the bowls and spoons.

"Sit down, sit down," said Tolstoy.

The only seating in the room was the two couches. Phil and Guy pulled them up to the table and sat together on one of them. Sirah sat on the other couch. Tolstoy opened up a nearby cupboard and brought out a bottle and four goblets.

"I've been saving this," he said.

Sirah chirped to him, and he chirped back.

"She would like to know if it is all right if she touches one of you," said Tolstoy.

"You know, that's the first time a lumen's asked," said Phil. He thought about it, but what was he going to say? "Of course."

Phil reached his arm across the table toward Sirah. She gently touched one of his outstretched fingers.

"Thank you, sir," said Sirah. "It is an honor to be graced by your presence and to be allowed to speak to you in your language."

"No need to be so formal, Sirah," said Tolstoy. "It is your way, though, I suppose."

Tolstoy opened the bottle and poured a deep red liquid into each goblet. "Now then, first things first."

Phil and Guy looked at each other, and grabbed their goblets, ready for the toast to Mr. Thicket. Tolstoy, however, proceeded to tell them about the stew in his pot.

"This stew can be a touch spicy for some," he said, dishing some out to each diner with a large ladle. "Just sip it gently at first until you get used to it."

When he had finished serving, Tolstoy sat down and took a big loud slurp of stew.

"Go on, dig in," Tolstoy said.

"Tolstoy," said Sirah. "I think our guests were expecting something before the meal."

"What?" Tolstoy asked.

"No, it's okay," Guy spluttered.

Phil quickly took some stew on his spoon and ate it in solidarity with Tolstoy. He didn't want his host to feel awkward. Sirah, however, didn't seem to care about that. Phil noted that the stew was spicy and delicious.

"Have you forgotten?" asked Sirah. "It's been so long since we've done it, since we dared believe."

"Forgotten what?" asked Tolstoy.

"Everyone, stop," Sirah said. "Now raise your glasses."

As they put their goblets in the air, Tolstoy's face changed.

"Yes, of course," he said. "It has been a very long time—but now the Malak have come. Now, more than ever, we have something to be thankful for and something to hope for."

"Together, then," said Sirah.

She breathed in heavily and then the four of them said loudly, "To Mr. Thicket!"

*****

"You know, he doesn't really like all the fuss," Phil said.

"What do you mean?" Tolstoy asked.

"Mr. Thicket," Phil continued between slurps. "He doesn't like it when people toast him. He says that it's not necessary."

Tolstoy and Sirah stopped eating, their eyes wide and their mouths open in disbelief.

"Yes, we know him," Phil said. "And we need your help to find him if you can help."

Phil sat back to see what their response would be.

"We should not be surprised that the Malak know Mr. Thicket," Sirah said. "Of course we will do everything we can to help you, but there may be little we can do."

"We know that Mr. Thicket has a hideout under a mountain," said Phil. "It's close to the Violet Wood."

"The Violet Wood is not far from here," said Tolstoy. "No wonder we are protected so well from the darkness here."

"Actually, Mr. Thicket is…" Guy began. Phil kicked him under the table and gave him a look telling him to be quiet. It was far better if these lumens knew nothing about Mr. Thicket's plans to turn the lumens dark. He had told them that most lumens would not understand that their loss of light was really for their own good and that Mr. Thicket was indeed their savior and protector, though not in the way they thought. He would bring the darkness as a way of giving them everlasting life, but lumens wouldn't understand this right away.

"Mr. Thicket is what, dear?" said Sirah.

Guy thought hard. "Mr. Thicket is… um… protecting lots of places like this."

"That is good news indeed!" Sirah beamed. "But as you can tell, we didn't even know he was close by, so we don't know how to find him."

"There was a door in the forest," said Phil. "But it was very hard to find, and Mr. Thicket had the key. The only other way we know about is near the top of the mountain. We flew on birds out of a hole near the peak. You wouldn't happen to have any birds around here, would you?"

"I'm afraid we don't," said Sirah.

"Can't you two just turn into birds and take us up over the mountains?" asked Guy.

"We would need a bird to touch in order to metamorph into one," said Tolstoy. "And the two of us have vowed to protect this village. We cannot stray too far. I'm afraid we aren't going to be much help."

"We can still get them to the surface and show them the pass to the Violet Wood," said Sirah.

"I'm surprised Mr. Thicket's home is so close to the eighteenth province, where there is such darkness," said Tolstoy.

Sirah slurped the stew in front of her. "You should not be surprised, my friend," she said. "Our protector and savior will always choose to make his home among those who are hurting. And make no mistake, those lumens that have lost their light are in great pain."

As they finished up their supper, Phil thought about their situation. At least they were close to Mr. Thicket's hideout. He was confident that if they came across any fully dark lumens, they might be more help than Tolstoy and Sirah. These two old lumens were nice, but they didn't know the real truth, and Phil knew it wouldn't help to tell them. He and Guy wouldn't be afraid of any darkness that was out there—he knew it all came from Mr. Thicket, and he was trustworthy and good.

"After you rest, Tolstoy will show you the mountain pass and get you on course for the Violet Wood," Sirah said. "I must remain here, but I have something for you that I pray you will never need to use."

Sirah grabbed Guy's wrist and pulled him toward her across the table. She reached inside her cloak with her other hand and produced a very small box. She placed the box in Guy's palm and looked him in the eyes.

"Use this only when all other light around you has faded," she said. "It is a last resort when all other options have been eliminated. Show this box to no one —not even to Mr. Thicket if you find him. If he sees this box, he will know that you were not supposed to show it to him. He will know that you have betrayed a trust that was not to be betrayed. Keep it hidden, and pray that you never need to open it."

"What's inside?" Guy asked.

Sirah let go of Guy's arm and smiled. She rose from the table and made her way to the door. "Tomorrow you will go with Tolstoy to the mountain pass."

Tolstoy stood up and then bowed low to Sirah. "Light will prevail, even in the darkest of places."

Phil and Guy stood up and, following Tolstoy's lead, bowed as well.

Sirah nodded and beamed at the boys. "I only wish our town would believe. Regardless, this is a happy day. Today I have seen the bright future of Azdia."

With that, she was gone, leaving Phil and Guy for the night with Tolstoy.

CHAPTER EIGHT
To the Cliffs

Del was up before the sun and left Sam and Emma sleeping on the sand. She stood nearby, looking out over the sea, trying to clear her head.

Since witnessing the capture of Mrs. Manters, Del had been wavering between confidence and doubt. She was supposed to be the chief of the Malak—the one to come and rescue Azdia. Blythe Thicket himself had told her that's who she was. Although she hadn't felt it at the time, she had felt it since—but not this morning.

She looked through gray mist at the rolling waves. She thought about a line from the riddle given to her by Blythe Thicket: "Over the sea to where the new birth falls." Should they try to follow the riddle rather than going to rescue Mrs. Manters?

As the thoughts swirled around, she wondered how they would possibly be able to find the Heir of Mordlum's mountain. They hadn't the first clue where in Azdia they were, and all they knew about his lair was that it was in the eighteenth province in a mountain range on the edge of the Violet Wood. Sam was right— they needed help.

She thought about Blythe Thicket and the love she had for him, how he always called her "little Del," and how playing a few games in his cottage made her feel as if there were no worries or problems anywhere in her world or his. She remembered her last few moments with him and with Crimson. She remembered their embraces and the way a hug from friends like Blythe Thicket and Crimson felt. She had felt confident and humble at the same time when she was around them. She wished desperately that she could see either of them.

Some of Crimson's last words clattered around in her mind: "You will return to Azdia, and I will find you when you do." She wanted Crimson to find her so badly. She could hear his voice in her mind, repeating over and over, "I will find you." She found herself whispering quietly out toward the sea, "Find me, Crimson."

"Do not be afraid," said a voice from behind her. "He will find you."

Del whipped around, but nobody was there. The voice had sounded so close and so familiar. It reminded her of Blythe Thicket's voice, but it couldn't be. There was no sign of anyone, and there was nowhere to hide. It must have been in her mind along with all of her other thoughts—but this voice had sounded as if it had come from outside of her—it had sounded so real.

Suddenly, she heard another voice.

"You're up early," said Sam. "Ready to go?"

Sam and Emma climbed over the rocks toward Del.

"You okay?" Emma asked.

Del, still shaken from hearing a voice and seeing no one, said, "Yeah, I'm fine. Let's get moving."

*****

The rocks over which they had previously scrambled gave way to a steady incline through the forest toward the distant cliffs. When the three of them reached the tree line, Sam and Del stopped.

"Let's go," Emma asked. "We've got to keep going, right? I think that's a little trail up ahead through the forest. Actually, it's all very beautiful isn't it?"

Emma was right. There was what looked like a very small trail, wide enough for them to travel single file through the undergrowth. She was right about the beauty as well. All the trees and plant life glowed in all kinds of colors. The treetops swayed and creaked in a cool breeze coming off the sea. It had cooled down quite a bit from the intense heat of the beach.

"Looks like mostly fir trees," said Sam, ignoring Emma.

"They're definitely alive," said Del. "Don't think you'd want one of those branches full of needles taking a swipe at you."

"Was it really that bad?" asked Emma.

"Yes," said Sam.

"If you startle them or make them mad or anything, they might attack you," Del added.

"But this forest looks so nice," said Emma, taking a few steps toward the trail.

"Just wait," said Del. "Please don't make us prove it to you. Believe me, I hope more than anything that nothing happens in this forest. We just need to think it through and take precautions."

"What kind of precautions?" asked Emma.

"I think maybe we just need to be respectful," said Del. "Don't touch anything if you can help it. Stick to the path. That kind of thing."

"And probably the most important thing," said Sam. "Stay as quiet as you can."

"Give me a break," sighed Emma, stomping toward the path.

"Emma, stop!" Del whispered urgently.

Emma stopped, turned back toward Del and Sam, and rolled her eyes. "Well, I guess you're the experts. So... don't touch anything, and keep quiet?"

"Yeah," said Del, moving past Emma and taking the lead into the forest.

*****

For the most part, the trail followed the coastline, allowing them to check their progress, which was slow. After several hours of walking, Sam whispered, "I don't think we're going to make it to the cliffs today. We need to think about where we're going to sleep and whether this trail is safe overnight."

"It might just have to be," said Del.

"You mean we're going to have to just sleep out here?" said Emma. "Sleeping on the beach was bad enough."

"Do you have any other suggestions?" asked Del.

"Aren't you supposed to be someone important here?" Emma said. "Where's the welcome? Where's the food? I guess there aren't lumen hotels or anything like that?"

"We didn't see any the last time we were here," said Sam.

As they spoke, some branches above them rattled together.

"Shh," Del whispered, glancing up. "We just need to keep going. We're going to be safer when the trees are asleep, anyway, so let's not worry about where we're going to sleep."

They continued walking in silence for the rest of the day. As evening fell, they found a place where they could sleep just off the trail that overlooked the sea.

"We're already pretty high up," said Del, looking down at the sea below.

"The cliffs must be massive," said Sam. "Way bigger than this drop, and this is already higher than the diving tower at the pool."

*****

Morning came quickly. Del woke with a start to see Sam and Emma both standing over her.

"Back to normal, eh?" said Sam. "Guess you finally decided to sleep in."

"Is it morning already?" Del croaked, stretching on the ground as if she were a cat waking from a long nap in the sun.

"It's been morning for a while," said Emma.

"Time to go now, though," said Sam.

Del got to her feet as pine needles bristled above them. They could see the cliffs stretched out into the sea. Perhaps they could make it there before dark. Without another word, she set off along the narrow path.

The steady climb through the forest was as uneventful as the previous day. They stopped only to take on water and to eat some of the provisions they had brought with them. Del hoped they would find some food somewhere —they were running very low.

By the early evening, the trees began to thin out. Del could see the light from the setting sun flickering through the glowing pine branches. They hadn't seen the sea in a while, but Del was confident the path had led them in the direction of the cliffs as they had continued on an upward incline.

The forest gave way to a meadow of long, golden, glowing grass waving in the breeze. It was immediately obvious that they were standing at the top of the cliffs. The sun was setting, and it looked as if purple and orange fingers were dipping themselves into the sea, which stretched out to meet the sky across the horizon.

At the far end of the cliff, looking as if it were about to fall off, was a single gnarled tree. It was not a fir tree like most of the forest had been. It didn't have any leaves either—it looked dead as far as Del was concerned.

She didn't care too much about the tree at the end of the cliff, however. It was what was next to the tree that mattered—a log cabin. It looked nice enough from a distance, though it was absolutely tiny. There were no signs of life around it and no sign of light coming from inside.

They couldn't make out any kind of trail through the meadow. If there had been one in the past, it had been overgrown with grass long ago.

"C'mon," said Del. "Let's check it out."

They waded through the grass. To their right was the cliff itself with its long drop-off. Below, Del could see the forest, and beyond that, a long, sandy beach stretched to nothing in the growing twilight.

Sam was steering clear of the drop-off—really clear. He walked on his own on the far side of the meadow. Del glanced over at him and realized something strange. A little beyond Sam, the meadow just stopped —no trees, just nothing.

"Guys, come over here," Sam called.

Emma and Del jogged over to Sam.

"There are two sides to the cliffs," said Sam. "We're on a peninsula—it sticks out into the sea. We can see both sides. And—look!"

Sam pointed down over the edge of the other side of the cliffs in the opposite direction of the beach. Below them on the other side of a bay was a lumen town. There were many houses and a few ships docked in a harbor. All of the buildings were concentrated on the coast with the majority of them hugging either side of a river that spilled into the bay.

"That's where we need to go," said Sam. "We'll be able to get help there."

"Absolutely," said Del. "But not today, that's for sure —it's too far."

Light was fading fast, making it difficult to make out any signs of lumen life in the town below.

"Let's check out the cabin," Del said, starting to move away from the edge of the cliff. "And keep low. We have no idea what we might find here."

The three of them crept hunched over through the tall grass, which they hoped would do a decent job of hiding them from any potential enemy that might be around. They arrived at the cabin door.

"Do we knock?" Emma whispered.

"There's a window," said Sam. "We should look."

They slid along the side of the cabin. Del popped her head up to the window and looked inside.

"Everything's dark," she whispered. "I can't see anything. I don't think anyone's inside."

They returned to the door, and Del pushed it open slightly. They passed through the door, leaving it open, allowing for some of the fading light from outside to pass through the larger opening.

*****

Del wasn't sure if she was relieved or disappointed to find the cabin empty. They wouldn't have any help from anyone, but nothing sinister was waiting for them either. She felt much better about making their way to the town to find help, even though her only prior experience with a lumen town had not been a good one.

The town of 1875 had been going dark, and Del had been attacked on the street by a crazy lumen named Pyria. Pyria's sister Cinder had been the only reason Del had survived that day, and without Cinder's help, they wouldn't have been able to navigate the streets safely. Even Cinder, who had helped them greatly, had not been particularly nice about it. She made fun of Crimson and cast doubt on everything that Del had been beginning to believe about Azdia, the Malak, and Mr. Thicket. Eventually, Del had discovered that Cinder had been wrong about everything.

Emma, Del, and Sam had to duck their heads in the small cabin—it was clearly built for lumens. Del glanced around the empty room. It was simple. There was a table with four chairs around it and another two chairs in the corner. Everything was made of basic wood, including two interior doors. The space was so cramped that when Del opened the first door, it touched the corner of the table.

Del peered through the open doorway. The second room was a tiny kitchen, and it was a mess. Cupboards had been left open, dishes had been smashed on the floor, and food had been left out for what smelled like days or maybe weeks. Sam and Emma appeared at Del's side.

"Something happened here," said Sam.

Del moved past the other two back into the main room.

"Where are the people who live here?" asked Emma.

"I don't know," said Sam. "But whoever they are, they haven't been here in a while. I'm guessing they won't be back anytime soon either."

"Good," Del announced. "At least we'll have their beds to sleep in. Come here!"

The third room was a bedroom with four beds. They were small, designed for lumens, but they would be more comfortable than the floor. The mattresses had been stripped bare, but there was a pile of blankets in one corner of the room.

"Do you think someone was here looking for something?" asked Sam.

"Could be," said Del. "I think we'll be safe here for one night. We can head for the town in the morning."

Each of them claimed a bed and settled in.

*****

"Wake up," came a whisper in Del's ear.

Moonlight shone through the bedroom window.

"It's still night," Del said.

She looked over at Sam, but he was sound asleep. It hadn't been a girl's voice that had whispered. In fact, it had been a lower voice than Sam's, now that she thought about it. Must have been a dream, Del thought.

She rolled over to go back to sleep, but for a brief moment her eyes remained open. She saw blankets that were peeled back and an empty bed.

"Sam, wake up!" Del shouted. "Emma's gone!"

CHAPTER NINE

Guy's Fear

The next morning, Tolstoy gave a bottle of glow-water and a pack of food to each of the boys before leading them out of his house and along the streets of the secret village. Though it was impossible to tell, being underground and all, it must have been very early—there weren't any other lumens out on the streets of town.

The three of them stopped at a sheer stone wall at the edge of 1300.

"Only Sirah and I know about this way out," he said.

Tolstoy looked around on the ground as if searching for something. "There," he said, carefully adjusting his feet.

"There's no way out here," said Guy. "Just a wall."

Tolstoy winked at them and touched the wall. He wrapped his cloak around himself several times, but as his inner gold glow intensified, it still shone through his clothing. His skin began to change, then everything else about him, until he had completely transformed into a very large rock, perfectly balanced where Tolstoy's feet had been.

A small bit of rocky ground under Tolstoy gave way, dropping a few inches. Phil heard a click, then a faint rattling of chains. Part of the wall dropped slowly away, folding down like a drawbridge. Chains lowered the rock door until it lay flat in from of them.

Tolstoy transformed back into a lumen, and the three of them ran through the gate. The chains pulled the stone back into place, and if it hadn't been for the glow from Tolstoy, they would have been in total darkness.

"Ingenious, don't you think?" said Tolstoy. "Only a rock is heavy enough to open the door, but what are the odds that a lumen will turn into a rock in exactly the right spot to open it?"

Tolstoy laughed to himself as Guy and Phil just stood staring blankly. Phil wasn't particularly impressed.

"Right then," Tolstoy began. "Up the stairs."

He walked a few paces past Phil and Guy and then began leading them up a narrow and very steep staircase.

*****

Phil was ready for a break. He felt as if he had been climbing a mountain, not a staircase. When they reached the top and Tolstoy swung open a door to the outside, Phil realized why he felt that way. They had climbed a mountain—they had just been inside it.

Tolstoy allowed the boys to take some food and water from their provisions before setting off. He led them along a path that had been cut into the face of the rock. There was a terrifying drop off the edge, and Phil and Guy stayed as close to the side of the mountain as possible.

Tolstoy had said that the Violet Wood wasn't far, but it was always difficult to tell what lumens meant when they said that sort of thing. Did he mean a few hours of walking, or would it be more like a few days?

Phil hoped that approaching the Violet Wood from the mountains might help them remember which mountain belonged to Mr. Thicket. Perhaps there would be a place somewhere along the mountain passes where they could look out over the Violet Wood and spot Mr. Thicket's hideout.

A cool breeze blew across the face of the mountain. The air was damp. Gray clouds hung overhead. As Phil looked out from the path, all he could see was gray mountains. There were no trees, just gray. Nothing looked particularly ominous—just lifeless. They trudged on.

"What if we can't find him?" asked Guy after they had already been walking through the mountains for what seemed like half a day.

"We will," Phil answered, but he wasn't sure if he believed what he was saying.

It was beginning to rain lightly when Tolstoy stopped. Before them was an archway made of rock that soared high over the path. It looked as if it belonged to a castle ruin, as though they were about to pass through an ancient gate.

"This is as far as I go," said Tolstoy. "I wish I could help you find him, but I am sworn to protect the village and must return before nightfall. We all vowed to never go beyond the gate into the eighteenth province without the permission of the council."

"But—" Phil began.

"You will be okay," said Tolstoy. "We are close

enough to the Violet Wood now. Through this gate and around the next bend you will find a bridge. Cross it and follow the path. On the other side of the next mountain you will see it."

"Why can't you just come with us?" asked Guy.

"A vow is a terribly serious thing," Tolstoy replied. "I must abide by it."

"But don't you think the council would understand?" asked Phil.

"No," said Tolstoy. "They wanted me to escort you out of town blindfolded so you could tell no one about us. I have already taken a huge risk keeping you overnight and taking you this far. If I don't get back soon, I will be missed, and I am already in enough trouble with the council. Sirah will only be able to cover for me for so long."

Guy opened his mouth as if to protest again, but Phil stopped him. "We understand," he said. "Thank you for everything."

"You are the Malak," said Tolstoy. "And I know you will rescue us from the darkness. May you find Mr. Thicket soon!"

*****

Phil and Guy said goodbye to Tolstoy and passed under the stone archway. Around the next bend in the path, there was indeed a bridge that spanned a wide gorge between two mountains. It was a suspension bridge made of wood with ropes for its railings.

"Do you think it's safe?" Guy asked.

"I hope so," Phil said.

Phil looked along the bridge and noticed several of

the boards were missing—broken away. The ropes were a little frayed close to the edge as well.

"It doesn't look safe," said Guy.

Phil took a step onto the first board. It creaked and bent a little bit. He held tightly to the rope railings and put his full weight on the first board. It didn't break.

"I guess this board's okay," Phil laughed.

Phil went a little further along and then turned around. The bridge swayed slightly in the breeze.

"I don't know about this," said Guy.

"We'll be fine," said Phil. "We just need to make it across and then around that mountain."

Guy took a step onto the first board and jumped back to the rocky path. "This is a bad idea."

"Come on," said Phil. "We've got to get across now before it starts raining harder."

Guy took a reluctant step back onto the bridge. He winced as though he were in pain as the board creaked under his feet.

They made their way slowly across the bridge, carefully stepping over the places where there were missing boards, always holding tightly to the ropes. A gray mist filled the gorge below them, and dark gray clouds swirled overhead. The wind and rain were picking up.

They had gotten to the mid point of the bridge when a strong gust of wind caused the bridge to swing violently, almost knocking the boys off their feet.

"Whoa!" Phil said, steadying himself by tightening his grip on the ropes.

Guy was nowhere near as calm as Phil, however. Guy was usually brave. He had kept his cool during a storm when their boat had been completely destroyed and when they were attacked by terrifying black-winged creatures. The only time Phil had heard Guy scream out of real fear was when they had flown at top speed on Mr. Thicket's birds. Now, on a bridge rocking in the wind, Guy let the same scream go.

Another gust of wind blew through the gorge as the clouds above them got darker. A storm was coming right at them.

"It's going to be okay," Phil yelled over his shoulder. "We'll be okay."

"How do you know?" Guy shouted back as the bridge swung some more. "We're going to die out here."

"We've got to keep moving," said Phil.

Guy didn't respond. Phil shuffled his feet along the bridge, which continued to swing in the ever-increasing wind.

"Just one step at a time," Phil yelled after a few paces, glancing back at Guy.

Guy had not moved a muscle. He was in the dead center of the bridge, his knuckles white from gripping the ropes so tightly.

"Come on, Guy!" Phil shouted. "You've got to move."

"I can't!" Guy yelled.

"You have to! We can't stay out here."

Phil made his way along the bridge to his friend. He placed his hands on Guy's hands.

"We're in this together," Phil said. "I'm with you. We're getting off this bridge."

Phil began loosening Guy's grip on the ropes. He felt Guy relax a little, even though the wind continued pushing them around. Phil slid Guy's hand along the rope.

"Okay," Phil said. "Now your feet. You can do it."

Guy shuffled forward one step.

"That's it," said Phil. "Now a bit quicker. Don't look at anything except me. Just follow me and we'll be okay."

Phil kept his hands on Guy's hands and backed along the bridge, guiding Guy the whole way. As they shuffled slowly across, Phil looked over his shoulder every now and again to make sure he had his footing.

The wind howled, rocking the bridge from side to side. The clouds continued growing darker. They were losing light fast.

"We need to pick up our pace," said Phil.

Guy nodded. He seemed to be regaining his composure.

They kept moving, a little more quickly. Guy was relaxing. The worst was over, it seemed, even if the storm around them was picking up. They were going to make it, Phil thought. Hopefully, they could find shelter on the other side before the storm got any worse.

Flashes of lightning lit up the dark clouds above and the mist below. Thunder boomed. They were still on the bridge. A giant clap of thunder cracked as a massive lightning bolt flew past them. Guy's grip on the ropes tightened as his high-pitched scream rang out. Phil screamed as well, gripping Guy's hands.

They were almost to the other side. They were so close. Phil summoned all the courage he had and tried to loosen Guy's grip, but Guy was not budging.

"You have to, Guy," said Phil.

Guy wouldn't look at Phil. He looked down into the mist. Phil leaned over as he spoke directly into Guy's ear. "We're almost there. We're going to make it."

Lightning lit up the gorge again. The eyes of both boys were trained on the mist below, which from the flash of lightning changed in an instant from the dull gray to a bright white and back again. Phil could have sworn he saw something in the mist.

"Come on, Guy," Phil ordered. "We're going."

Phil grabbed Guy's wrists and pulled with all his might, but Guy wasn't moving. He was stronger than Phil, and his whole body was tensed up.

"Enough!" Phil yelled. "There's something down there. We have to get off this thing, now! No more being a baby! You have to stop being afraid."

"I'm not afraid!" Guy exploded.

As he yelled, he let go of both of the ropes and batted Phil's hands away. For a few seconds, neither of them were holding on. Those few seconds were all that the storm needed. Thunder boomed and lightning struck as a great gust of wind swung the bridge faster than it had moved before. Both boys lost their footing.

As Phil fell, he managed with one hand to grab the rope that held the floorboards of the bridge together. With his other hand, he reached for Guy, who had already fallen too far from the bridge to grab any part of it himself—but the bridge was already swinging away from Guy. Phil wasn't even close. The mist below enveloped his friend, whose high-pitched scream was drowned out by the sounds of thunder and Phil's own cry: "No!"

CHAPTER TEN

Messages and a Map

Del and Sam scrambled out of the cabin and scanned the meadow. Everything glowed in silver and gold, and the grass swayed gently. There was no sign of Emma at first.

"Where is she?" asked Sam.

Del raced around the side of the cabin and saw her walking away from them, directly toward the cliffs.

"Emma!" Del called. "What are you doing up in the middle of the night?"

Emma didn't respond. She just kept walking. In the moonlight, her golden hair seemed to dance with the same glow as the grass that surrounded her. She shimmered as she walked, surrounded by the light of Azdia.

Del and Sam started to run toward Emma. Emma didn't change her pace at all, nor did she turn back anytime that Del or Sam called her name. They reached her just as she was one step from plummeting to her death.

Del grabbed her, and Emma went completely limp, collapsing into Del's arms.

"She's asleep," Del said.

"Do you think she was sleepwalking?" Sam asked.

Before Del could answer, Emma's eyes fluttered open. "What are we doing outside?" she said.

"Sam thinks you might have been sleepwalking," said Del.

"Really?" said Emma. "My parents told me about it happening a few times before, but I was really little."

"Well, it happened tonight," said Del.

"And you almost walked right off the cliff," said Sam.

"The cliff?" Emma repeated, obviously still groggy. "No, I wasn't going to the cliff, I was about to turn, and you stopped me."

"What are you talking about?" Del asked.

"I was dreaming," said Emma. "We're supposed to find something here, and I was walking to it in my dream. Where was I when you stopped me?"

"Right here," said Del, standing up.

"And I was about to turn…"—Emma thought for a moment—"that way."

All three of them looked in the direction Emma pointed. The gnarled tree with no leaves was no more than ten paces from where they stood. Part of the tree grew out of the grassy part of the meadow, but half of its roots jutted out of the ground and wrapped around massive sections of rock. It was as if the roots were holding the top part of the cliff face together and keeping it from falling into the sea below.

"Why am I not surprised that you're pointing at a tree?" said Sam.

The three of them walked up to the tree.

"Now what?" asked Emma.

"You're asking us?" said Del. "You're the one with

the dream."

"I don't know," said Emma. "You woke me up too early, I guess."

"You'd rather we let you fall off the cliff?" said Del.

"Do you think the tree is alive?" asked Sam. "It doesn't seem to be glowing, and there aren't any leaves." He placed a hand on the trunk, which immediately lit up. "Never mind," he said.

He had barely gotten the words out before three branches, as fast as anything, swooped down from above. The ends of the branches turned into vines that slithered like a snake quickly attacking its prey. One of the vines wrapped itself quickly around Sam's wrist. Del jumped toward Sam to help him, and Emma jumped back away from the tree. Their movements were slow compared to the vines. Another wrapped itself around Emma's waist, and another got Del's arm.

Emma was screaming her head off. Another vine came down and covered her mouth, muffling the sound. She continued to struggle to get free, as did Del and Sam, but it was no use. The tree pulled Del closer to its trunk. If she didn't know better, she would have sworn that it was looking at her, examining her in some way.

Then she thought: *This is Azdia: that is exactly what this tree is doing.*

The examination didn't last long, however. The vines lifted the three of them off the ground and held them out over the cliff. Del looked down. The drop must have been as long as three football fields. Her mind raced, trying to think what she would do when the vine dropped her and her friends. She immediately grabbed ahold of the vine with her free hand, clinging tightly.

Crack! It sounded as if a tree branch had snapped

off. Another crack sounded, and then the roots of the tree began to move very slowly. Their movement was accompanied by a creaking sound and the sound of rock grinding against rock. It wasn't only the roots that were moving—the roots were moving the boulders that they held as well.

The roots were acting like fingers on the invisible hand of a giant, slowly but easily moving the boulders aside as though they were pebbles. When the creaking and grinding sounds stopped, the vines lowered Del, Sam, and Emma into a cave that had been revealed behind the rocks. The vines gently set their feet onto solid rock and released them.

Del looked up at the rocks above her. There was no easy way to climb back up to the meadow and cabin above. They had left everything in the cabin. They had no provisions and no supplies with them. Day was beginning to dawn, and it looked as though their only option was to walk into a dark cave.

"You said we were supposed to find something," said Del to Emma. "Let's hope it's something good."

"At least the tree didn't kill us," said Sam.

*****

They moved single file into the cave and found themselves in quite a large cavern. The walls and floor were solid gray rock, but overhead were the roots of the grass from the meadow glowing in shades of pink, yellow, and turquoise. The roots on the ceiling provided plenty of light for them.

The first thing Del noticed was what must have been thousands of tiny pieces of paper strewn across a large table and scattered around the floor as well. There were pictures drawn on each piece of paper, as though a little child had been drawing for days on end.

In one corner, there was what looked like a telescope, but it was wide rather than long. There was a square piece of black wood next to the strange telescope, and there was a round hole in the wall the width of the scope. The morning light was just beginning to shine through the hole.

One of the walls had three doors, and each door was labeled with numbers over the top of it. The first door had 13–14 over the top of it, the second had 15–17, and the third had only the number 18. On another wall was a large map. Del, Sam, and Emma walked over to it to get a better look.

The map was covered with numbers. The numbers thirteen through eighteen were in the largest script on the map.

"This is a map of Azdia," said Sam. "Those big numbers show the provinces, and look at all the towns —they're there as well."

"There's eighteen and the Violet Wood," said Del, pointing. "This is how we'll know where to go."

Emma wandered over to an opening in one of the walls. "You can see the town from here," she said.

Del and Sam joined her at the opening and looked out. The three of them turned together and looked at the far wall at the three unopened doors.

"I guess we have to check what's behind them, don't we?" said Emma.

"I'll do it," said Del.

Emma and Sam stood by the window as Del approached the first door. She glanced at the wooden sign hanging above it. Inscribed on the sign was 13–14. She turned the doorknob and pulled. She heard a kind of humming and jumped back, startled.

Del turned to Sam and Emma and said, "Birds."

Del put her head inside the room and then pulled back.

"There's tons of them," she said over her shoulder. Sam and Emma joined Del, and together, they walked slowly into the first room.

On two walls facing each other, there were small cages from floor to ceiling, and each cage had its own number. Some cages were empty, but some contained gray birds about the size of a pigeon. All of the birds looked identical, and each had a tiny tube attached to one of its legs. Each cage had a small dish, some containing bits of seed, others empty. Each cage also had a tube that stretched from the cage up to the ceiling. All of the tubes—there must have been at least fifty of them—went to one place. Above their heads was a large reservoir of water.

"That's a smart way to give them all water," said Sam.

The sight was all rather un-Azdian: gray birds, no color, no glowing, cages, tubes. Of course, Del had only a very limited experience with lumens, but Del was surprised to see any caged animals in Azdia. She had a feeling that this was not the way Azdia was supposed to be.

"These are carrier pigeons," said Emma suddenly.

"They're what?" asked Del and Sam together.

"Carrier pigeons," Emma repeated. "At least I think that's what they are. I saw a show that had carrier pigeons in it last year. My dad told me that way back in the olden days, people used to use them to get messages to people. That's what the tube things on their legs are for. That's where the message goes."

"And that's what all the little bits of paper are out there, I guess." said Del. "They're messages."

"Do you think the numbers on the cages are towns?" asked Sam.

Del looked more closely at the numbered cages, knowing that if Sam asked a question like that, he was working on a theory.

Sam pointed. "Look up there."

At the top of the cages on one wall was the number 13, and on the other wall, 14.

"The number at the top is the province," Sam continued. "And the number on the cage is the town in that province. It looks like each town gets more than one bird, because some of the numbers are there more than once."

Sam was getting excited as he spoke and figured things out on the fly. "There are five cages for 1301, 1302, and 1303. Then you've got 1304, 1305, and 1306 with three cages, and 1307 with six cages. And that's it for thirteen. I bet if you check the map there are only seven towns in the thirteenth province."

They ran out of the room to look at the map. Sam was right. They found the thirteenth province and the seven marked towns, 1301 through 1307. Sam ran back across the room and opened the second door that was marked 15–17. He went inside and came back out quickly. "This room's the same, just three walls have cages instead of two."

He swung the final door open and checked inside. "Whoa!"

"What is it, Sam?" said Del.

"It's packed full," said Sam. "There are way more cages and way more birds."

"That makes sense," said Del, who was still standing with Emma by the map. "Eighteen has way more towns than any other province."

Sam joined the girls in front of the map. "We know we're somewhere on the coast," he said. "If we can find out what town that is across the bay, then we could use the map to get to the Violet Wood."

"Or we just find someone in town who can lead us there like Crimson did," said Del.

As they searched the rooms and the cavern some more, they found that most of what was there was for the care of the birds, including a few sacks of birdseed. They tried eating it. It wasn't very good, but Del was surprised that she didn't despise it. Maybe she was just that hungry.

What they didn't find in their search was a way out. They returned to where the vines had dropped them into the cave, and everything had changed. Del's heart sunk as she looked at the rocks in front of her. The tree roots had put the boulders back in place. They were trapped.

CHAPTER ELEVEN

Saved Again

Phil hung onto the ropes of the bridge as it swung violently. He stared helplessly down into the misty gorge where he had seen Guy disappear. Lightning flashed, and he could have sworn he saw something. Yes, there was something down there. It was flying toward him. Any second, he would see it fully.

Phil pulled himself up onto the bridge to try to steady himself. If something was about to attack him, he needed to get ready, or better, get to the other side of the bridge. Lightning flashed again. Whatever it was was still flying toward him. It was big. He wouldn't stand a chance.

Before Phil could move any farther, the mist parted slightly, and up shot his assailant. His heart skipped a beat at what he saw. How could it be? How could he have found them? How could he have known?

Guy, terrified but alive, sat perched atop a large cream-colored bird, sitting behind their savior—Azdia's savior. Phil looked on in wonder at the sight of Mr. Thicket, his long blond hair blowing wildly in the wind.

The bird flew past Phil, high into the air, up to the

dark clouds. In one hand, Mr. Thicket held reins to direct his bird, and in the other he held what looked like a glowing piece of glass. Was it what Phil thought it was?

Lightning flashed through the gorge again, but this time, the bolt headed straight for Mr. Thicket, Guy, and the bird. Mr. Thicket held his one hand high in the air, and the lightning struck his outreached hand. The Crystal Seed absorbed the bolt of lightning. Mr. Thicket let out a cry, but it was not a cry of pain. It was joyful, as though he had just won some great victory. He had a huge smile on his face.

Mr. Thicket hid the Crystal Seed inside his cloak and steered his bird back down toward Phil. Phil instinctively let go of the rope railing and held his arms up to Mr. Thicket, who grabbed him and hoisted him up onto the bird to sit in front of him. Guy was hanging on around Mr. Thicket's waist, cowering.

"That's twice now that I've had to rescue you," Mr. Thicket said.

"Thank you," was all Phil could say.

They soared higher through the black storm clouds. They increased in speed, faster and faster, until they were completely clear of the storm.

"Where are your friends?" Mr. Thicket asked.

"We don't know," said Phil. "We need your help to find them. We were trying to find you."

"Very well," said Mr. Thicket. "They are in Azdia, then? Sam and Del?"

"Yes," said Phil. "And my sister Emma."

"Let's get indoors," said Mr. Thicket. "I'll take you home."

"Under the mountain?" Phil asked.

"Yes," said Mr. Thicket, pulling out the Crystal Seed from under his cloak and holding it in front of Phil. "Don't worry, my boys. We'll find them. If we work together, we'll definitely find them."

*****

Phil was relieved to be out of the wind and rain, flying with Mr. Thicket up above the storm, just under the thin gray clouds. He felt lighter than air sitting in front of the protector and savior of Azdia. He knew that he and Guy would be okay even though he could hear Guy whimpering and almost feel his shivering at the back of the bird.

Phil's thoughts went to his sister. He had tried to stop Del from taking her to Azdia. He remembered trying to grab Emma and then her getting sucked through. Del and Sam had dove in after her before he could react. He had been quick to follow but not quick enough, barely touching Sam's hand while holding tightly to Guy's. Why had Del been so determined to come back? And why had she wanted so badly to bring Emma with her? Why hadn't he been faster or stronger? None of that mattered now. They just needed to find them and get them home.

The Crystal Seed was right there in front of him in Mr. Thicket's hand. The seed was their way home, and the one who had sent them back the last time had it. They just needed to find Del, Sam, and Emma and then use the seed to go home. At least it wouldn't be like last time, where they had to find the seed first, using a riddle they didn't understand, and then trick Old Blythe to even get a chance of getting back. This time, Mr.

Thicket had the key to the portal home.

They hurtled toward one of the high peaks. It looked familiar. It was Mr. Thicket's mountain. Just below the top, a small opening presented itself. They flew right into it at top speed. All went dark except for the swirling green light of the Crystal Seed. The bird was in a steep dive inside the mountain tunnel. Guy wasn't screaming, but behind him, Phil could feel Guy's grip tightening around Mr. Thicket's waist. He hoped the man would still be able to breathe by the time they reached the bottom.

Seconds later, the bird was circling around inside a large open cavern. Torches lined the walls. A welcoming party of lumens, all without light, waited for them. Eleven other birds sat on perches along one wall. Sculptures lined the other walls. A large table was set in the middle.

The bird landed, and two lumens approached to help them dismount. Mr. Thicket lowered Phil and then peeled Guy off himself and got him to the ground as well. Guy looked terrible, as though he had been in some kind of fight.

"You going to be all right?" Phil said.

Guy nodded once and looked down.

Mr. Thicket jumped off the bird. "Let's see about you getting cleaned up a little bit, shall we?"

He clapped his hands, and a lumen appeared in front of him.

"Make preparations for a good meal," Mr. Thicket ordered. He turned to two other lumens. "Take Master Phil and Master Guy to their rooms so that they can dry off." Looking at Phil and Guy, he added, "I hoped for the day when you would return, though I had hoped it would be all of you. In your rooms, you will find suitable fresh clothes. Change and be back here as soon as you can for supper."

The lumens led Phil and Guy along the familiar hallway to the exact same rooms they had occupied before.

Before going into his room, Phil said, "You sure you're going to be okay?"

Guy coughed. "Yeah, I'll be okay."

Phil opened his door, but before he entered, Guy said, "D-don't tell anybody, okay?"

"You're the toughest guy I know," Phil said.

Guy managed half a smile and went into his room. Phil went into his as well.

*****

Almost everything was the same as the last time Phil had been here. The room was spacious and decorated nicely with a bed, dresser, desk, and a couple of comfy chairs. There were two lamps burning brightly, giving plenty of light. The only major difference in the room from last time was that over in one corner was a large bathtub. It was full of water with steam rising out of it. Next to the tub was a small chair with a towel hanging over it.

A set of clothes had been laid out on the bed. They were simple but dry: a pair of black pants, a tan shirt and sweater, socks, and underwear. Everything looked to be about his size. He supposed the lumens must have made the clothes by hand.

Phil took off everything and got in the bath. It felt fantastic. The water didn't glow at all. It felt a lot more like home than Azdia, except that the tub wasn't as nice as home. It seemed to be made out of some sort of metal and wasn't the most comfortable thing in the world to lie down in, but it was warm, and it was clean. Phil dunked his head under. He found a bar of soap next to the tub on the seat of the chair. They had really thought of everything.

As he sat soaking he began to get really hungry. He got out, toweled off, and put on the lumen-made clothes. Although not necessarily what Phil would have chosen for fashion, they were at least dry.

He left the room to find two lumen attendants waiting.

This was a nice touch, he thought. *Wouldn't want to get lost on the way back to supper.*

Phil knocked on Guy's door, and Guy promptly opened it and came out into the hallway.

"I'm starving," said Guy.

The old Guy was back.

"Bath?" asked Phil.

"Yeah."

"Me too."

The boys followed their attendants down the hall. The smell of delicious food wafted over them.

"I meant what I said before," Phil whispered to Guy. "Toughest guy I know."

*****

The table in Mr. Thicket's great hall was full of food. There were several containers of hot soup, loaves of bread, and many varieties of cheese, meat, and fruit. There was far more than they could eat, and it all looked fantastic.

Next to each of their ornately carved chairs was a high stool and a little ladder leading to the top of it. A lumen scrambled up each ladder and stood on top of each stool, ready to serve. Phil knew the drill from the last time they had been here. Just point at what you want, and the lumen on the stool would put it on your plate.

Del had seemed uncomfortable with this and with the fact that the lumens were dark. Phil knew better, though. The dark lumens were happy, and they loved to serve. They loved Mr. Thicket. He had given them everlasting life, after all.

Guy seemed to embrace being waited on as well, probably because he was almost always hungry. He pointed at pretty much the entire spread and soon had a pile of food on his plate along with three different bowls of soup.

"I know we're not supposed to toast to you," Phil said to Mr. Thicket. "And don't worry, I'm not going to do that. But I just want to say thank you. You saved us again."

"It is what I do, and what I love doing, my boy," Mr. Thicket replied. "You're welcome."

They ate and drank. Somehow, Guy finished everything in front of him and pointed for more cheese and meat afterward.

"Why don't you tell me what happened," said Mr. Thicket.

"Well, we weren't going to come back," said Guy.

"At least, not right away," Phil lied, not wanting Mr. Thicket to think that they never wanted to come back when he so clearly wanted them there with him.

"Del really wanted to come back right away," said Phil.

"Made up a crazy story about you not being Mr. Thicket," said Guy through a mouthful of food.

"We think she must have had some weird dream, or maybe her being sick did something to her," said Phil.

"Was she still sick once she returned home?" asked Mr. Thicket.

"No," said Guy. "You cured her, though, right? You said it would take time to get fully better."

"It was crazy," said Phil. "She said that Old Blythe was actually Mr. Thicket and that she spent a long time with Old Blythe. Then he sent her home and told her she had to return to Azdia because she was the chief of the Malak. She really believes it. I figured if we just didn't come to Azdia for a while, she'd come to her senses. I mean, you were the one who helped us, not him. You saved us before, you helped us get home, and now you've saved us again."

"You're right about Del," said Mr. Thicket. "At least, mostly. When she got back to the cottage, it was clear to me that Old Blythe had put some kind of spell or curse on her, bewitched her in some way. I blame myself for sending her with the task of distracting him. I just didn't know what else to do. I knew if I had been the one to keep him occupied, he would have been suspicious, and we might never have found the Crystal Seed. That's why I sent Del on what may have been too difficult a task.

"She even tried to attack me when she returned, but I got her away from that dangerous Old Blythe and brought her here. I tried to reverse whatever he had done to her, but the more I tried, the more she seemed convinced that somehow Old Blythe was me. Nothing I did seemed to work. I went back to Old Blythe's cottage thinking that if I could capture him, perhaps I could force him to reverse the effects on her. But he was gone.

"I searched everywhere for him without success. Del got worse. She would dream about Old Blythe and about a red lumen, and then she would wake up and believe that it had all been real. I had hoped to set her free from her delusions so she could see the truth, but in the end, all I could do was send her home and hope that everything would go back to normal. Alas, it sounds as if her delusions continued."

Phil didn't know whether to be angry at Mr. Thicket for sending Del with Old Blythe in the first place or to be thankful for everything he had tried to do for her after the fact.

"Del thinks the light has to return to Azdia, and she thinks she somehow is supposed to bring it back," Phil said. "And she's out there."

"You know there were prophecies about this," Mr. Thicket said. "There would be one who would pose as the protector of Azdia but would really lead to the destruction of the lumens."

"You think that's Del?" asked Guy.

"We must find her," said Mr. Thicket. "The salvation of Azdia depends on it. We must find her and—"

"And Sam and Emma too, and we can all go back home, together?" Phil offered.

Mr. Thicket nodded.

"How will we know where to look for them?" asked Guy.

"I may have a way," said Mr. Thicket. "But not tonight. You both look exhausted, and everything can wait until you've slept."

They finished the meal, and Phil and Guy were escorted back to their rooms. They were indeed exhausted. Phil said goodnight to Guy in the hallway, went into his room, and collapsed on the bed.

CHAPTER TWELVE
Into the Fortress

Before meeting Crimson, Kita had never met a lumen who had wanted to accomplish something quickly. He was determined to get to the nearest town, 1501, as soon as possible and find a ship to go across the sea. They had to find Del Ryder.

They had tried to find birds in the forest that would have been large enough to carry them, but they hadn't had any luck. Kita wondered if Verdi, Cinder, and Crimson could simply transform into birds, but they explained to her that 1501 was too far for them to transform and stay in that form. The meager provisions of water and berries collected in the forest wouldn't sustain that kind of metamorphing. They would have needed far more to eat and would have needed to stop for rest too often for Crimson's liking.

They had been about to give up looking for faster transportation and simply begin walking when they came across a herd of massive creatures that Kita had only ever heard about. It turned out that Crimson had ridden these great beasts before. Two feldroes out of a herd of at least twenty agreed to take them most of the way to 1501. Crimson and Kita rode on one feldroe with Cinder, Verdi, and Tabby on the other.

Along the way, at each rest break, Kita began trying to learn her abilities. Verdi had no patience with her, but Crimson and Cinder each took turns giving her advice and trying to encourage her.

She made no progress, however, and was beginning to feel as though she would never be able to metamorph. Her saving grace was Tabby. Most lumens, if they have the chance, learn to metamorph for the first time into a winx because lumens and winxes are able to bond with one another so quickly, and winxes are always more than happy to help. As Kita became more and more frustrated with herself and her inability to metamorph, at least holding Tabby made her feel better.

They developed a rhythm of riding the feldroes during the day and resting and practicing metamorphing at night. This continued until Crimson announced that the feldroes would take them no further.

"They wish to return to the forest—they aren't much for towns," he said. "And we'll be at 1501 soon."

The feldroes left them, and the Company of Light continued on foot.

*****

Kita could see the ancient walls of the fortress-city of 1501 in the distance. During the dark times of long ago, the lumens of the fifteenth province had built the walls in their desperate fight against the forces of Mordlum. No one knew how many battles had happened at this spot, but the walls had always held firm—1501 never fell to Mordlum in a straight fight. Kita had learned from a young age that the more the lumens of the fifteenth province had prepared for war, built up the walls, and fought Mordlum off, the dimmer their lights had become. In order to make sure they could continue to fight, they had organized themselves into an army with ranks and officers, and a commander over the fighting force.

With the ranks and officers came corruption. Rumors of spies among them were rampant, and in the end, one of the high-ranking officers betrayed the lumens of Fifteen. Mordlum and his forces were let into the village-fortress by one of the lesser gates under the cover of night. Once inside, Mordlum removed what light remained from every single lumen in the village. From then on, during the time of darkness, 1501 became one of Mordlum's capitals. Because of 1501's placement on the Great Sea, Mordlum built an even bigger harbor and great ships to go across and conquer the lands on the other side of the sea.

Kita was nervous but excited. She had never previously been outside of her own province, and now she was a member of the new Company of Light going into a famous fortress. After that, she would be going across the sea to find the chief of the Malak in their fight against the growing darkness.

*****

They arrived at the main gate of 1501. The walls loomed above them. A lumen appeared in a high window, near the top of the wall. He peered down at them, squinting his eyes suspiciously. "State your names and business," he said.

"I'm Crimson, and this is Verdi, Cinder, and Kita," said Crimson. "We need a ship to sail across the Great Sea to New Azdia."

"There are no more ships here," the lumen barked down.

"What do you mean, there are no more ships?" Crimson asked. "There is a whole fleet of ships. You have the largest harbor in Azdia."

"The ships all left, and most of the lumens as well, on account of the…" the lumen trailed off.

"If there are no ships, then we need a place to stay for the night," Crimson replied. "We have been traveling, and we are tired."

"We have no room for strangers at the moment. You'll have to move along."

"If most of the lumens left on the ships, then you should have plenty of room!" said Crimson fiercely. "Now let us in."

"I am not authorized to open this gate for anyone who is not from the fifteenth province, and I know you are not!" the guard barked back.

"The darkness is winning when we stop helping each other," said Crimson.

"The darkness doesn't win or lose," said the guard. "It just happens. And when it's a darker time, we all need to be more careful. You should have stayed in your own town and waited for the darkness to pass. That's the best thing to do."

"But surely the lumens of 1501 would know better than anyone that the darkness must be resisted," Crimson shot back.

"The lumens of 1501 know better than anyone that the stories of old are just stories," said the guard.

"But the walls," said Crimson. "The great harbor. What of them?"

"What of them?" the guard retorted. "They're here. Our ancestors were builders and sailors. The walls were built to keep everyone safe during the dark time, and they worked, the same way they're working now. Now, good day." The lumen's face disappeared from the window, and his hand reached out and closed a wooden shutter.

"Now what do we do?" asked Kita.

The company stared at each other blankly.

"Could we fly in if you changed into birds?" asked Kita. She loved the idea of flying.

"We could try," said Crimson. "But if they've got lumens in the watchtowers, we'd be taking an awful risk of being shot down. At best, we'd be tracked and caught when we landed."

"What if we swam in?" asked Cinder. "We just walk around the town to the Great Sea and we swim to the harbor."

"That's not so easy either," Crimson replied. "The walls extend into the harbor, and there are six great iron gates that go under the water and prevent anything from coming in or out."

"So you shrink yourselves down to fit through the bars of the gates," said Kita.

"It's too dangerous," said Crimson. "We might have to metamorph into fish to be able to swim that far, and then we'd have to shrink as fish, change back to regular size, and then change back to lumens. We don't have that kind of energy on the provisions we have left. You will need to learn that we cannot solve every problem simply by metamorphing. It is a powerful ability, yes, but it must be used cautiously."

Kita was surprised to hear Crimson say this. She had heard wild stories of him single-handedly shrinking four Malak, and of him turning into a flying creature to fight off two creatures of darkness. This didn't sound cautious to her. She had signed up for adventure and expected to have the Crimson of adventure. Where was he?

"So what *are* we going to do?" Kita asked.

"Simple," said Crimson. "We're going to try a different gate."

*****

The Company followed the great wall of 1501 until they reached another gate. Not being the main gate, this one was smaller than the first. There was still a small wooden shutter higher up on the wall.

"Let's try something different this time," Crimson said. He walked to the gate and knocked. The shutter opened.

"State your names and business." The same greeting, a different lumen.

"My name is Crimson. This is Verdi, Cinder, and Kita. We come in the name of Eleanor of old and in the name of Mr. Thicket, and we come with a vital message. I demand to see your commanding officer at once."

The lumen above them disappeared, and the wooden shutter closed.

"Well, that worked well," said Cinder. "So onto the

next gate, then?"

"Just wait," said Crimson.

The wooden shutter opened, and the lumen looked down and said, "You've already been to the main gate. They didn't let you in there. I'm not going to let you in here."

"I tried to be nice at the main gate," Crimson replied. "Now, didn't you hear what I said? I demand to see your commanding officer. You do have a commanding officer, I'm sure."

The shutter closed again.

"We wait again?" asked Cinder.

"Yes," said Crimson as he sat on a nearby rock. "I think this one might take a little longer."

The others sat as well. They had all been walking for a very long time. Each of them reached into the packs they were carrying to get some water. Suddenly, bells rang out inside the fortress. The wooden shutter did not open again. The gate did.

*****

The Company put away their provisions and got to their feet. A group of twelve lumens, each wearing helmets and carrying spears, awaited them on the other side of the open gate.

"Come with us," one of them said. The group of twelve surrounded the company and escorted them through the gate and along the empty streets of the fortress.

"Excuse me," Cinder piped up. "Where exactly are you taking us?"

There was no response.

"Excuse me," Cinder said again.

Nothing.

"Hello!" Cinder stopped walking. "I'm not going anywhere until someone tells me what's going on."

"Keep moving," said a lumen from behind.

"No," said Cinder.

The one who had spoken lowered his spear and pointed it at Cinder. "Move!" he shouted.

"No," said Cinder again. "Not until someone tells me where you're taking us. If you're throwing us in jail, fine. I just want to know."

One of the lumens in front turned to face Cinder. He had a stern look on his face. "For some reason, your request has gone right up the chain to the commander," he said. "That could be good for you, or it could be really bad. My vote is for bad. Happy? Let's move."

The group continued along the streets. Kita could see lumen faces looking at them through the windows of houses as they passed. She wondered at the anger of these lumens. It was so out of place. She had never before seen a lumen even hold a weapon, and she had never before seen lumens with such a dim glow. She had been nervous about crossing the Great Sea, but now she was just plain scared. She was just glad that she was with Crimson.

They arrived at a house larger than any house Kita had ever seen, made of orange brick with a thatched roof. Two lumens with spears stood guard outside a white fence that surrounded the house.

The stern lumen who had turned around stepped toward the two guards, and they whispered to one another. The two guards led the entire group through the gate of the fence, along a well manicured path, and up a flight of stairs to a large covered porch. Black double doors opened, and four more guards stepped out onto the porch. One of them said to the twelve original guards, "You're not needed anymore."

The twelve turned and marched back along the path and through the gate. The two fence guards followed them, presumably to return to their posts. The four new guards took the Company inside.

*****

"The commander wishes to welcome you to 1501," one of the guards said.

"A strange kind of welcome," said Cinder.

"You can't be too careful these days," said the guard. "Follow me."

The Company followed the guard through a series of rooms all connected by beautifully carved wooden doors. The other three guards followed in behind. The inside of the house was like nothing Kita had ever seen. There were paintings from floor to ceiling, and even paintings on the ceiling. The trim around everything was gold and was made to look like wings. Some gold wings looked as though they were tucked in, as though the walls were somehow the invisible body of a bird sitting on a perch. Other wings were stretched out across walls like the span of a great bird in flight. The furnishings were beautiful as well. Tables and chairs of the highest quality had been carved to look like various kinds of creatures, so if you sat on one of the chairs, you would look as if you were sitting on the back of some animal of the forest or the plain.

The guard and Company stopped in front of massive

double doors. They were emerald green and studded with gold feathers.

"This is the commander's chamber," said the main guard. "Whatever he decides to do with you will be done."

He opened the doors.

"Send them in," a voice called. "And guards—stay outside with the doors closed."

The Company walked into the commander's chamber, and the doors closed behind them.

CHAPTER THIRTEEN

Towns in Trouble

As soon as the boulders sealed them inside the cavern, Emma panicked. "What are we going to do?" she asked. "We can't stay in here. There's only birdseed to eat. I don't want to die in here."

"Calm down," said Del. "It's not that bad. We can figure this out."

"Maybe we can figure out how the messages work, and we can send a bird for help," said Sam.

"How are we going to figure them out?" said Emma.

"I don't know," said Sam. "But it's worth trying."

They went over to the table, and Sam began sorting through papers.

"They're mostly pictures and numbers," said Sam. "There's some writing on them, but it seems like lumens communicate through pictures—like in ancient Egypt."

"They're called hieroglyphics," said Emma.

"I know," said Sam.

Del thought about how much Sam knew. He read a lot, and Del knew that Sam especially loved all things ancient Egyptian or ancient Greek, as well as anything to do with space, which wouldn't really help them much now.

"Do you really think you're going to find anything helpful?" Del whispered to Sam.

"Maybe," said Sam. "It seems like on every message there is a number and also a picture of a cliff with a star on it. I think we are at the cliff with the star, and the number is always one of the towns on the map. I think maybe that's the 'to' and the 'from' for the message."

"Okay?" said Del.

"I'm working on something, all right?" said Sam.

"Okay, okay—what do you need us to do?" Del asked.

"Look for numbers that are the same," Sam said. "We should put all the messages from the same towns together to see if there is anything we can find that might help us."

Del, Sam, and Emma got busy sorting. As the day continued, they looked at hundreds of papers, each with their own numbers, pictures, and symbols. They made piles for every town, but they couldn't figure out how the symbols worked. They took breaks from the papers every now and again to eat birdseed and to try to find a way out. Nothing presented itself, and no one showed up to help them.

The light outside faded. They were tired, and eventually they fell asleep on the floor under the table that was now covered in neatly piled papers.

*****

It was the middle of the night when Del awoke and saw Sam in the corner looking at the telescope-like instrument.

"Sam, what are you doing?" Del whispered loudly.

Sam dropped the piece of wood that had sat beside the telescope-thing, and it echoed as it hit the stone floor. Emma sat bolt upright and hit her head on the bottom of the table so hard that a bit of wood popped off the edge of the table and fell to the ground.

"Ouch!" said Emma, rubbing her head.

"You broke the table," said Del, picking up the piece of wood and trying to fix it back onto the table edge.

"Wait," said Sam. "I've seen that shape."

Del looked at the piece of wood in her hand; it was a rather odd shape. It had jagged edges, and it occurred to Del that there was no way that Emma could have broken this off the table simply by knocking her head. It looked as if it had been cut, fabricated to fit into the table's edge and hidden there.

Sam stood beside the map, pointing. Indented on the wall, cut into the rock, was the exact same shape as the piece of wood that Del now held. Del brought the piece over and slotted it into the space that it was clearly made to fit. She tried jiggling the piece of wood, and to her surprise, the rock around it moved. She turned it more deliberately, and a small section of rock turned with it. She turned it as far as she could until it would not turn anymore. Then, nothing happened.

"That's weird," said Del. "What did I just do?"

"I think…" Sam began. He pushed on the rock wall, and a large section of it gave way, swinging away from him as if on giant hinges. "I think it's a door, and we just found the key."

"We wanted to find a way out," said Del. "I guess this is it."

"Or it leads somewhere terrible," said Emma.

"I don't think anyone would hide a key to a dungeon or something here," said Sam. "I actually think the thing in the corner might be used for sending signals somewhere. If this tunnel doesn't work out, then we can just come back—I might be able to figure it out."

"Let's go down the tunnel," said Del.

All three of them stood looking into the opening. No end to the passageway could be seen. It appeared to just go straight on and on.

"I think we should put the piece of wood back," said Sam.

"I think you're right," said Del who was closest to the key. As she went to grab it, she heard something that distracted her. It was the flutter of wings. She whipped around to see a pigeon fly into the room through the opening. It sailed over to the table and landed there, scattering some of the papers.

Sam, Del, and Emma walked slowly toward the bird. It seemed unconcerned by their approach.

"One of us is going to have to get the message from its leg," Sam whispered.

"I'm not doing it," said Emma.

"Me neither," said Sam.

"Fine," said Del. "I'll do it."

Sam and Emma stopped near the end of the table as Del moved closer to the bird. Del reached out to grab the tube on the pigeon's leg, but before she could get it, a second bird landed on the table, causing the first bird to flap its wings and jump back a few inches. More papers flew off the table and scattered over the surface. Startled, Del jumped back as well.

Del looked over at Sam and Emma. "What's going

on?"

Sam and Emma shrugged.

Del inched forward, grabbed the leg of the nearest pigeon, opened the container on its leg, and pulled out the slip of paper. She unrolled it. On the paper near the top was a picture of a cliff with a star and the number 1303. In the middle of the paper was a symbol. It looked like a house with flames coming out of the top of it. Del quickly grabbed another pigeon and got its message. It had the cliff with the star as well, the number 1302, and an identical house on fire symbol.

She held up the two messages for Sam and Emma to see. "They're the same," she said.

"What do you think they mean?" Emma asked. "Houses on fire?"

"I don't think it can mean anything good," said Del.

"We've seen this before," said Sam. "We grouped messages by number, but I'm sure I've seen that symbol before, I think in almost all of the towns of Thirteen."

Sam rummaged through some papers on the table.

"Look here," he said. "This one is from 1306. Del, check that pile there. Emma, check that one."

They each sorted through different piles of papers. Sure enough, Del found a house on fire message from 1304, and Emma found one from 1305. The only towns in the thirteenth province that they couldn't find a house on fire paper for were 1301 and 1307.

"Something terrible is happening in the thirteenth province," said Sam.

"Do you think the town across the bay is 1301?" Del asked.

"It could be," said Sam, glancing at the map on the wall and then out the opening. "1301 is on the coast, and everything looks peaceful and quiet down there. Of course, we have no way of knowing if we are even in the thirteenth province. There are plenty of towns on the coast in fourteen and fifteen on the map."

"We still should try out the passageway, I think," said Del. "See where it leads."

"We have to take care of the birds first," said Emma. She went into one of the bird rooms and returned with dishes of birdseed and water. She placed them on the table, and the two birds started eating.

Sam and Emma went into the passageway, and Del removed the key from the stone keyhole. She put it back in its place on the edge of the table and joined the other two. They went several steps down the passageway. Del's eyes adjusted to the dimmer light. She still couldn't see any end to, or even any bend, in the path ahead.

"How far do you think we should go before we turn back?" asked Emma.

"Until it's a dead end, I guess," said Del, looking over her shoulder at the others. "Oh, no. Go back! The door's closing!"

Emma, who was behind Sam, turned and ran back as the stone door swung closed.

Boom. She got back just as it slammed shut. Sam and Del arrived and began searching for a way to re-open the door. There was no handle, and none of them could find a seam in the rock. It was as if there had never been a door there at all. They were stuck in darkness. There was no going back. The only way was along the endless passageway.

*****

The passageway was damp and cold and completely dark. They felt their way along it, not knowing where it might lead. Hours passed. The tunnel eventually took several turns, sloping down for most of their journey, sometimes quite steeply. Finally, they turned a corner, and a dim light appeared ahead.

"Thank heaven!" sighed Emma.

The narrow tunnel widened into a small cavern. The source of the light was coming from an opening on the far side. They went into it. It was another tunnel, but this one had flaming torches lining the walls. Someone had definitely built this and had used it recently.

This new tunnel had a steady upward incline and got progressively less cold and damp than the other. After another long trek along the upward tunnel, they met their first choice. The tunnel before them split into two.

"Which way?" Sam asked.

"I don't know," said Emma. "We've been down here for hours. I can't even think."

"Let's go to the right," said Del.

They did, and after a few steps, there was another branch in the road. They could see ahead of them that there were several other openings leading off this main tunnel. It was as if they were on a main street and there were all kinds of side streets running off it.

"How are we supposed to know where we're going?" asked Emma.

"We aren't," said Del. "We just have to keep going."

"And hope we find something helpful," said Sam.

Aside from the children feeling lost, which was nothing new for being in Azdia, not much happened in the underground maze. In fact, "maze" is probably not the best word to describe where they were, because it was all quite well-organized. There were several wide well-lit tunnels, and there were much narrower tunnels that contained less torchlight. They initially stuck to only the wider passages. The narrower ones were just too small; a lumen would have easily been able to walk through, but Del wasn't sure if Emma would manage to squeeze herself in.

After walking the main tunnels for a while and getting nowhere, they stopped to regroup.

"I feel like we've been walking in circles," said Emma.

"We have," said Sam. "But I think we've actually covered all the larger tunnels."

"We've got to try the smaller ones to see if there's a way out," said Del.

"I'll go into one and check it out," said Sam. Del was surprised at his bravery in offering, but of course, every now and again, Sam would get brave in the face of something that seemed quite terrifying to Del. Del didn't particularly like closed-in spaces, and the smaller they got, the more afraid she got.

Sam chose the closest small tunnel and crawled inside. Del looked in after him. In front of Sam, there was flickering light shining down from an opening in the ceiling. Sam turned over on his back to look up into the opening. He looked back at Del.

"There's a door up there," he said. "There's another overhead opening farther along the tunnel, though. I'm going to check it out."

Sam wriggled along the tunnel and quickly arrived at the second overhead opening. He turned onto his back to look up.

"Another door," he said. "And there's more openings

father along. Should I keep going?"

"Come back," said Del. "I don't think Emma will be able to make it that far. We should try this first door. She might make this one."

Del squeezed herself into the tunnel and shimmied into the first overhead opening. Her face was next to a small torch, which was set back into the wall of the small vertical opening. Over her head was a perfectly round door with a small knob in the center. She reached for the doorknob and turned it, then pushed. The door moved up.

She called back to the others, "The door opens. C'mon."

Del pushed harder on the door, and it swung right up, staying flipped open. Above her head was a small space and then planks of wood. She pulled herself up and rolled to one side to make room for Emma and Sam.

Sam's head popped up through the hole, and his body followed. Emma came next—she had managed to squeeze through.

"Where are we?" Emma asked.

"I think we're under a building," said Del.

Sam moved along the ground, following the crawlspace to the place where the side of the building touched the ground. "This way," he called, and he pushed on the side, which gave way easily. They were out.

Sam rolled away, out of sight. Del and Emma crawled quickly to catch up to him, and then they rolled out from under the building. Before she had a chance to look around at anything, Del felt heat around her. The building they had been under was on fire. The three of them scrambled to their feet and turned in a circle, taking in their surroundings. They were in the town, but every building—everything around them in fact—was burning.

CHAPTER FOURTEEN

Dark City

Phil and Guy met in the hallway after being awoken by their lumen attendants, who led them to the great hall for breakfast. The meal was as lavish as any other they had had while in Azdia and far better than anything Phil ever got at home.

Mr. Thicket was absent for most of the meal. He turned up near the end but did not sit down to eat.

"I trust you've had plenty to eat this morning and are well rested," he said. "I've got a big day planned for us. Are you ready for some flying?"

"I'm not flying anywhere," Guy said.

"I understand," said Mr. Thicket. "I can give you a drink that will help calm your nerves, or I can just take Master Phillip, and he can fill you in later."

"I'll be okay if you want to stay here," said Phil, although he wasn't sure if Guy would be okay on his own.

"I'll stay" said Guy. "Phil can go."

"Very well," said Mr. Thicket. He clapped his hands. "Prepare two birds."

Two lumens scurried over to the wall of perches.

They climbed up to the birds and began fitting them with harnesses and reins. Once ready, the two birds flew down from their perches and landed near the table.

"You're sure you don't want to come?" Phil asked.

"I'm sure," Guy said.

"My lumens will get you any food you like anytime," Mr. Thicket said to Guy. "And you're free to explore. My lumens will help you find your way around. Some of them are getting quite good at speaking our language, and most of them understand it now."

"Where are we going, anyway?" Phil asked.

"You'll see," said Mr. Thicket, pulling himself up and onto his bird. "A place that is quite wonderful."

With the help of a small stool and one of the lumens, Phil got up onto his bird. They took off, circled the room once, and shot up through the same tunnel by which they had entered, leaving Guy behind.

*****

The Violet Wood stretched out below them, only it didn't look anything like it had the last time Phil had seen it. The beauty and grandeur of the old forest had been stripped away. Trees had been ripped from the ground and left to rot. Even the purple bark that had shone like glass was chipped and cracked beyond recognition. Phil noticed that many of the trees were missing their roots as though they had been carefully removed.

Mr. Thicket flew close to Phil and shouted, "Look ahead, my boy—beyond the forest."

Phil squinted at the horizon and could see buildings ahead. Was that the town he had visited before? Was it

1875?

"I wanted to show you my pride and joy," Mr. Thicket called. "The future of Azdia. Ahead of you is Tamavaros."

"Who?" said Phil.

"Not who. Tamavaros is the name of the city. It was once known as 1875—I believe you visited it when it was but a shadow of what it is now. Tamavaros is a great city—the first of the new great cities of Azdia."

They flew closer, and Phil began to see what Mr. Thicket meant. 1875 had been a small town—when they had been there before, it hadn't taken them long to cross it. Now it was vast and impressive. The most noticeable thing about Tamavaros was the towering wall that ran along the edge of the nearest buildings. It looked as though it were made of smooth black glass. Phil could see lumens patrolling on top of the great wall.

They flew over it and then above the city, and as they did, Phil could hear a great cheer rising up from below them. The lumens of the city knew Mr. Thicket and were clearly happy to see him fly overhead.

The last time Phil had seen 1875, its streets had been empty, and the buildings had been burnt out or run down. There had been a fear and a sickness gripping the place. Mr. Thicket had been removing the light from lumens, and the ones with light had assumed that something terrible was happening to them. They didn't realize he had been giving them everlasting life. By the looks of this great city, they now understood.

There were new buildings everywhere, built from the same glassy black substance as the walls. To Phil, the city seemed to have a kind of beauty to it. Lumens were busy working, constructing new buildings, it seemed. Everything was neatly ordered. The streets were perfectly straight. It was nothing like it had been.

They flew to a tower that rose above the rest of the buildings. From its top, they looked out over the whole city. Phil could see the edge of the Great Lake. Remarkably, the city walls extended almost to its shores. The new city was massive.

"What do you think?" Mr. Thicket asked.

"It's magnificent," said Phil.

"The lumens here prepare for a new day. They are ready to take everlasting life and give it to all who will receive it. They are at my command and can be at yours as well, my boy."

"Is everyone here happy?" Phil asked.

"They will never die," said Mr. Thicket.

"What will happen to the lumens who don't... understand?"

"Some lumens will, sadly, end up being sacrificed, but they have a choice. Those who do not choose life will die eventually anyway. If they resist us, they will simply meet their end sooner. It is sad, but in the end, look at what will be." Mr. Thicket waved his arm out over the great city and smiled.

Phil couldn't help but be impressed.

"You said they can be at my command as well?" Phil asked.

"They will listen to you," said Mr. Thicket. "They know you are with me. I will establish other cities, and I will need someone wise to help me. You could be truly great, my boy."

"Really?" Phil asked.

"Of course," said Mr. Thicket. "What is now mine

can very soon belong to you. All this can be at your command."

Phil relished the thought of it. His friends already did what he said most of the time, but the idea of an entire city of lumens just waiting for him to tell them what to do—what a thought. He looked at Mr. Thicket. This man had a plan. He was in control. He was using his power to help others, and he wouldn't let anyone stand in his way. He would make tough choices when he needed to. This was the kind of man Phil wanted to be.

*****

Phil and Mr. Thicket spent their day inspecting construction work in the city. Mr. Thicket encouraged his workers who were doing well and yelled at the ones that were, in his words, "too lazy." He had a few lumens taken away because of their shoddy construction work. "We can't have any weak links in our great city," he had said.

The day had been long but awesome. Phil was so impressed to see Mr. Thicket at work. He had rescued all of these lumens and given them a purpose. They had built something amazing.

As the gray light of day faded, their birds carried Phil and Mr. Thicket back toward his mountain. The ride back was silent, except for the wind, which whipped across Phil's cheeks. Flying down the same familiar tunnel into Mr. Thicket's great hall, they landed in the same place from where they had first taken off.

Another meal was awaiting them, and lumen attendants stood around, ready to serve.

Guy loped into the room accompanied by two other

lumens.

"Finally," Guy said. "You've been gone forever."

"Everything okay?" Phil asked.

"Yeah, just really bored," said Guy. "Seems like the only thing to do around here is eat."

"I don't think I've ever heard you complain about that before," said Phil.

"Well, I couldn't eat another thing," said Guy.

"A shame, really," Mr. Thicket chimed in. "It looks as if they've outdone themselves for supper. Come join us anyway. Phil here is probably famished after our day."

"I saw 1875," Phil said. "They're rebuilding it. You should see it, Guy. The lumens there are so happy. It's so different than when we went there. It's called Tamavaros now, and Mr. Thicket is going to build other great cities like it all over Azdia."

They sat down at the table. Guy immediately pointed at a bun and a few pieces of meat. His lumen servant grabbed what he wanted and put it on his plate. Phil looked at him incredulously.

"Well, I can't just sit here and watch you eat, can I?" said Guy.

Phil laughed. "That's the Guy we know and love."

Guy turned to Mr. Thicket and said, "So, how are we going to find Del, Sam, and Emma?"

"Tomorrow," said Mr. Thicket. "Phil and I have had a long day. I'll explain the plan tomorrow."

"That's what you said yesterday," said Guy.

"I know," said Mr. Thicket. "Be patient Master Guy. Tomorrow will be here before you know it."

CHAPTER FIFTEEN

A Gift Received

The commander of 1501 sat on an elaborately carved wooden throne on a raised dais reached by three stairs. The walls around them were bare save for two banners that hung on either side of the dais. Each banner pictured the silhouette of a woman's head in profile, her hair blowing wildly away from her face. Although this was all there was in the room, Kita was immediately filled with hope in seeing the banners.

Eleanor, she thought.

The commander sat straight, looking regal, as if he were more than a commander of a lumen city, maybe the great king of some vast nation. He glowed with a deep green and wore a green cloak, which was fastened together with a large gold pin that was in the shape of a wing.

Next to the commander was a very old lumen. She had a wrinkled, kind face and glowed silver with piercing silver eyes. The silver lumen wore a similar cloak to the commander, but it was fastened with a different pin—this one looked like a miniature cliff with a star near the top of the cliff. She held a walking stick in her hand and had a large brown satchel slung over one shoulder.

"Could it be?" the commander whispered. The silver lumen nodded at him.

The commander cleared his throat and then chirped in the lumen language: "Welcome, friends. I apologize for how you may have been treated, but we have been on high alert for some time. While many lumens have closed their doors for fear of the darkness, we are cautious for a different reason, though my guards have instructions to say nothing. In 1501, we are preparing for war. We know of the darkness in Eighteen and have received reports of whole towns being burned in Thirteen to the north. We expect the forces of darkness will be upon us soon, and we intend to fight. Your presence is a sign of hope for us. We wait for Del Ryder to come and defeat the darkness."

"You know of Del Ryder?" said Crimson.

"And we know of you, if you are indeed Crimson," said the commander.

"I am," said Crimson. "Then you believe the tales of her and me meeting Mr. Thicket?"

"Perhaps you'd better explain, Treola," said the commander.

"If you stand against the darkness," Kita blurted out, "Then why weren't you at the Old Oak? Why weren't you there to convince the others?"

The commander stood up from his throne and said, "You don't think we tried? Our delegation was turned back at sword point by Panak's supporters."

"So why didn't you fight back?" Kita bit back.

Crimson laid a hand on Kita's arm.

"Would you have lumens take up arms against one

132

another?" asked the commander. "We need someone who will be able to inspire hope again. That is not me, and it is not any of you. We believe it is a new chief of the Malak. We believe it is Del Ryder. Now, Treola, please explain the rest."

Kita remained silent as the old silver lumen, Treola, stepped forward. "I was a resident of Koht Valgust."

Every lumen knew about Koht Valgust—the hidden place of solitude that Eleanor had used as a communication center during the dark times. She had taught the lumens how to use birds and light to send messages to one another. Few lumens knew its location other than it being somewhere in the north.

Treola continued: "Very few know that Koht Valgust has always been a place that Eleanor and Mordlum would visit to receive the news of Azdia and to learn where they must visit next to further expel the darkness. Mordlum's last visit was terrible. He was the one with news. We all knew of the growing darkness, of course, but he told us that he suspected that his heir was behind it, the Heir that he thought had been destroyed.

"Worse, however, was the news that Eleanor had been captured. Mordlum believed it was the Heir himself who had her. He was going in search of her, but he told me that if he was unsuccessful, then another would be coming—a new Malak, one who had been to Azdia before—one named Del Ryder. He said that she was the true hope in the face of darkness. She would come to rescue us all, as Eleanor had before her.

"Long after his visit, I received a message from him that he had yet to find Eleanor and had lost any way to return to his world. I sent out birds with messages to every town I could informing them that Del Ryder was coming to restore the light. Only one bird returned. One bird from 1501, with a message that said, 'When nowhere is safe, we will protect you until she comes.' I didn't think I would need protection—that was, until they found us. I was returning to Koht Valgust from a trip to a nearby town for some supplies, and when I got home there were dark lumens, spies for the Heir, everywhere—blocking my way in.

"I returned to the town and spread the word that all needed to flee. Most boarded ships, intending to go across the sea. I would not go with them, however—they had long since lost hope. I knew I needed to come here and join those who truly believed. When I arrived, there were already rumors of Del Ryder appearing at the Old Oak with a lumen named Crimson. Now you have come, and surely, Del Ryder will be here soon."

"We believe Del Ryder will be heading across the sea," Crimson said. "We are here to see about a ship to take us to Old Azdia."

Treola shook her head. "Mordlum was insistent. He charged Del Ryder with rescuing Eleanor should he fail, and he was sure Eleanor was somewhere on this side of the sea."

"If that is true," said Crimson, "our greatest duty is to assist her in that rescue, and I know where Del would be heading. She would be going to the Violet Wood. She met the Heir of Mordlum there and would return to that place if she believed he had captured Eleanor."

"This is insane!" Cinder piped up. "I'm from 1875, and the darkness got really bad there. The wood is completely dead now. We cannot go there."

"As the new chief of the Malak, Del Ryder would have a plan," said Treola. "If you are sure, Crimson, that she would go to the Violet Wood, then we must join her there."

"I don't know if she would have a plan," said Crimson. "But if she does what Mordlum told her to do, it would mean she's beginning to believe in herself. She's foolish, but she's also brave. Del Ryder needs our help, but it may be to save her from her own impulsiveness."

"I know a lumen or two who've been known to be a bit impulsive," said Verdi.

"I was younger then," said Crimson.

"That was the Crimson who saved Del Ryder and her friends," Verdi reminded Crimson.

"She may already be at the Violet Wood," said Treola. "It was some time ago that Mordlum visited me."

"It is a dark day when we must concern ourselves with more than today and tomorrow," said the commander. "We must eat, and you will all need rest. We can give you provisions and weapons for your journey to the Violet Wood."

"But," Kita piped up, "the Violet Wood is terribly far. If Del Ryder is already there, will we not be too late?"

Treola whistled, and from high above flew a golden-feathered bird, its wingspan as wide as Kita was tall. It wasn't the largest of birds in Azdia, but it looked powerful and fast. Treola, who was slight but still a little bigger than Kita, held out her arm, and the large bird landed on it, almost knocking Treola to the ground.

"We will fly there," she said.

"We'll need much larger birds to ride," said Kita.

"We will change into birds," said Treola.

"Impossible," said Cinder. "We can't sustain that kind

of metamorphing for that long."

"We can with this," Treola said, pulling something out of her satchel. She held what looked like the end of a tree root in her hand. "These are the very last of the roots of an ancient forest, a forest that was planted far in the north using one of the Crystal Seeds—the Seed of Transformation. With these last roots, we can extend our powers of metamorphing. We will be able to last long enough to reach the Violet Wood, but perhaps not much farther than that."

"Kita here has not yet learned her abilities," said Verdi.

"I've been practicing," said Kita defensively.

"And how's that been going?" said Cinder.

"Well, I've come close to changing," Kita started, not wanting to admit that she hadn't even been able to get Winx fur to grow on her arm.

"Close isn't going to help us when we're fighting the Heir of Mordlum," said Cinder.

"She's small enough to ride on one of us," said Crimson.

"We should leave her here," Cinder protested. "If Treola comes with us, we won't need Kita. She just slows us down anyway, and she'll really slow us down if she's riding on top of one of us."

Crimson held up his hand, asking for silence. "It is often from the most unlikely places that light will come," he said. "Keep practicing, Kita. You will get it, and you will come with us tomorrow."

*****

After eating a fantastic supper, Treola showed Verdi

and Cinder to their bedrooms and then led Kita and Crimson to an empty room. "We will practice together," she said.

Verdi had reluctantly agreed to allow Kita to keep Tabby in order to practice changing. Any time Tabby was near to Kita, she would immediately turn an affectionate purple. Their relationship was growing.

"Now, Kita," said Treola, "give it a try—concentrate."

Kita stood in the center of the room and held her winx. She focused on her care for Tabby as she had been taught. As she held her, Kita got flashes in her mind of the parts of a Winx—the fur, the face, the bone structure, the muscles. She tried in her mind to imprint those flashes on her own body. She could feel herself getting tense.

"Now let go," said Treola.

Kita tried to let her mind go blank and allow her body to move into the form that she had focused on. Nothing happened.

"It's no use," said Kita. "I'm not going to get it."

"It's okay," said Treola. "Let's make it easier. Put Tabby down and just put one hand on her. What do you love about her most?"

"I suppose that she likes me," said Kita.

"Anything else?"

"She's soft," said Kita. "But that sounds stupid. Here we are about to go to war against the darkness, and I'm talking about how I like winxes because they're soft."

"We cannot lose the simplest and perhaps most important parts of who we are and what Azdia is," said Crimson. "We will fight the darkness because that which makes us joyful, no matter how small, must be protected."

"Our connection to winxes reminds us that there is unconditional love," said Treola. "When I see Tabby, I'm reminded of Mr. Thicket—of how much he cares for us, and how nothing will stop him from protecting us."

"You're saying that Mr. Thicket loves us the way we love winxes," said Kita.

"I'm saying we love the way he first loved us," said Treola.

Tabby purred gently as her fur moved beneath Kita's touch.

"Now, try again," said Treola. "And this time, just touch Tabby gently and think about what you love about her."

Kita closed her eyes and thought about how soft Tabby's fur was. She thought as well about how she would never want to see anything bad happen to Tabby. In her mind, she began to get flashes of the various parts of a winx, as before.

"Stay focused on what you love," said Treola.

Kita pushed the images of the winx anatomy out of her mind, and focused more on what she felt and what she knew. In that moment, she knew that she was beloved by someone greater than herself—greater than anyone, in fact. She no longer felt like she was only connected to Tabby the winx. A shudder came over her body, and she felt a power take hold. What was most strange about it was that the power felt like a person.

She had been taught about his protection and about how he cared for Azdia and all its creatures. She had been taught that their care of Azdia was all about reflecting Mr. Thicket's care. But there, in an empty room in the heart of a fortress, she knew deep within herself, as if for the first time, that Mr. Thicket loved her. It was as if she was the only creature in all of Azdia, and all that existed anymore was her, Mr. Thicket, and his love. A single tear trickled down her cheek.

She lifted the hand that was not on Tabby and wiped the tear away. Kita opened her eyes, looked at Treola and Crimson, and instantly felt silly and somehow exposed.

"It's okay," said Crimson.

"Is that how it is… for every lumen?" Kita asked, realizing that she hadn't changed.

"Some get a stronger connection to him than others," said Treola. "But yes. Our connection to everything living in Azdia—to the light, to everything—is actually a connection to him."

"But why don't you just tell every young lumen before we are supposed to learn our abilities?" Kita asked.

"We do tell you," said Crimson. "But like so many things about Mr. Thicket, what we say about him often only begins to make sense after you've experienced something about him."

"Does it get easier?" said Kita.

"Yes… and no," said Treola. "There is far more to him than is contained in all of Azdia, so the more you learn, the more languages you receive, the more you metamorph, and even the brighter your light, the more there is to know about Mr. Thicket."

"It's all so confusing," said Kita.

"This is why, for now, you need to receive your abilities as a gift," said Treola. "Learn them, yes, but also simply accept them. You're so close."

"But, I didn't change at all," said Kita.

"Oh, but you did," said Treola. "Try taking off your boots."

Kita kicked off her boots, and all over her feet was the softest of fur.

"I guess some lumens change feet first," Crimson said.

Kita couldn't believe it. She had done it. She had changed—just a little. But she hadn't thought at all about her feet changing. That's when it hit her. She hadn't done it. Mr. Thicket had changed her—she just let him. More tears started forming in her eyes, but her heart was full—full of gratitude.

"That might be enough for tonight," said Treola.

"Okay," said Kita.

CHAPTER SIXTEEN

Fire and Nightmare

The heat from the flames was intense. Fire was everywhere. Smoke filled what should have been a sun-soaked sky above. They needed to act quickly, but Del hadn't the first clue what to do.

"Follow me," Emma said to Sam and Del, trying to sound brave. She started running in a direction where the fire seemed marginally less fierce. Fortunately, the buildings were spaced fairly far apart so that they were able to dart between the buildings without being too close to the flames.

The town was empty. There were no lumens to be found—just buildings on fire. Del held her breath as much as she could. Her eyes stung. She kept her legs moving, following Emma, and checked behind her to make sure Sam was keeping up.

Del's heart pounded. She wasn't sure if Emma was leading them further into the fire or if the town was just really big, and it was taking them longer than she'd hoped to get out.

Sam was coughing. Del looked over her shoulder. He had stopped running.

"Emma!" Del called.

Emma stopped, and the two girls turned back. Sam was hunched over and through his coughs said, "I don't think I can keep going."

"You have to, Sam," Del said, pulling on his arm. Emma grabbed his other arm, and the three of them continued scrambling through the smoke and fire.

"I think I see—" Emma started.

"What is it?" asked Del.

Just ahead of them was a wheel on fire, spinning slowly. It was big. If the three of them stood on each other's shoulders, it would still have been larger than them. Attached to the wheel was a series of buckets, and dripping from the buckets was water.

They raced toward the wheel of fire, knowing that at any moment it could come crashing apart and the buckets would fall. As they got closer, the source of the water became clear. A river rushed past them. There were several wooden bridges in view, each of them ablaze as everything else in the town.

"Get in the river," Del ordered. "It's the safest place."

Sam looked as though he were going to pass out. He'd probably inhaled too much smoke. Del and Emma pulled him toward the water.

"He's not going to be able to swim," Emma said. "Look at him."

"It's our best chance, though," said Del, looking at the water. The light of the flames reflected off the rushing river in what looked like beautiful multicolored patterns.

They dragged Sam right to the river's edge, and Del stared at the water. She looked deeply. For a second, she thought she saw a face smiling up at her. Her heart skipped a beat, and she felt as if she had suddenly been transported to Blythe Thicket's cottage—she had such a feeling of safety. She blinked, and the face disappeared. Thousands of the tiniest glow bugs sparkled and danced where the face had been.

"What is it, Del?" Emma asked.

"Nothing," said Del. "It's just that—the water—it's glowing."

"Is that good?" asked Emma.

"It's very good," said Del.

Sam's eyes rolled into the back of his head as the two girls lifted him a bit and guided his body into the rushing river. He was quickly pulled from their grasp, but to Del's delight, his head stayed above water. The water cradled him and carried him off toward an unknown destination.

Del and Emma both jumped in to the river and were whisked away as well.

"Drink the water!" yelled Del, taking a big slurp.

As soon as her lips touched the water, Del felt alive. Drinking this water took her back to the forest where she had first met Crimson and had first drunk glow-water. Her mind jumped to each time she had feasted: aboard the Zephyr with Hollow, Verdi, and Egreck; with the Heir of Mordlum; and finally, with Blythe Thicket in his little cottage on the edge of the Violet Wood. Had she really just seen Blythe Thicket's face in the bottom of the river? She wanted to believe she had, but it had all happened so quickly.

The burning village was all around them. The river took them under several burning bridges. Each time, Del was afraid that hot ash or chunks of a bridge would fall off right on top of them, but that didn't happen. It was as if the river protected them as it raced them away, hopefully to some safe haven.

A safe haven did not await, however. Instead, the river spilled them out into the sea. A heavy wind was blowing the smoke from the fire inland, so for the first time, they could see a beautiful blue sky overhead.

Del and Emma swam over to Sam, who had woken up. Del could tell immediately by his eyes and the strength he seemed to have back that he too had drunk some water from the river.

The wreckage of the village was a frightful sight. Black smoke rose high into the air, and flames leaped back and forth between buildings. Del wondered how on earth they had managed to get out.

"It's like we're in the middle of a war," said Sam.

"Let's hope we're in the middle," said Del. "I'm hoping we're not at the end. I'm hoping we're not too late."

*****

They swam as quickly as they could through blackened debris, close to what remained of the docks that had previously lined the harbor. The effects of the glowing water from the river began to wear off. Del could feel the muscles in her arms and legs begin to tighten in the cold, black water of the sea. She imagined Sam was doing worse than she was. They needed to get to shore, but not to a shore on fire. She pulled herself through the water and tried not to think about what creatures could be lurking below.

The struggle to get to a safe shore did not take long, although in Del's mind—and in her limbs—it felt like hours. Del, Sam, and Emma made their way to some rocks a safe distance from the nearest burning buildings and pulled themselves up out of the water. They lay for a moment, all three of them breathing hard.

They had nothing but the cold, wet clothes on their backs. Their only saving grace was that the air itself was warm and dry with a blazing sun overhead, and they were still close enough to the burning village to feel some heat coming from the massive fire. They would dry off quickly, despite their blue lips.

Without supplies, they wouldn't be able to get far. Del didn't feel like moving anyway, and by the looks of Sam and Emma, they were just as exhausted as she was. They lay on the rocks, trying to bake themselves dry. It worked, but Del didn't feel as though she was getting any energy back. If anything, the heat from the sun and the flames, along with the sound of the lapping waves, was putting her to sleep.

*****

"Del, Del."

Hands shook her awake. She must have drifted off on the rocks.

"Sorry," Del said instinctively. "Was I asleep?" She opened her eyes slightly, sensing that brightness would hit hard if she opened them fully. She saw the outline of a window framed with light.

"C'mon, Deli, you're going to make us late!" said a voice.

Del felt blankets around her. She sat up. "Where am I?"

"Get up already!" The voice belonged to her sister.

Del was in her own room, in her own house. What was going on?

"You better get ready," Suzanne said as she turned and marched out of Del's room.

Del jumped out of bed and grabbed her phone. It was 8:37 a.m. The date read Monday, August 31st. It was the first day of school. She checked her text messages. Nothing this morning yet, but all her messages from the day before were there. She sent a quick message to Sam: "You there?" There was no response, but that wasn't unusual. A message popped up from Suzanne, which was unusual. "Get down here. We're waiting for you."

Del quickly changed her clothes, matted her hair into something that didn't look horrible, and headed downstairs. Something was not quite right.

Her mother greeted her at the bottom of the staircase. Tears streamed down her cheeks. "Isn't it wonderful, Del?" her mom said. "Your dad's come back. He still loves us."

Del's mom hugged her. Tears started to form in Del's eyes as her mother held her close.

Del's mother led her into the kitchen. "He brought your friends to celebrate," she said.

"What?" said Del. "Which friends?"

Seated at the kitchen table were Phil, Guy, and Mrs. Manters. What was this? What was she doing there? What were any of them doing there? But it wasn't the presence of Mrs. Manters, Phil, or Guy that distressed her the most. At the head of the table was a man with blonde hair and beautiful blue eyes. It was him. It was the Heir of Mordlum.

"Isn't it wonderful to be one family again?" Del's

mother said.

"No!" Del yelled. "What is this? What are they doing here? What is he doing here?"

"Sit down, my dear," said the Heir of Mordlum. "I should have told you before, but I suppose it is better this way. Far better to break the news to you in our own home. Now, come and eat. Your friends here are hungry too."

Del noticed that Suzanne had completely disappeared. "Where's my sister?"

"She went to school with her boyfriend," the Heir answered coolly. "Nice boy."

It was at least plausible that Suzanne would have gone off with her boyfriend and that the Heir of Mordlum would think Jerk was "nice."

"Come, sit," the Heir said again.

"No," Del insisted. "Phil, Guy! What are you doing here?"

Neither of them responded, but Del's mother, who had strangely enough put on an apron and started scrambling some eggs, jumped over to Del and pushed her toward the table.

"Now, listen to your father," she said. "He's come back to us. Go and sit with him. At least listen to what he has to say."

"He's not my father!" Del yelled. "He's evil!"

She ran over to Mrs. Manters, who didn't move a muscle. "Tell them," said Del. "Tell them about the Heir of Mordlum."

Del looked down at Mrs. Manters' chair and, for the first time, noticed that she was tied to it. Phil and Guy were tied to their chairs too. Mrs. Manters slowly turned her head toward Del and stared at her with blank eyes. It was as if she were not really there. She spoke, but it was barely recognizable as her voice. "I am sorry. I am so sorry."

Del turned to run away, but the door to the living room had disappeared. She turned back. The back door was gone too, and so were the windows. There were only walls. Del couldn't get out.

"Why are they tied up?" Del said.

"Precautions, my dear," said the Heir. "Now, come, sit. There's no other way."

Del took a step toward the table.

"Del, stop!" It was another voice.

Del turned in place. Emma stood next to Del's mother.

"Del, none of this is real," Emma said. "Come with me. I can get you out."

Del's mom reacted first to Emma's sudden appearance. She sprung at her, tackled her to the ground, and said, of all things, "You weren't invited!"

As they struggled on the floor, Emma began to glow as if she were a lumen. The glow increased in intensity, with light shining from her chest and neck as if through her necklace. Del's mother moved to strike Emma but was stopped either by Emma's own strength or possibly the light.

"Del, you've got to trust me," said Emma, pulling herself up.

"You can't," said Del's mother. "You need to stay here with me and your father. We're a family again. You can't leave. You'll be just like him if you leave me."

Del walked toward Emma, determined to go with her. She wasn't scared of the light coming from her.

"Don't leave me," Del's mother said. "Please stay."

Mascara ran down her mother's cheeks. She lay on the floor, a mess, weak.

"Don't leave me," her mother said again.

Del got close to Emma, and they grabbed each other's hands.

The Heir of Mordlum rose to his feet and held out his hand. In it was a Crystal Seed. Did he really have one?

"They are my prisoners, Del," he said, motioning to Phil, Guy, and Mrs. Manters. "But I'll let them go in exchange for you."

"I'll free them," Del said defiantly.

"Come and get them, then," said the Heir.

Del pulled away from Emma and rushed toward the table. Lightning shot out of the Crystal Seed toward Del. Emma jumped in front of Del but somehow was not struck by the lightning. A hole had opened up in the middle of Emma's chest. The center-piece of her necklace disappeared, and all the lightning was absorbed within Emma. When the lightning stopped, Emma was fine.

A sickly smile crept across the Heir of Mordlum's face. "Thank you," was all he said.

Mrs. Manters' blank eyes dropped. "All may be lost."

Emma grabbed Del in a huge bear hug, and light enveloped them.

Del's mother looked up at Del from the floor.

"Please take me with you," she said.

*****

Del woke up. She was on the rocks near the sea, a stone's throw from the smoldering town. Emma lay next to her, holding Del's hand. Sam was snoring a few feet away.

"What was that?" asked Del.

"It was a dream," said Emma. "A really bad dream."

CHAPTER SEVENTEEN

Dreamroot

After a long sleep, and after a huge breakfast, Phil and Guy waited for Mr. Thicket to tell them what they were going to do to find their friends.

Mr. Thicket reached into his cloak, pulled out the Crystal Seed, and laid it on the table in front of him.

"Before I can tell you how we will find your friends, you must understand something about the Crystal Seeds," he began. "This is not the only Crystal Seed, as you know. There are seven Crystal Seeds altogether, including the one in your world. They are the source of all the magic of Azdia, and each one possesses a different power. This one is the Seed of Light. It gave Azdia and its creatures their light. It can attract light and also emit it. Its most powerful form is lightning.

"The seed in your world, which you used to travel here, is the Seed of Connection. It binds Azdia together into one. It can open up bridges that can be traveled through to any place in Azdia. Every other seed can summon the Seed of Connection to open up a bridge and travel back to it. We could summon a bridge using the Seed of Light and send you home right now, but we need to find your friends first, of course.

"There is a Seed of Transformation and a Seed of Language. These are the seeds that give lumens their abilities, but they also allow the bearer of them to transform themselves or other things at will or to communicate in any language they wished.

"The Seed of Healing can make things well. If you have this seed, you can heal anything or anyone you wish.

"Then there is the Seed of Protection. Anyone who possesses this seed cannot be harmed. It is this seed that has provided a cloak of protection over much of Azdia for the ages. This seed gives lumens the instinct to protect all life in Azdia.

"Finally, there is the Seed of Dreams. This seed is the most mysterious of them all. While the others all seem to have a function that can clearly be identified as good, no one ever knew how the Seed of Dreams helped anyone. All that was known was that it held sway over the dreams that lumens had when they slept, but I've discovered its true purpose."

"Do you have that seed too?" Phil asked.

"No," said Mr. Thicket. "But we're coming to that in a moment. The Seed of Dreams is a communication tool. The one who has it can enter the dreams of others in order to give them a message, and it works across great distances.

"When I rescued Del from Old Blythe's cottage, I thought that perhaps he also had the Seed of Dreams and had been using it on her to influence what she believed was real. But after I sent her back home, I discovered what he had really done.

"I had overlooked something very obvious when it

comes to the Crystal Seeds: things grow from seeds. There are places in Azdia where the trees originally grew from a Crystal Seed. The Violet Wood was an ancient forest—and what did the trees look like?"

"Purple glass," Phil said.

"Glass or?" Mr. Thicket prompted.

"Crystal?" asked Guy.

"Precisely," said Mr. Thicket. "The Violet Wood grew from a single seed, which was then dug back up and hidden. The Violet Wood grew from the Seed of Dreams, and the roots of the trees can be used in much the same way as that seed."

"What are you saying?" asked Phil.

"I'm saying that Old Blythe used Dreamroot to communicate with Del while she slept, but that we might be able to find her by doing the same thing."

"Is that why the forest was dying?" asked Guy.

"I think so, yes," said Mr. Thicket. "It takes a lot of Dreamroot to be able to enter someone's dream. Many trees must be destroyed, and as Old Blythe did so, it affected the entire forest until all the trees lost their leaves and died."

"So it wasn't because the trees' lights were going out?" asked Phil.

"No, not at all," said Mr. Thicket. "Their roots had been systematically removed. Once the forest had been decimated, I and my lumens collected all the Dreamroot we could to keep it out of the wrong hands. Now, come with me, and I'll show you how I think we can find your friends."

They left the table and, with several lumens following them, walked into the corridor system. They took passageways that they had never seen before, past several closed doors and a number of other passages leading this way and that. They turned many times on their way to wherever they were being taken. Had they been on their own, Phil was sure that he and Guy would have gotten lost.

Mr. Thicket stopped outside of a large wooden door. "This is what I'm calling the dream room," he said, opening the door.

They walked in and were hit with a musty, earthy smell. Hanging from the ceiling were hundreds of tree roots. There was certainly no glow to the roots. There were lumens coming and going by a door on the far side of the room. They looked as though they were preparing some kind of stew or soup in a large black pot.

"We find that if we boil the Dreamroot, it works quite well," said Mr. Thicket.

"So you've done this before?" asked Guy.

"Oh, yes, but we must be sparing," Mr. Thicket replied. "I know this looks like a lot of Dreamroot, but we only have a limited supply. If only we had the Seed of Dreams itself."

*****

Mr. Thicket led Phil and Guy out of the room full of Dreamroot and into another room that had a row of beds. It looked a lot like a hospital ward or an army barracks that you would see in old movies. All the beds were wooden, and they were spaced just a few feet apart.

"Like most things in Azdia, it helps if you have a connection to the one to whom you are trying to send a message. This is where I need you, my boys. We have to hope that one of your friends is asleep when we try this. Each of us will drink some of the potion made from the Dreamroot. It will put us to sleep, and I will be able to connect to your dreams. I don't have full control over the dreams, but I have some influence. We will, in some ways, share a dream, but each of us will experience it a little differently from the others.

"In the dream, you both need to think of your friends and really concentrate. If one of them is sleeping when we are, we may be able to influence their dreams."

This was all astonishing to Phil. The room looked a little creepy to him, and of all the things that he'd experienced in Azdia, he was more wary about this than anything. "What if something goes wrong?" he asked.

"I won't lie to you," said Mr. Thicket. "The shared dream can certainly turn into a nightmare, especially if one of us or one of your friends resists. But nothing terrible can happen. At the worst, we just all wake up."

"But how are you going to find out where they are?" asked Guy.

"I will do the talking," said Mr. Thicket. "I'll try to get one of them to say something that can point us in the right direction."

"But Sam and Del won't trust you," said Phil.

"Ah, but that is the beauty of dreams," said Mr. Thicket. "I don't need to be myself. I can be someone else in the dream. I will have a few moments when we first make a connection to find a setting for the dream and to choose someone to be. Once we know who we are connected to, I will choose a place where the person is comfortable and a different person to be; I'll be the person they most wish to see—someone they will give clues to."

"It all sounds risky," said Guy.

"It isn't really," said Mr. Thicket. "Your friends won't know that anything is going on. If things go badly in the dream, they will simply wake up and think they had a bad dream. We can always try again if we don't get the information we need."

"But this just doesn't seem right," said Phil. "Invading someone's dreams, looking into their mind. Can't we find another way?"

"Other than flying all around Azdia, there is no other way," Mr. Thicket said. "This will give us a starting place, and it's not an invasion. We won't be looking at their dreams. We are planting a dream within them in the hopes that we can find them and rescue them."

Phil still didn't feel great about this, but he wasn't in charge. All they could do was go along.

Each bed had a small table next to it, and on each table was a cup. Each of them chose a bed to lie upon.

"Remember, each of us will experience the same dream a little bit differently," said Mr. Thicket. "You may see and hear things that I don't see or hear. Say nothing, but notice everything. After we wake up, we will share what we experienced. It may be one of you that sees the clue to their location. Now, concentrate on your friends. Think only of them as you drink."

They took their cups, drank the Dreamroot potion, and were asleep an instant later.

*****

Phil's eyes adjusted to the light. He was sitting at Del's

kitchen table across from Guy. Mr. Thicket sat at the head of the table. Del's mom was cooking something— breakfast, he guessed.

"You look like yourself," Phil whispered. "It's not going to work."

"Del won't see me this way," Mr. Thicket whispered back. "Remember, we will each see and hear different things."

"But who are you supposed to be?" Guy asked.

"The person she most longs to see," said Mr. Thicket. "Her father. Now, stay quiet, boys. No matter what happens or how strange it gets, say nothing. It is just a dream. Let me do all the talking."

Del's mother looked over at the table and smiled. Then she looked toward the living room. "I should go and get Del," she said as she walked out of the kitchen.

"This isn't going to go well," said Phil.

"Shh. Not another word," said Mr. Thicket.

Del and her mother walked into the kitchen. To Phil's eyes, Del almost shone. Had she always been this beautiful, or was it just the dream? In that moment, he realized just how much he missed his friend. Instantly, he was taken back to when the two of them had been alone in the forest of the Old Oak, where the trees had attacked them. It had been the time he had felt closest to her. He knew she was wrong about Mr. Thicket, but he longed to have the trust between him and Del rebuilt. Phil desperately hoped this plan would work. They had to find Del, Emma, and Sam. They just had to.

"Isn't it wonderful to be one family again?" said Del's mother.

"No!" Del yelled. "What is this? What are they doing

here? What is he doing here?"

It was just as Phil had feared. She recognized Mr. Thicket. They were sunk before they had even begun. Mr. Thicket didn't miss a beat, however.

"Sit down, my dear," he said. "I should have told you before, but this is much better. Far better to break the news to you in our own home. Now, come and eat. Your friends here are hungry too."

"Where's my sister?" Del said.

Phil thought it a little strange that Del would care at all about Suzanne.

"She went to school with her boyfriend," Mr. Thicket answered calmly. "Nice boy."

Nice boy? Phil thought. Someone hadn't done his background check.

"Come, sit," Mr. Thicket said again.

"No," Del insisted. "Phil, Guy! What are you doing here?"

Phil glanced at Mr. Thicket. He gave Phil and Guy a look indicating that they should keep their silence.

Del's mother left her cooking to push Del toward the table. "Now, listen to your father. He's come back to us. Go and sit with him. At least listen to what he has to say."

"He's not my father!" Del yelled. "He's evil!"

Del ran to one of the empty chairs and pleaded with the emptiness. "Tell them. Tell them about the Heir of Mordlum."

She paused.

"Wait—why are they tied up?" she said, backing away from the table.

Phil looked down at his arms. There was nothing holding him in place. He moved his arms freely. He looked from Del to Mr. Thicket, whose mouth was moving, but no sound came out. Something was going terribly wrong with the dream.

Mr. Thicket's voice suddenly returned and turned to more of a command. "Now come, sit. There's no other way."

A look of resignation crossed Del's face as she took a step toward the table.

"Del, stop!" It was Emma. How did she get here? By the look on Mr. Thicket's face, he was wondering the same thing.

"Del, none of this is real," Emma said. "Come with me. I can get you out."

Out of nowhere, Del's mom tackled Emma to the floor and shouted, "You weren't invited!"

As if the dream had not already been strange enough, Emma stood up and began glowing with an intense light as though she were a lumen. She said, "Del, you've got to trust me."

"You can't," said Del's mother. "You need to stay here with me and your dad. We're a family again. You can't leave. You'll be just like him if you leave me."

Del walked toward Emma.

Del's mother kept pleading. "Don't leave me. Please stay. Don't leave me."

Del grabbed Emma's hand and looked defiantly at Mr. Thicket, who rose to his feet. He held the Seed of Light in his hand.

"They are my prisoners, Del," he said, motioning to Phil and Guy.

What is he doing? Phil thought.

Mr. Thicket continued. "But I'll let them go in exchange for you."

"I'll free them," Del said.

"Come and get them, then," said Mr. Thicket.

Del pulled away from Emma and rushed toward the table. Mr. Thicket held the Seed of Light out, pointing it at Del. Emma jumped in front of Del as though she were being shot by something, though if there was anything there, Phil couldn't see it. In an instant, Emma's necklace, then her chest, then her entire body was engulfed in light. Then it all died down, and at the end of it, Emma was fine.

Mr. Thicket locked eyes with Del and said, "Thank you."

Thank you? What was going on? What had they just witnessed? Had Mr. Thicket figured out where they were? Phil was so confused. He tried with all his might to look and listen for some clue that would help them, but he couldn't make any sense of this crazy dream.

Then, for a second, as he looked from Del and Emma to Mr. Thicket, he was sure that he saw someone else sitting at the table in the empty chair that Del had gone to. For the briefest of moments, he thought he saw the priest's wife, her arms tied to the chair, but she was gone in an instant. Why would that image pop into his dream? Then in the stillness of the moment he heard her voice, just one word: "Lost."

Emma and Del hugged and disappeared into light as Del's mother pleaded with them, "Please take me with you."

Mr. Thicket sat back down at the table with Phil and Guy. To Phil, Guy looked as if he had just been on a roller coaster or run a marathon or something.

"Not exactly as planned," Mr. Thicket said, "but helpful nonetheless. I had to improvise a little bit, but I think this might just work. Probably best if we wake up now."

Del's kitchen, her mother still weeping on the floor, faded away as Phil wondered what on earth Mr. Thicket was talking about.

CHAPTER EIGHTEEN

The Invasion Army

Sam still lay asleep on the rocks. Del was shaken.

"It didn't feel like just a dream," Del said.

"I don't think it was *just* a dream," Emma replied. "I mean, I think some of it was kind of real—not the house or the kitchen table, and not your mom, but the stuff he was saying. I think it was really him saying it."

"Emma, how were you…?" Del began.

"How was I in your dream?" Emma asked.

Del nodded.

"I'm not entirely sure. I was dreaming my own dream. It was wonderful until…"

"Until what?"

"It's going to sound silly, but my grandpa was there, but it wasn't really my grandpa. It felt like him but better, if that makes any sense. We were in a forest. I remember hearing the leaves rustling and branches creaking around us, but somehow it sounded like music—really beautiful music. Everything was glowing. Everything except one tree—the biggest and oldest-looking tree that was in the middle of a clearing.

"It all felt wonderful and important somehow. My

grandpa and I didn't talk until he said in a strange sort of voice, 'She needs your help.' He pushed me—pretty hard, actually—and all of a sudden I was in your kitchen."

"You said it was your grandpa and not your grandpa?"

"I know that's weird. You know how dreams are sometimes. It wasn't really him; I just felt like I feel when I'm around my grandpa, but even better, you know?"

"Like he loved you more than anything else in the whole world? Like everything was going to be okay forever?"

"Exactly."

"Emma, that was Blythe Thicket. That's exactly what he's like. You met Blythe Thicket in your dream, and he sent you to save me. Was there a rock in the clearing that you could walk up, like a kind of stage or a place someone could speak from?"

"Yes," said Emma vaguely. "How did you know that?"

"I've been there. You were at the Old Oak."

The idea of Emma meeting Blythe Thicket in her dreams caused a strange mixture of joy and resentment in Del. It was as though he were right there, somehow protecting them, even protecting Del in her dreams. Del longed to see him and wished she had dreamed what Emma had dreamed. She would give anything to be back in his cottage with Crimson without any cares or problems. She stood up and turned away so that Emma wouldn't be able to see her watery eyes.

"He's not my dad, you know," Del said. "That part of the dream wasn't real."

"I know," said Emma. "I knew right away—he could never be your dad."

Del appreciated the reassurance from Emma, but she wasn't really sure herself. What if he was her father? It was possible. She barely remembered her dad, and her mom had destroyed all the pictures. For a fleeting moment, Del wished that her sister were there with her. She wanted to stop feeling alone. She knew she had Sam, and Emma was actually a lot nicer than she'd ever expected, but it wasn't enough for her. She needed more.

"We have to rescue them," Emma said. "That terrible man has them—my brother… and…"

"And Guy and Eleanor," Del said. "We have to rescue them—all of them, but we're going to need help from somewhere. I wish Blythe Thicket were actually here and not just in your dreams."

Emma didn't say anything.

"Emma, how did you absorb the lightning from the Heir of Mordlum?" Del asked.

"I don't know. I think that was just one of those weird dream things. I jumped in front of you and it just kind of happened. Somehow, I knew that we'd both be okay."

Del accepted this. Even though the dream seemed to have elements of reality, it had still been a dream, and weird things happen in people's dreams.

"We better wake up Sam," Del said.

*****

"We probably shouldn't have just fallen asleep like that," said Sam once the girls managed to wake him.

He sat rubbing his eyes.

"We need to get out of here," said Del. "We need to find help."

"We don't even know where 'here' is," said Emma.

"Um, yes we do," said Sam.

"We do?" said Emma and Del together.

"It was written on every building in town," said Sam.

"Of course," said Del.

"You managed to see something on the buildings through all that fire?" asked Emma.

"Well, not every building," said Sam. "But lots of them—the ones that weren't totally burnt. Most buildings in Azdia have an address, and in lots of the towns, the first four numbers of the address are actually the number of the town; at least, that's what we were told."

"Why didn't we think of that before?" asked Del.

"I don't know," said Sam. "But as soon as I saw an address on a house, I remembered. We're in 1301. We know where we are, and we know where we need to go."

"But how are we going to find our way?" asked Emma.

"I copied the map down," said Sam. He reached into a pocket and took out a small plastic ziplock bag. Inside were his cell phone, some matches, and pencil and paper. "I wasn't totally unprepared for this trip, you know."

He unfolded the piece of paper to reveal a crudely-drawn map. Sam pointed at a dot and the number 1301. "We're here," he said. "And we need to get there." He pointed at the Violet Wood.

"The only major town on our way is 1307," said

Emma, looking at the map. "Maybe we should head there."

"The river we were in goes there," said Sam. "And according to the map, there is a road as well. And you know what else? The messages that came in from the birds?"

"With the fire symbol on them?" asked Del. "I guess we know what they meant."

"Yeah, but there wasn't a message from 1301 or 1307," said Sam. "1301 just got burned to the ground. I bet whoever set this fire is heading to 1307 next."

"So we need to get there first," said Del. "Maybe the lumens in 1307 are still okay."

"And maybe we can still get help there," said Sam.

"Let's get moving," said Del. "We should be able to walk around the town to the far side and rejoin the river there and then maybe find the road."

*****

It turned out that Del was right. They managed to make their way around the town without too much difficulty and found the river and road that followed it. The three friends made their way between several of the buildings still smoldering from the recent fire, which had now died down. They were looking for anything that might help them on what might be a long journey. They had the river water to drink, but they would need food. Del was already quite hungry, and she was sure Sam and Emma would be too.

They dared to enter one of the buildings that was still standing and no longer looked hot. Most of the inside was singed beyond recognition. They scrounged around and found a few crackers in a small metal tin that lay under some debris. Del took the tin and put it in her backpack.

"There's not much here," Del called to Sam and Emma, who had been searching on the other side of the building.

"Shh—come over here," Sam whispered.

Sam pointed to a blackened window where he had smeared away some of the soot. Del looked through. Dark lumens marched along the street. There were hundreds of them, but there were more than just lumens. A massive dark gray leg passed the window. Del looked up after it passed and beheld the huge beast with a neck like a giraffe and three antlers on top of its head —a feldroe. She and Phil had ridden these beasts before. This one looked fierce, menacing, but somehow not as wild as she remembered them. This feldroe looked as if it were under the control of the dark lumens.

Del kept her eyes fixed through the window. It took a long time for the army of dark lumens to pass by. As they went, Del counted sixteen feldroes, but there might have been more—maybe twenty. Neither the feldroes nor the army of lumens were the most devastating thing, however. Ear-piercing screeches could be heard from high in the air above.

"What is that sound?" Emma asked.

Del and Sam had both heard that kind of screech before. Del feared the worst, searching the sky as best she could through the soot on the glass, and she caught a quick glimpse of what was making the noise. Her suspicions were confirmed, and her heart sank. It was indeed the same kind of creature that had attacked them in the Violet Wood. It was the same kind of creature that had carried Crimson off.

"Sam, it's those things again," said Del.

"How many?" asked Sam.

"I only see one, but the screeching sounds like more," said Del. "Maybe four?"

"What are they?" asked Emma.

"We never found out what they're called," said Del.

"What about nightwings?" Sam offered.

"Whatever we call them, you don't ever want to ever meet one," said Del. "Basically, they hunted us."

*****

The feldroes, nightwings, and dark lumen army had finished moving through the town and looked as if they were going to take the road inland on exactly the same course that Del, Sam, and Emma were intending to take.

The three friends briefly considered abandoning their plan, but for some reason, the presence of the dark lumen troops gave Del a renewed sense of purpose.

"There's got to be a thousand of them," Emma said.

"Yeah, but that means we only have to be faster than the slowest lumen," said Del. "They're not looking for us. If we can stay hidden, then maybe we can get to 1307 before they do. We could warn the town and then get help."

Del's heart pounded. Maybe this was exactly what she was supposed to do: the chief of the Malak, racing against the darkness to bring hope to places in Azdia where the light still had a chance to shine.

They wasted no time, only going into one more

building on the edge of town that hadn't seen the same level of destruction as the others to find some extra provisions. They found half a loaf of bread, some berries, cheese, four bottles that they could fill from the river if necessary, and two carrying bags. Del carried one with half the provisions and added in the tin of crackers they had found in the other building. Emma carried the second bag, leaving Sam, who had been struggling the most, free of any extra burden.

The three of them were only a few minutes behind the army. The army stuck to the road the whole time. Del, Sam, and Emma stayed just off the road, hiding behind bushes and rocks.

Their main concern was not being seen from above by the nightwings. They took great care to find shelter that covered them from above. They did manage to catch some glimpses of the terrible beasts, and after hours of walking, they were able to tell the creatures apart by markings on their wings, variations in their claws, and what were certainly battle scars. By the time the army was stopping for the night, Sam had been able to distinguish six different nightwings.

With the army beginning to make camp, the friends had a decision to make. They could stop as well and get some much-needed rest, or they could keep going and try to get out in front of the army.

"I'm exhausted," said Emma.

"We all are," said Del. "I think we need to rest, but we can't rest for too long. We don't know how long they will take a break, so we will need to sleep in shifts."

"This is also our best chance to find out how big the army really is," said Sam. "We could count how many lumens there are."

"We should do that while they're asleep," said Del. "Why don't you two get some rest first? I'll wake you up when most of the lumens are asleep."

"They're sure to set up a night watch as well," said Sam. "Don't do anything stupid, Del."

"I won't," Del said. "Don't worry."

They found a spot away from the army, behind some rocks with a bush providing a canopy for them. Sam and Emma were asleep in almost no time.

Del wanted the first watch. In truth, she did not want to sleep at all. She didn't want another nightmare. It had been scary, and she had this feeling that maybe the Heir of Mordlum could somehow use the dreams to get information from her.

Del left their hiding place and snuck up onto the rocks. From there, she was able to get a good look at much of the lumen army. Four feldroes stood at attention in the four corners of the camp, each with two lumens armed with torches and bows perched on top of its head.

Del watched and waited. Once she was sure that most of the lumens were asleep and that Sam and Emma had had a long enough rest, Del returned to their hiding place and woke them.

The three of them moved in a circle around the camp, staying out of sight but also remaining close enough to be able to get an approximate count of the lumens.

It took a long time to count them all, especially since the whole time they had to worry about the sentries on top of the four feldroes. They had to guess a little bit on the numbers where there were clusters of dark lumens sleeping next to—and in some cases, on top of—one another. There were six nightwings, twenty-four feldroes, and somewhere around twelve hundred lumens.

After they had fully circled the camp, they sat together, horrified.

"He's the one who sent them, you know," said Del. "The Heir of Mordlum is killing off Azdia. We have to get to 1307 before this army gets there. This is why we're here, I'm sure of it."

"You need to rest first," said Emma.

"I'm fine," said Del. "We need to get moving. We have to get to 1307 to give them as much time as possible to get ready."

"They might already know this army's coming," said Sam.

"But they might not," Del replied. "And we're wasting time talking about it."

Del walked away, expecting the other two to fall in line. She believed what she was saying, but she still wasn't sure if she could believe in herself. She thought of Phil, Guy, and Eleanor. The more she thought about her friends, the more she wanted to stop the Heir of Mordlum. If he had infiltrated her dream to scare her or to deter her, he had failed. The thought of her friends in trouble only spurred her on to help them and to help any of the innocent creatures that the Heir seemed bent on hurting.

Eventually, Del turned to look back. Sam and Emma were lagging behind, having to run to keep up with her. Had she been running? She couldn't remember. She stopped.

"We need a break," said Sam.

"We just started," said Del. "We've got to get there

before them."

"What are you talking about?" said Emma. "We've been jogging for hours. We have to stop."

Del had lost all track of time. She had been so focused that the hours had felt like just a few minutes. Strangely, she didn't feel tired. She felt energized, like she could run to 1307 in a flat-out sprint.

Emma and Sam collapsed onto the ground. Emma pulled two water bottles out of her bag and handed one to Sam. They downed the water quickly. Del pulled out her water bottle and took a few sips. She felt strong as the liquid trickled down her throat. She pictured the scene from her dream again and became anxious to get moving.

"Have you had enough rest yet?" she said.

"We need a few minutes," said Sam.

"And maybe a bit to eat," said Emma, pulling out some bread and cheese.

"Okay," said Del. "Let me know when you're ready, and we'll go. We have to keep moving."

CHAPTER NINETEEN

A Dream Explained

Guy and Phil jumped up from their beds, but Mr. Thicket moved slowly. He looked exhausted and haggard, his hair almost white rather than its usual vibrant blonde. Through thick breathes, he puffed, "Give me a moment, my boys. Everything will be okay."

The dream had taken a lot out of Mr. Thicket. Phil hadn't expected that, and he wasn't entirely sure that Mr. Thicket had expected it either.

"Something strange was at work," Mr. Thicket said. "I couldn't hide my true identity from Del in the dream, as you likely saw."

"Are you her real father?" asked Guy. "Because it seemed like that's what you were saying."

"My dear boy, no," said Mr. Thicket. "I chose to be her lost father because it is best, in dreams, to tap into the deepest of emotions when you are trying to send a message or discover something. But for some reason, she still knew my true identity. With her mother being in the dream, I thought I should play the role of being her father. It is best not to alter the dreamer's reality—it would only agitate her and possibly wake her too early."

"You said we were your prisoners," Phil challenged.

"I know what I said," said Mr. Thicket. "At that point in the dream, I could tell we weren't going to find any clues as to where they were, so I had to do something else. I provoked her."

"But——" Phil tried to interject, but Mr. Thicket continued.

"I provoked her so that she would be sure to come and find us. She believes I am evil. It would have done no good to challenge that notion for the time being, as deluded as it is. Instead, I decided to use it, to play into it. You heard her. She is going to come here to rescue you. And when she does, we will rescue her."

"What about my sister?" said Phil. "What was she doing in the dream?"

"I'm not entirely sure," said Mr. Thicket. "But I think she may have been there as part of Del's imagination. She likely used Emma as a way of protecting herself and as a way of escaping the dream."

"It was all so confusing," said Guy.

"We were all confused," said Mr. Thicket. "I'm sure Del was as well."

"I wish we knew where they were," said Phil.

"I will send out patrols to look for them," said Mr. Thicket. "But you know her. Del is determined. She will find her way here. My lumens will be on high alert so that when they see your friends, they will bring them here. They will watch the mountains, the Violet Wood, and all the paths that lead here. Do not fear. It won't be long before you see your friends again."

Phil was uneasy. Mr. Thicket seemed to have an explanation for everything, even when things went wrong. Could Del really be that wrong about him?

Doubt had begun to creep in about Mr. Thicket. Phil wanted to believe him, and he desperately wanted to be someone important like him. He started to get the feeling that he would end up having to choose between Mr. Thicket and Del.

"I actually feel tired," said Phil. "How long were we asleep?"

"Not long at all," said Mr. Thicket. "You boys will need more rest."

"Is it okay if we head back to our rooms?" Phil asked.

"You may," said Mr. Thicket. "I need you boys to trust me, to have faith in me. Azdia is a confusing place. Things are not always what they seem, and not everything is black and white. But I am on your side. You boys know that, don't you?"

Phil and Guy nodded.

Mr. Thicket clapped his hands twice, and four lumens appeared at the door.

"Take them to their rooms," Mr. Thicket said.

*****

Guy joined Phil in his room, and immediately, they began talking about the dream.

"It was weird that Mr. Thicket was tired, right?" said Guy.

"I know," said Phil. "I mean, I'm kind of tired, like sleepy, but he looked bad. And what happened to his hair?"

"Do you think he's telling us the truth?" asked Guy.

"He's for sure not telling us everything," said Phil. "But I think he still wants to help us."

"I don't think he's as good as we thought he was,"

said Guy.

"No, I guess not," said Phil. "But I think, somehow, that's the point. Mr. Thicket never said he was totally good. Parts of the darkness seem bad, but the real reason for the darkness is good, you know?"

"Yeah," said Guy. He paused and then continued. "Phil, I saw something in the dream. Something really weird."

Phil said nothing but let Guy continue, anticipating what he was going to say. "It was only for a second—actually, less than a second. She was there, and then she was gone. The priest's wife."

"In the empty chair that Del spoke to? I saw her too."

"She was tied up, Phil. Tied up. And Del thought we were tied up too. She saw us tied up. And Mr. Thicket said we were all his prisoners."

"But Mr. Thicket said that just to get Del to come find us, and when she does, he'll help her—he'll help all of us get home."

"Did you hear a voice?" asked Guy.

"Lost?" said Phil.

Guy nodded. "Why would she be there and tied up?"

"I don't know. Maybe Mr. Thicket put her in the dream for Del, thinking that it would give her even more of a reason to come here."

"But wouldn't Del just think that was really weird… unless…"

"Unless the priest's wife is in Azdia," Phil concluded.

"And why would she be tied up, Phil?"

"Maybe she's somewhere else. Maybe Mr. Thicket didn't even see her."

"Maybe he's got her tied up somewhere in the tunnels."

Phil's heart felt as if it had dropped into his stomach. What if Mr. Thicket wasn't Mr. Thicket? What if Del had been right all along, and he and Guy were prisoners of the Heir of Mordlum?

"We've got to look around some of these passageways," said Guy. "We've got to find out what's really going on."

"Okay," said Phil.

They walked over to the door and opened it a crack. At the end of the hall was one of their lumen attendants, who turned toward the door as soon as it opened. The lumen smiled at them and gave them a nod.

"But they're so happy," Phil whispered.

"They might be our prison guards," said Guy. "Let's find out how many lumens are here and then just go to my room."

Phil and Guy entered the hallway. It stretched in two directions. They walked toward the lumen they had seen smile. From around the corner came another lumen, who stood awaiting them, also smiling. Phil looked over his shoulder. At the other end of the hallway, two other happy lumens appeared.

The boys opened Guy's door, and as they went inside, Phil nodded politely at the lumens.

"Four guards," said Guy once the door was closed behind them.

"They aren't guards," said Phil. "They're always with us to lead us around, but that's just because we don't know where we're going."

"We've never tried to go anywhere when we're supposed to be in here sleeping, though."

"I don't think there is any way out except that

hallway, so I don't know what you think we're going to do."

"I guess we just try walking past them and see what they do. Then, I say we just make a break for it."

"Or we tell them we're hungry. They'll believe you if you tell them that. If they take us to get some food, that's when we look for a chance to sneak away."

"That's not going to work."

"If it doesn't, then at least we'll get something to eat."

"You make a good point," said Guy. "Let's try it."

*****

They left Guy's room and walked up to the nearest lumen attendant.

Phil said, "We're really hungry. Could we go down and get something to eat?"

The dark lumen smiled and nodded, signaling for them to follow him and another lumen. As they walked along the hallway, Phil began to think about how the dark lumens, while always happy, seemed to have something missing. It was more than just not being able to transform or learn another language. They seemed to lack any individual personality. They were always polite but seemed to limit their interactions with Phil and Guy. They always smiled, but it was starting to get a little creepy.

More and more, Phil was starting to think Guy might be right and Del might be right for that matter. What if they really were being held captive by Mr. Thicket? What if he really wasn't the real Mr. Thicket after all? They had to find out.

The two lumens led them into the Great Hall. It was

quiet and dim. Only a handful of torches remained lit. The twelve birds were on their perches but asleep. One of the lumens that had led them into the hall scurried away through one of the doors. The other stood staring and smiling at Guy and Phil.

"What now?" said Guy.

"Will the other lumen bring some food?" Phil inquired.

The remaining lumen nodded.

Phil remembered what Mr. Thicket had told him when they had stood on top of the tower in 1875 watching the lumens as they rebuilt it. "All this can be at your command." He walked over to the table. It was completely clear. Every other time they had seen the table it had been set up as though for a royal banquet.

"You're not expecting us to eat right off the table are you?" Phil looked at the lumen. "You better get it set or wake some others who can give you a hand."

The lumen bowed to Phil and ran through a door. Quick as a flash, he was back with two plates and some utensils. He put them in place on the table and then scurried back through the door to collect more things that would be needed to set up for a meal.

Phil backed slowly closer toward a door on the far side of the hall—a door that they had seen Mr. Thicket come through but had never entered themselves. Guy followed Phil's lead. The lumen, preoccupied, didn't seem to notice the boys making their way across the hall. There was no sign of the other lumen.

Once they reach the door, Phil stood with his hands behind his back and felt for the doorknob. He turned it, and he could tell the door would open. The lumen setting the table looked as if he was almost done. He glanced over at Phil and Guy and then disappeared to go and get the last of the wares for the table.

"Let's go," said Phil, swinging the door open.

He and Guy passed through the door. A torchlit hallway stretched before them. Phil closed the door quickly and looked for a lock on the door. There wasn't one. He scanned nearby for anything to brace the door.

"We're going to have to run," said Phil. "Come on."

Phil took off down the hallway with Guy close behind. The narrow hallway twisted and turned with no offshoots or doors leading off from it. Phil heard the door behind them open and close, and he picked up his pace, sprinting fast. He and Guy were fast runners, but Phil had no idea how fast a dark lumen would be. He imagined that he and Guy would be able to outrun them. Fortunately, he was right.

They continued running until they came to a staircase that led down. Phil started down the stairs, but Guy stopped him.

"Phil, look," he said. Guy pointed to a small hole in the rock just to the right of the staircase. "Do you think we could hide in there?"

Phil looked into the hole.

"Let's try it," Phil said.

Guy went first, just squeezing through the hole. The hole led to a small tunnel, which opened up enough to allow the boys to crawl on their hands and knees along it. Just as he began thinking they had perhaps made a big mistake running away and an even bigger mistake crawling into a dark tunnel, they heard what sounded like shouting. They couldn't make out the words, but some kind of argument was going on.

There was still a bit of torchlight coming from the

main tunnel, and there was another very faint glow coming from ahead of them. They kept moving forward toward the muffled argument. As the glow got brighter, they began to be able to make out the words and the voices.

It was definitely Mr. Thicket and someone else. Who was the other voice? It was a woman.

"You have no right," the woman said.

"Rights have nothing to do with it," said Mr. Thicket. "The very thing I need is going to be brought right to me. You have made a terrible mistake."

"You may hurt us, but in the end, you will not win," said the woman.

Guy and Phil continued shuffling along the tunnel. The woman continued, "Good always prevails; light will always overcome darkness."

"I'm afraid you, like all the Malak, are confused about light and dark," said Mr. Thicket. "I am rescuing Azdia from the light. I am giving its inhabitants everlasting life through the darkness I bring. I am their savior."

"You will not fool me with your deceit," said the woman. "Your darkness takes away any real life the lumens have. I know what you are up to. I know what you have become, and we will do everything to resist you."

"I am the savior of Azdia, and all of Azdia will see me that way," said Mr. Thicket. "I will reign over the lumens as their lord and king."

"There is only one Mr. Thicket—and it is not you!" The woman's voice was forceful and determined.

Guy and Phil reached the source of the light in the tunnel: a small opening in the floor. Both of them peered through the hole. There, below them, was Mr. Thicket. Across from him was a large cage, something you would expect to see at a zoo to house some wild animal. But inside the cage was an old woman. It was the priest's wife.

Phil looked on in disbelief. She was his prisoner, and now Phil knew that so were he and Guy.

"We can't stay here," he whispered to Guy.

As soon as the words were out of Phil's mouth, Phil regretted it. Mr. Thicket looked up and locked eyes with Phil. His face twisted into a sickly smile.

"I imagined you boys suspected, but now you know," Mr. Thicket said. "Sadly, this is sometimes what it takes to save the world." He motioned at the cage and continued. "You will both need to choose your side. Save Azdia and save your friends—you can all go home, safe and sound—or be my enemy. Eleanor here chose to be my enemy."

Eleanor? Mrs. Manters is Eleanor? Phil's mind was reeling as he stared in disbelief. He had chosen to support someone evil. Old Blythe really was Mr. Thicket, and the man Phil had stood by and admired was the Heir of Mordlum.

Neither Phil nor Guy answered the Heir of Mordlum. Instead, Phil pushed past Guy and started making his way further along the tunnel, feeling his way in the darkness. Guy followed.

The Heir of Mordlum's voice echoed through the tunnel as they crawled as fast as they could. "Your choice is made! There is no escape for any of you. My lumens will find you. You cannot hide, and you cannot escape."

CHAPTER TWENTY
City's Edge

Determined to stay ahead of the lumen army, Del pushed Sam and Emma to keep a fast pace as they continued following the river toward 1307. They had no real idea how far they needed to go, and as was usual in Azdia, it was hard to keep track of how much time it was taking them. Del thought the sun was setting for the sixth time in their journey as they stopped for a break, though she wasn't sure. They had taken some breaks, and now Del was starting to allow longer and more frequent stops, both because it seemed as though Sam and Emma needed them and because they hadn't seen any nightwings in a while.

They were down to their last few crackers. It wouldn't be long before they would have have to start scrounging for wild berries or other plants to eat. At least they had the river, full of glowing life. Perhaps, under the rejuvenating power of the water, the three of them could continue to stay ahead of the army.

"We need to sleep," said Sam, slipping to the ground. "A real sleep. Not just a couple of hours."

"We need to stay ahead of that army," said Del.

"We don't even know where the army is anymore," said Emma. "It might not even be heading where we're heading."

"It's heading there for sure," said Del. She was determined to be the chief of the Malak. Warning the lumens of 1307 was the least she could do. "We've got to give them as much time as we can."

"I don't know how you're doing it," said Sam. "Me and Emma can't keep going. We have to have a real break."

"Fine," said Del. "You sleep; I'll keep watch."

The truth was, Del hadn't slept deeply since her nightmare. The dream motivated her to keep going, but she didn't want another one.

Sam and Emma lay down, and within seconds, Sam was snoring. Emma wasn't too long after him. Del decided to just let them sleep until one of them woke up. Hours passed; Del wasn't sure how many, but the sun had long since disappeared.

Emma stirred, and her eyes fluttered open. Del was sitting next to them, hugging her legs and rocking gently back and forth. After the hours of waiting, she was finally getting tired herself.

"Del," Emma whispered.

"Yeah?" said Del.

"You need to sleep too, you know," Emma said. "You don't have to worry. I'll be right next to you."

"I just don't want the Heir to find anything out," said Del. "I think it's better if I just nap here and there."

"You need real sleep," said Emma. "I can protect you."

"You don't know that." Del yawned as she spoke.

"Fine," said Emma. "Just take a nap, then."

"Yeah," Del yawned again. "Just a nap."

And with that, Del was asleep.

*****

Del blinked her eyes open and tried to focus as the light of day filtered through the glowing leaves of a nearby tree.

"Don't get mad," said Sam. "I let you both sleep a little longer than you'd want—but you needed it, and we'll be okay. There's no sign of the army."

Emma sat up and rubbed her eyes. "I'm guessing you slept well?" she asked Del.

"Yeah," said Del, groggy but fully rested. "I don't think I dreamt at all."

"I think I met Blythe Thicket again," said Emma.

"What?" said Sam. "You met Blythe Thicket? And what do you mean 'again'?"

Del and Emma proceeded to fill Sam in on Del and Emma's strange, shared dream and Del's theory about Blythe Thicket being in Emma's dreams. Then Emma started in on her latest one.

"It started off wonderful. I had the same feeling as I had before, except this time, I knew he wasn't my grandfather. We were walking in the same forest by the big oak tree."

"The Old Oak?" Sam asked.

"Yes, the Old Oak," Emma continued. "Anyway, Blythe Thicket turned to me and said, 'I'm glad you recognize me.' Then he said, 'She'll be okay tonight,' and I knew he was talking about you. We walked for a while, not saying anything. Then he said, 'Pay attention,' and he pushed me, like before, and suddenly,

I was in my old dreams that I always have. I was beside a lake, and snow was falling over it but not on me. Then I was looking out over a desert or something—there wasn't anything living, anyway. But something else was there too—a lumen, but she didn't say anything; she just pointed out at the horizon. The rest is still kind of hazy."

"You can't remember anything else?" Sam asked.

"Wait," said Emma, closing her eyes. "I didn't go straight to the lake. There was something else in between being with Blythe Thicket and being at the lake."

Emma tightened her eyelids, held her breath, and appeared to clench every muscle in her body, clearly trying to picture her dream.

"What was it?" Del asked.

"There was a door, I think," said Emma. "It's all hard to picture. There was a weird-looking forest. I know there's more, but I can't see it."

She let out a deep breath and opened her eyes. "I'm sorry," she said and then fell to the ground. She had fainted just like she had on the beach.

Del and Sam jumped to her side.

"Emma!" Del said. "Emma, wake up! You need to wake up!"

As Emma started to come around, shrieks could be heard in the skies.

"We've wasted too much time," Del said. "We've got to go."

A nightwing appeared overhead. Del didn't think it had seen them. She and Sam helped Emma to her feet, and the three of them began to run. Del took the lead again. She moved swiftly and made sure they did not stick to any paths, keeping under the cover of trees and rocks as much as they could.

Del's focus and drive returned, and she kept the other two moving. They only took an occasional break for food and naps for the next two sunsets and sunrises.

They spoke no more of dreams, nor of Blythe Thicket, nor of the Heir of Mordlum. Everything was about getting to 1307 before the lumen army.

*****

For most of their journey to 1307, they had found shelter amongst trees or rocks. The last stretch, however, was wide open. A great plain stretched before them with a broad road cutting through it, leading toward a walled city far in the distance.

This was it—their last push. After eating their last crackers and drinking some water, Del, Sam, and Emma set off. Without any great places to hide on the plain, they decided they may as well walk along the road. They were in the open for the first time.

The plain was much larger than it had seemed at first, and their trek across it was taking forever. Gray clouds had settled in overhead, making the late afternoon much dimmer than usual. Behind them, light from the setting sun peeked through the clouds, making it difficult to see exactly where they had emerged from the forest hours earlier.

Del kept looking back, expecting to see the lumen army in pursuit. She didn't see any sign of them, however—that is, until they were about three quarters of the distance across the plain to the city.

"A nightwing," Sam said suddenly.

Del and Emma turned and looked up at the darkening clouds. The creature wasn't directly overhead. It had emerged from the clouds in the distance. A second one followed it out of the clouds.

"There's another one," said Emma.

"No," said Del. "It's all of them."

All six nightwings flew just under the clouds towards Sam, Del, and Emma.

"Do you think they see us?" said Sam.

"Off the road!" Del ordered.

They raced off the road and into a patch of long grass. Del dove to the ground, and Sam and Emma followed. They lay flat so that they could no longer see the nightwings. They could definitely hear them, though. Their screeching was terrifying.

"We can't just hide here," said Sam.

"They're going to find us," said Emma.

"They're not looking for us," said Del. "They're here for the city."

"I'd say the lumens in the city know they're coming now," said Emma.

"But we still need to help them," said Del.

"What can we do against those things and a whole army?" said Emma.

"She's got a point," said Sam.

"I don't know," said Del. "But this has been the plan. We have to get to that city before they do."

Del got to her feet but stayed hunched over so that the grass still provided some cover.

"Follow me," she said.

She led Sam and Emma further away from the road.

"We'll try to stick to this tall grass," said Del. "We'll be less likely to be seen. But we're getting to that city."

The sun dipped below the distant tree line. Del looked back across the plain that they had covered. Firelight flickered near the trees. They kept moving. Del looked back again. Why was there fire near the forest? It was the lumen army—somehow, they had caught up.

In an instant, their mission changed. It wasn't about warning 1307 about an impending attack. Now, they needed to get to the city for their own sakes. They needed to get there before the army and hope that its walls would be strong enough to protect them all.

*****

Torches began lighting along the heights of the walls of 1307.

Del, Sam, and Emma began running through the long grass toward the city. They could still make it there before the army, which was still a great distance away. They just needed to hope they were not spotted by the nightwings.

They didn't let up in their run across the plain. The army had not gained any ground on them, but it was still moving along the road at a strict march. Now that they were closer, Del could see that the city walls were much higher than they had looked when they first saw them. Del hadn't realized just how long it was going to take to reach the city from the edge of the forest, but they were nearly there now. She figured another ten or fifteen minutes of good running and they'd be safe.

She was relieved to see the massive main gate of the city begin to open.

"We're going to make it," said Emma.

Once the gate was fully open, lumens began to pour

out of the city. They carried swords, shields, spears, and bows—they were ready for battle.

"Maybe they didn't need a warning," said Sam.

"Wait," said Del. "Stop running."

The three of them stopped in their tracks and crouched in the grass.

"What is it?" said Sam.

"Those lumens aren't glowing," said Del.

"What do you mean?" said Emma.

"Look at them," said Del. "The lumens coming out of the city are dark—we can't go there."

"It's all been for nothing," said Sam.

"We're going to be captured," Emma sobbed.

"Don't panic," Del said. "It'll be okay. I just don't totally know how yet."

"They don't know we're here," said Sam, "and we have no light on us. They are easier to see than we are."

"But there's nowhere to hide out here," said Emma.

"If they're not looking for us, they probably won't find us," said Sam.

They scrambled through the grass again, away from the road, the city, and the lumen army that was coming from the forest. When Del felt they were far enough away from where the army and the lumens from the city would meet, she signaled to Emma and Sam, and the three of them lay in the long grass again.

A loud horn sounded as the city lumens and the army met in the field outside the city gates. The dark lumens greeted one another with cheers, and the six nightwings continued to screech above. The cheers of the lumens gave way to a chant. It wasn't in the lumen language, but Del didn't think it sounded English either. She could hear "Dae-gan, Dae-gan!"

A nightwing flew up from behind the walls of the city, joining the other six that circled over the now single massive army outside the city. The seventh nightwing had a rider—a menacing-looking lumen in full armor who was wielding a spear that was as long as the nightwing itself.

The lumen rider's voice raised above the others as he flew.

"Light is gone from Thirteen!" he shouted in English. "The age of Eleanor and Mordlum is over. No compassion will be shown this time, and we will all live forever!"

At this, the dark lumens all cheered, and the feldroes bellowed loudly. As the nightwings continued soaring in circles over the army, led by the lumen rider, the chant rose up again: "Dae-gan, Dae-gan, Dae-gan!"

Del wasn't entirely sure what she was witnessing, but she knew it was not good.

CHAPTER TWENTY-ONE

Flight and Fury

Despite Crimson and Treola calling it a night, Kita had barely slept. Instead, so encouraged by her progress, she convinced Verdi to let her keep Tabby with her so she could practice metamorphing. She managed to get winx fur to grow up her legs, and one time she managed to shrink a little bit—not down to the size of a winx, but still, Kita had felt like she had done okay.

By morning, she was by no means ready to try changing into a bird. The others would have no difficulty, however, and they all gathered in a courtyard outside after they had met for a bite to eat in the dining room.

The courtyard behind the commander's house had walls around it, and all the guards had been dismissed to the outside. Treola stood behind a small table that held a pitcher and four glasses. The golden bird from the day before was perched on one end of the table.

"Each of us must drink this tonic made from the roots of the trees of transformation," Treola said. "We fly today to the Violet Wood and to Del Ryder."

Treola held her glass high, and the liquid within it swirled with golden light. Crimson, Verdi, and Cinder all took their glasses. "To Mr. Thicket!" they cried together.

"And to Del Ryder!" Treola shouted.

"To Del Ryder," said the others. Crimson wore a proud but concerned look.

They drank their draughts, and Cinder said, "I know we have to do this, but we are basically returning to my home. When I left, there was nothing left besides dark lumens—sick and confused, turning on those of us who still had light and driving us out. By now, the Heir of Mordlum must have an entire army. What are we against them?"

Crimson turned toward Cinder, looked her straight in the eyes, and said, "We are the Company of Light, and today we add to our number. Treola flies with us, and we will not fail. I have seen the enemy, and I was rescued by Mr. Thicket himself. He will not let us down. He will protect us."

"He didn't protect Pyria," said Cinder.

"We've all suffered losses," said Verdi. "But we cannot let Del Ryder go it alone."

"I know," said Cinder.

"We must not delay any longer," said Treola. "Kita, you will ride with me."

She touched the golden bird and in a flash was transformed into a glowing silver version. She had managed to make herself a little bit bigger than the one on the table so that Kita would be able to ride and hopefully not slow them down too much.

The three remaining lumens touched the bird and transformed. Crimson was red, Verdi green, and Cinder a deep blue. Kita climbed onto Treola.

"We will be ready when we need to be," said the commander. "To Mr. Thicket and to Del Ryder!"

The birds took off with Crimson in the lead, followed by Verdi, Cinder, and finally, Treola with Kita on her back.

*****

The fortress of 1501 quickly became a dot on the horizon below and behind them as they soared high near the clouds above the Azdian countryside.

Kita figured that these lumens had all transformed into birds before—metamorphing into a bird was something most lumens did as soon as they had mastered changing into a winx. And why not? You got to soar high above everything and be completely free.

This was the closest Kita had ever come to flying herself, and she loved it. It was exhilarating but also a little terrifying, not being a bird herself. She had no wings, so if she fell off Treola, that would be the end of her. She held tightly around Treola's neck, gripping some of her feathers.

Their flight was swift. Kita thought about how unusual it was for lumens to be in a hurry. She also had a growing sense of dread mixed with excitement. Flying was wonderful, and she was excited about Del Ryder and about fighting for light of her land. Her growing dread, however, concerned her. What if they failed?

The sky was filled with thickening gray clouds. There were times when it was quicker and easier to fly straight through the clouds rather than swoop around or under them. When a particular cloud was wispier, Kita was able to make out flashes of Cinder's blue tail feathers, but when the clouds were a darker, thicker gray, Kita would lose sight of everything.

A large cloud loomed ahead. Crimson headed straight for it. He disappeared, and in a flash, the others were gone as well. Treola flew into the cloud, and nothing could be seen but gray. Moisture formed on Kita's arms and face. She noticed Treola getting wet as well. They were inside a rain cloud. Treola pressed on and then finally broke through on the other side.

Where were Cinder's blue feathers? Where was everyone? The leaders had vanished. Kita scanned the sky quickly, and then Treola went into a dive.

"Look down there," Treola said.

Kita held tight as the dive continued. She squinted to see the others, who were all below them and farther ahead. Perhaps Treola's eyesight was sharper as a bird, because Kita never would have spotted them. She quickly realized how they got so far away. They had all dove as well, and the speed of the dive was like nothing Kita had ever experienced.

As they made up the space between themselves and the others, the reason for their dive became apparent. They were being chased by something, and now Treola was in pursuit of their predator: a great black creature, its featherless wings stretched like a kind of skin from its body into sharp points. As they got closer, Kita could see claws protruding underneath the creature's massive body, and from their angle, the creature's fierce face could be made out as well.

The black creature was almost upon Cinder. Treola increased her speed. How was she able to move so fast with Kita's extra weight?

The creature's jaws snapped at Cinder, and several feathers came off in its mouth. It spat them out in disgust. One more snap and Cinder would be gone.

Treola dove, getting close to the creature. She reached out a talon and touched the end of its wing as it flapped up. The creature was startled, and looked back, locking eyes with Kita as though she were a rider in control of her steed. Kita could have sworn a wry, evil smile came across the creature's mouth.

The creature turned back to bear down on Cinder, snapped again, and just missed her. She had one more chance.

"I'm going to have to metamorph!" Treola shouted. "Try to hang on."

"What?" Kita protested, but there was nothing she could do.

Treola began changing in midair, as she flew. She tried to keep beating her wings, but for a moment, she was unable. Heat came from Treola's body as her silver glow increased. Together, she and Kita went into a freefall. Kita held tight to Treola's feathers, closing her eyes in fear.

Then, the feathers in Kita's hands disappeared. She slid along the body of a creature that looked just like the black one that Treola had just touched, except Treola had become a shimmering silver version.

"Grab on," Treola cried.

But Kita couldn't grab anything. She slid straight off and fell. Treola's talon flashed out but missed her. Out of the corner of her eye, Kita saw a flash of red.

"I've got her," Crimson called. "Now go, Treola. Save us!"

Crimson's dive was far faster than Kita's fall. In an

instant, she was sitting on his back looking up at the sight above. Treola flew faster than any bird, straight for the creature who had an open mouth bearing down on Cinder. Treola made it just in time, hitting the creature headfirst. A flurry of wings, talons, and teeth lashed at each other, as Cinder flew away to safety, circling close to Crimson.

Verdi had peeled away and was trying to get into the fight. He flew straight for the melee of wings and talons. Treola's silver head turned toward him, and in the lumen language, she yelled, "No! Do not come in here!"

Her voice changed to a great roar as the other creature bit hard into her neck. Verdi flew past the fight to circle with Crimson and Cinder. Treola got one of her talons free and slashed across the body of the beast. It cried in pain and let go of its hold on Treola. She furiously attacked with both talons, and turning to the birds, she said, "Fly, my friends! Fly!"

"No," said Crimson. "We must help her. I've fought these things before."

Crimson, with Kita as rider and flanked by Verdi and Cinder, flew at great speed toward the fight.

"Don't metamorph," they heard Treola cry. "You must save your energy."

"Listen to her," said Crimson. "Stay as birds, but fight as hard as you can."

The three birds flew at the black winged creature, scraping at it with their talons and beaks. Their help was just enough to give Treola the upper hand. She swung her tail around and lashed at their opponent with one final blow. It fell from the sky, lifeless, and hit the ground with a loud crash.

The birds and Treola followed it down. Once on the

surface, Treola quickly transformed back into herself. A terrible wound was on her neck, and blood was pouring out.

"Quick," said Crimson. "Kita, you must save her."

She had healed a few creatures before, but not yet another lumen. Still, Kita knew what to do. If the connection was strong enough, a lumen could heal others through touch and by offering powerful words of love and caring. Kita dismounted from Crimson and approached Treola, laying her hands on her neck. She felt the warmth of the blood. Tears formed in Kita's eyes. How had she come to feel so attached to Treola in such a short time? She didn't know, but now that Treola needed healing, Kita was thankful that they had made such a connection.

"You will be well," Kita said with a smile. "I care for you, and you are valued to me, not because of what you have done, nor because of your standing, but only because you are."

Treola smiled back as a tear trickled down her cheek. "You could have left me, you know?"

"No, we couldn't," said Kita. "I care for you, and you will be well."

Kita felt the blood stop flowing. She shifted her hands a little bit.

"There," Kita said again. "You will be well. All will be well."

"Thank you," Treola sighed. She looked exhausted.

Kita removed her hands. Only a small scar remained.

"You will need rest," said Crimson.

"We will all need some rest," said Treola. "We cannot make it there in one trip. It's too far. But you mustn't metamorph. You must stay as birds to keep the effects of the roots of transformation."

"We'll stop here, then," said Crimson, "and then fly again after some sleep."

"Crimson, if you can carry Kita, I can carry Treola," said Verdi. "We can still make it."

"That's the spirit," said Treola.

"Cinder, when we wake, you will need to lead," Crimson said.

"Don't worry," said Cinder. "I know the way from here."

CHAPTER TWENTY-TWO

Lost and Found

Del, Sam, and Emma watched the army of dark lumens in horror. They hadn't found a message with a house of fire from 1307 because it was a dark city. It had never been on fire. The lumens within it were on the side of the Heir of Mordlum. Del feared the worst. They were quite likely too late to save Azdia, and she had no idea what to do next.

Azdia's fate was not their greatest concern, however. The road that would lead them to the Violet Wood went straight into the city and, according to Sam's hand-drawn map, continued on the other side. They would have to walk for hours, possibly even a full day, to get to the other side of the city. It's not as if they could walk close to its walls, either. They needed to keep their distance—they could not risk being seen. They also had no food. They did, however, have some water in their bottles and wouldn't need to find their way past the army to the river.

"We can't just stay here in the grass," said Sam. "It's too dark to check the map, but if I'm remembering right, we should be able to cut across that direction and meet up with the road."

"Are you sure?" asked Del.

"Pretty sure," said Sam. "After the city, the road kind of curves back up and follows some mountains, I think. If we go that way, we should eventually see the mountains, and then we can just head straight for them and hopefully find the road."

"Okay," said Del. "That's what we have to do."

"What are we going to do for food?" Emma asked.

"We're just going to have to find something," said Del. "Hopefully berries or something."

They crept through the long grass away from the city walls, the road, and the army, which was still celebrating into the night. Eventually, they reached a treed area where they felt they could stop and rest until daylight returned.

*****

As day broke, Del, Sam, and Emma soon realized that the small treed area was actually the beginning of another forest. Its trees didn't glow, but they did look a lot like the tree that had grabbed them on the edge of the cliff. It hadn't glowed either—until they touched it. Had that tree been friend or foe? Had it helped them at all by grabbing them and putting them in that cave under the cliff? Del wasn't sure.

The forest was a good distance from the city, but they could see some activity just outside the city walls. It looked as though the lumen army was setting up camp. Perhaps there wasn't enough room for all of them inside.

Sam got his map out.

"If we head through this forest, we should meet up with the road on the other side," he said.

"I don't like the idea of going into this forest when there's no path to follow," said Del.

"Me neither," said Emma.

"Let's just walk along the edge of it, away from the city, for a while and see if it at least thins out a bit," said Sam.

That's what they did, leaving the city behind completely. The forest, however, remained as thick as ever. Del was convinced that at any moment, the gnarled branches were going to transform into vines, wrap around them, and take them prisoner.

Hours passed until eventually, they came upon a patch of berries. The berries were juicy, blue, and almost as large as Del's fist. Del figured she would rather die from poisoning than die of starvation. They tried them, and they tasted delicious.

The three friends were sitting and enjoying a bit of water and a feast of the oversized blueberries when— *snap*. The sound had come from the forest, like someone had stepped on a branch.

"What was that?" asked Emma.

All three of them got to their feet and squinted into the forest. That was when Del saw it. It was the top of a very familiar hat sitting on top of a short, stocky man. The man moved away from them at a slow pace, but it had a rhythm to it. Del knew that rhythm. She knew the hum or whistle that matched that rhythm perfectly.

"It's him," Del said. "It's Blythe Thicket."

She grabbed her backpack and raced into the forest.

"Del, wait!" Sam called.

"Mr. Thicket!" Del called. She stopped and looked

around. He was gone.

Sam and Emma caught up to her.

"He was there," said Del. "I was sure I saw him for a second."

"I didn't see anything," said Emma.

"Me neither," said Sam. "Del, there's nothing here. It was probably an animal or something. We should go back to the berry patch."

They turned to go back, but the edge of the forest seemed to have disappeared.

"How?" said Emma.

They hadn't run more than about ten strides. How could they have lost the berry patch? Sam ran back to where the edge of the forest should have been.

"It's as though we're right in the middle of the forest," said Sam.

Del and Emma walked over to Sam.

"What's going on?" Emma said.

"Look!" said Del, pointing. She had spotted the hat again for a brief second, but then it disappeared behind a tree. "He's there!"

Del started running again.

"There's nothing there," Emma yelled. "Del, stop."

Del reached the tree where she thought she had seen Blythe Thicket, and once again, there was nothing. She scanned the forest as Sam and Emma caught up.

"Del, there's nothing…" Sam started.

But Del had spotted him again for the briefest of moments. This time, he was farther away, deeper in the forest. She started running again, moving as quickly as she could.

"Mr. Thicket!" she yelled. "It's me! It's Del! Come back!"

She lost track of Mr. Thicket's hat as she ran. Where was he? Was he really there, or was her mind playing tricks on her? She stopped again. He was gone. There were only the trees around her.

"He was here, you guys," Del said once Sam and Emma had caught up. "You have to believe me."

The problem was, Del wasn't sure if she believed it herself. Had she seen him or just wanted to see him?

"There's nobody here," said Sam.

"I'm sorry," Del said, looking around at the trees. "We're lost, aren't we?"

Sam nodded.

Suddenly, an arrow whizzed by Del's head and stuck into a tree behind her. Instinct kicked in as she dropped to the ground. Three more arrows followed in quick succession, all hitting trees. Sam and Emma dropped as well.

Del popped her head up and saw two dark lumens racing toward them. They had swords in their hands.

"Run!" Del yelled as she jumped back up and took off. Sam and Emma followed her through the forest, trying to keep up. More arrows flew past them as they ran.

The forest thinned out a little bit. Instead of a canopy of leaves overhead, they were back to the familiar gray cloud cover. A stream flowed through a clearing, and not far from them, there was a bridge over the river. That meant there had to be a path.

Del, Sam, and Emma began running toward the bridge. Del spotted four dark lumens, each equipped with a sword on the other side. There was no way Del, Sam, and Emma would make it to the bridge before the lumens.

Del turned and ran straight into the stream. It wasn't deep, but the current knocked her off balance. Sam and Emma followed, but none of them fell. Arrows whizzed past them, and they waded through the knee-high water to the other side.

The lumens from the bridge turned and made their way to cut them off. Two more lumens appeared in the trees directly ahead of them. They held swords in their hands as well. Del, Sam, and Emma were running out of options.

Del raced along the bank of the stream in the opposite direction to the bridge. Emma was right behind her. Sam, however, was lagging behind the faster girls and was only just pulling his feet out of the water. He wasn't going to make it. One of the sword-bearing lumens had moved to head him off. Del stopped to go back for him.

"No, Del!" Sam yelled.

An arrow flew straight at her and struck her in the leg. She collapsed.

Emma stopped, turned around, and raised her hands in surrender to the dark lumens. It was the only thing they could do.

That was when Del heard a chirp from above. It didn't sound like a lumen chirp—it was much more bird-like. Del looked up, and indeed, there was a giant blue eagle in a steep dive heading straight for them.

The bird was glowing and beautiful, and a little terrifying. It swooped down and hit two of the lumen attackers with its talons. They fell to the ground and did not get back up—they were completely knocked out.

A second bird, this one gray, swooped down, barreling toward the two lumens closest to Sam. This bird had a rider—a lumen, old-looking, with a striking silver glow. Finally, a lumen of light.

The gray bird took out two more lumens with one swoop. As the dark lumens went sprawling, the silver lumen jumped from the bird's back, caught a sword that had been knocked out away from one of the dark lumens in mid-air, and landed ready to defend Sam. In an instant, the old silver lumen had disarmed another dark lumen. She clocked him good and hard on the head with the hilt of her sword, and he fell flat on his face.

As she did this, a third bird, this one glowing red and ridden by a pink lumen, dove at the five dark lumens who were all in a pack racing toward Del. With barely any effort, the red bird had knocked them out as well.

The birds circled back to deal with the archers in the forest, dodging more arrows as they flew.

The silver lumen ran to Sam and helped him get to Del and Emma.

"Are those birds lumens?" Del asked through gritted teeth.

"Yes," said the silver lumen. "That red one is—"

"It's Crimson, isn't it?" Del said.

"It is," the silver lumen continued. "And I believe you know Verdi and Cinder as well. Now, let's see that leg."

"That's Cinder?" said Sam.

Treola nodded as she examined Del's leg. "This is the Company of Light, at least most of it. Now, the arrow hasn't gone very deep, thankfully."

She pulled hard on it, and it ripped out of Del's leg. Del howled with pain.

"I'm glad to see Del Ryder is not alone," said the silver lumen.

"Do we know you?" asked Del.

"No, but I know of you," said the silver lumen. "I am Treola, and I am at your service, Del Ryder, chief of the Malak. But we need Crimson to get over here to heal your leg. He has a connection with you, and I do not."

"Sam can do it," said Del.

"He's not a lumen," said Treola.

"He's done it before," said Del.

"Never," said Treola. "It is a power that only lumens possess."

Del searched the trees. The birds were just starting to make their way back after dealing with the archers.

"Crimson's probably the best one to do it anyway," said Sam.

Del grabbed Sam's hand and put it over her bleeding leg. "No Sam—it's you. It's always you and me."

Del held Sam's wrist, keeping his hand on her leg. Sam nodded.

"Everything's going to be okay," said Sam. "We all care about you, I care about you; No matter where you go or what you decide to do, I will be right here with you. Even if you go to fight against the Heir of Mordlum, I'll stand next to you. I'll be there for you all the time, and my family will always take you in."

Tears welled up in Del's throat at the last thing Sam said, but she stopped herself from crying by biting her lip. She knew he really meant it, and she knew it was true. Sam's family would always take her in. Her own family felt loveless, but Sam's home had always been a safe haven for her. Some of that was Sam himself, but it was his mom and dad too.

She wondered if she would ever stop longing for a family like that. It wasn't that she wanted a normal family, if there was any such thing. She wanted an abnormal family—she wanted a family like Sam's. They were abnormally loving and kind. That, more than anything, was what she wanted.

"Hey, Del—let go, okay?" said Sam.

Del had been squeezing his wrist hard. She let go and then inspected her leg, looking through the hole in her pants left by the arrow.

"Not even a scar," said Del.

"Unbelievable," said Treola. "Very strong words indeed."

The birds landed. The pink lumen hopped off onto the ground, and the birds metamorphed. Crimson ran to Del and gave her a huge hug.

"You're here," Del said. "I can't believe you're here."

"I told you I would find you when you returned to Azdia," he said. "Good to see you again as well, Sam."

"But how did you find us?" said Del.

"We know about your mission to rescue Eleanor from the Heir," said Crimson. "Treola learned of it from Mordlum himself."

"You've seen the priest—I mean Mordlum?" Del exclaimed. "Where is he?"

"Alas, I do not know," Treola said. "I only know he was continuing to search for his wife. When I first met Crimson, he believed you would know where Eleanor is being held and you would be heading here."

"Then we spotted you as we flew over," said Crimson. "And just in time it would seem."

"But we're lost," said Del. "We have no idea where 'here' is."

"What do you mean?" asked Crimson. "This is the very edge of the Violet Wood."

"It can't be," said Sam.

"The trees don't look like the ones in the Violet Wood," said Del.

"That's true," said Crimson. "But just along that path, you'll see it. These younger trees give way to the large purple ones of the ancient forest."

"But it just can't be," said Sam. "It should have taken us days, and we didn't even pass through the mountains."

"Those mountains?" said Crimson with a nod of his head.

Del looked, but some trees blocked her view. She moved to one side to get a clear view. Rising above the forest were snow-capped peaks.

"But those mountains should be over there," said Sam, pointing in the opposite direction. "We never walked through the mountains. We were just in this forest for a day, and that's it."

"Well, we're all here now," said Crimson.

Verdi and Cinder came over and shook hands with Del and Sam.

"You have to show her," said Crimson to Verdi.

"I guess so, but I've already been sharing her way too much," said Verdi. He opened up his satchel and pulled out the winx.

"Tabby!" Del squealed with delight, recognizing her immediately. She grabbed her out of Verdi's hands.

"I have missed you too," said Del, holding the winx up to her face and feeling the soft fur. Tabby immediately imitated Del's syllables with her purring and turned a full purple color.

"You definitely do have a connection," said Treola.

Verdi glared at Del, clearly unhappy to give up Tabby

to her.

"We better not stay right here much longer with all these dark lumens around," Crimson said. "But before we get going, introductions are in order."

"This is Kita," said Treola. "She is not yet able to language learn, so you won't be able to communicate—but she is loyal and strong."

Del and Sam nodded at Kita.

Crimson glanced over at Emma.

"Oh yeah, right," said Del. "This is Emma—Phil's sister."

"Very good to meet you," said Crimson, offering her a hand.

Emma shook it but said nothing.

"I suppose it's all a little overwhelming meeting all of us," said Treola.

"It's not that," said Emma, almost in tears. "It's my dream, and her. She's the one beside me at the end of it. It's her."

Emma pointed at Kita.

CHAPTER TWENTY-THREE

Finding the Heir's Lair

Treola was quick to respond to Emma's declaration that she had seen Kita in a dream: "How remarkable. Now, when we find a place to rest for the night, I will want to hear all about this dream of yours—just not now. As Crimson said, we can't stay here. Let's get moving."

Before leaving the river and the bridge behind, the company collected weapons from the dark lumens that still lay unconscious. It would have taken too long to retrieve the arrows, but they now had a sword for each of them.

As Crimson had promised, it wasn't far along the path from the river to the purple trees of the Violet Wood. The first purple tree they saw wasn't standing tall like Del remembered them, however. It was lying on its side across the path, blocking their way and blocking their view of anything that was on the other side. The trees were indeed massive. Del could barely reach the top of the trunk if she stood on her tiptoes.

"Give me a boost," Del said.

Emma helped her get up on top of the fallen tree.

From the top, Del looked out at the remnants of the Violet Wood. She counted three trees that she could see that were still standing. Most trees lay on their sides. They looked as though they had been uprooted, but there were no roots on any tree—the roots looked as if they had been cut off.

The rest of the company helped each other get up on top of the trunk.

"What happened here?" Sam wondered aloud.

"The whole forest has been cut down," said Crimson.

"Harvested," said Treola. "For the roots and the lumber. This is a dark time indeed."

The members of the company jumped back down to the forest floor. It was easy to find a good place to hide among the fallen trees. There were plenty of branches strewn all over, and the trunks made the forest into a kind of massive maze. It would be terribly difficult for any enemies to find them, but it would be equally difficult for the company to find their way through the forest.

They stopped at a good spot where the ground was covered with moss, which would be quite comfortable for sleeping. The lumens had brought some food with them. If they rationed it carefully, it might be enough for them all.

As they sat in a circle on the moss, Treola took one of the water bottles in her hand.

"It is good for us all to be together," she began. "Now we truly are the Company of Light, as of old: Lumens and Malak together. We were meant to meet at exactly this time. I don't want to think what may have happened had we been a moment later. As I said before, it is a dark day when we must worry about the passage of time. But worry we must, and with every moment that passes, it is another moment where our beloved and faithful Eleanor remains a captive of the Heir of Mordlum.

"Our task, set by Del Ryder herself, is to rescue the original Malak and any other Malak who may be held in the Heir's clutches. We must not fail. We will not fail, for we have someone on our side who does not fail. We have a great protector and provider. We have one who has always kept us safe and will never abandon us, even though the darkness grows. To Mr. Thicket!"

Everyone picked up a bottle or a small cup. The shout went up, and for a brief moment, Del didn't care who heard it—she was sure the others didn't care either.

"To Mr. Thicket!"

There was no great feast, but Del was thankful for what they had.

"Good thing Guy isn't with us," said Sam. "All our cheese would already be gone."

Del laughed, and at the mention of Guy's name, Emma's face went a little more pink than usual.

Just like a winx, Del thought as she laid her hand on Tabby's back.

"Now, Emma dear," said Treola. "We must hear about this dream of yours. Is that all right?"

"Yes," Emma replied. "I think so."

"It's not just one dream," said Del. "She has lots of them."

"I see," said Treola. "Has Mr. Thicket been in any of these dreams?"

"Some of them, I think," said Emma. "At least, that's what Del thinks—I don't know what he looks like."

"Perhaps Mr. Thicket has recovered the Seed of

Dreams," said Treola excitedly.

"What's the Seed of Dreams?" asked Sam.

"It is one of the seven Crystal Seeds that give Azdia its power," Treola replied. "Surely you know of the Crystal Seeds."

"We knew there were more than two," said Del. "But we didn't know there were seven of them."

"Then you don't know about their powers?" Treola asked.

"Blythe Thicket told me that when all the seeds come together, they are more powerful than anything," Del replied. "He said he had to hide them in the dark times, but he didn't really tell me anything else."

"Each seed possesses a different kind of power," Treola continued, looking very serious. "And anyone who possesses a seed can use that power for good or evil. If someone possessed all of the Crystal Seeds, they would be unstoppable. It is said that they could make anything happen simply by willing it. No matter what happens, the Heir of Mordlum must not find the seeds."

"What do the seeds do?" asked Sam.

"The Seed of Light can control light," said Treola. "It gave all light to Azdia. The Seed of Language gave Lumens the ability of language learning and allows the holder of the seed to communicate in any language. The Seed of Transformation gave lumens the ability of metamorphing and allows the holder to turn themselves or other things into whatever they wish. The Seed of Healing governs the way we can heal each other. The one who has that seed could heal anyone or anything instantly. There is a Seed of Protection that has kept Azdia safe all these years. If you have that seed, you will always be safe. There is the Seed of Connection which binds Azdia together and allows anyone to travel to any place in Azdia if they use it. That seed is connected to each of the other seeds, so if you have another seed, you can travel back to the Seed of Connection. But with the Seed of Connection you can go anywhere you like."

"That's the one in the graveyard," said Sam.

"In your world, yes," said Treola. "Finally, there is the Seed of Dreams. It governs our dreams as we sleep, but its true purpose was kept secret for years. The one who has the Seed of Dreams can influence the dreams of others with whom they are connected. It can be used to communicate with someone in their dreams, and you do not need to be near them to do so—it works across great distances."

"But where are all the seeds?" asked Del.

"Each seed was entrusted to a keeper, and Mr. Thicket kept one or two himself," Treola replied. "Not every keeper kept track of their seeds, though. Some seeds were rumored to be lost, including the Seed of Dreams. Emma, if you've seen Mr. Thicket in your dreams, that may mean that he has recovered it—and he may be trying to tell you something."

"I wish I knew what," said Emma. "They're just strange images, mostly: snow, bright light, trees, a door, and vines, and… it's Kita right?"

The lumens that could understand nodded on Kita's behalf.

"Whatever Mr. Thicket may be telling you, it will become clear in time," said Treola.

"I have a question," said Sam. "Where is Mr. Thicket? I mean, why doesn't he show up and help us?"

Treola cleared her throat. "Ah, Samuel. Just because we don't see Mr. Thicket doesn't mean that he isn't helping us."

Sam nodded as though this made perfect sense, but Del wasn't so sure. She still didn't know if she had really seen him in the forest, and even if she had, hadn't he led them straight to a bunch of dark lumens that were waiting to kill them? If Blythe Thicket was really around, he should show himself. He should really be with them and help them. When she had been in his cottage with Crimson, it had been so great. Why didn't Blythe Thicket just make it like that all the time?

"He might be helping us," said Del. "But it would be far better if he were here. He should come."

"How is it that you walked through a forest on one side of the mountains and ended up on the edge of the Violet Wood?" Treola asked. "How is it that you were able to survive this long? How is it that we managed to rescue you just in time?"

"Luck, I guess," said Del.

"No, no, Del Ryder," said Treola. "That was Mr. Thicket."

"Look, I love Mr. Thicket," Del continued. "He's amazing when I'm with him. But shouldn't things be a whole lot better if he can do things like make you show up at just the right time? Shouldn't he just fix everything? Why doesn't he just bring back the light if he's the amazing protector and provider?"

"That's not quite how he works," said Treola. "In fact, no one quite knows how he works. It's all a bit of a mystery—but he has a plan."

"Did he plan for Eleanor to be captured?" Del snapped.

"I don't think so," said Treola. "There are most definitely things in Azdia that work against him. He didn't intend for this forest to be cut down, I can tell you that."

"So we could fail, then, couldn't we?" Del concluded. "He won't protect us for sure. He can't protect everything."

"But he does have a plan," Treola repeated, calmly.

"But no one knows what it is," said Del. "And whatever it is, it sure doesn't seem to be working!"

"No one can know the ins and outs of his plan," said Treola. "But we can know the outcome—light. We cannot judge whether it is working or not. Who would have ever known that his plan in the darkest of times was to put forgiveness on display rather than vengeance? Love instead of condemnation?"

"If he really is so great, he would show up now and help us," said Del.

Del could hear herself saying the words, but she wasn't quite sure where they were coming from. She loved Mr. Thicket, but somehow, she was angry at him as well. Why had she been put in this position? Why had he made her into the new chief of the Malak? If it had been him in the forest, why had he only shown her the back of his hat? Why hadn't he talked to her? Why hadn't he just walked over to her and told her everything was going to be okay?

"Mr. Thicket alone can decide when it is best to be with us and when it is best to help in ways we cannot see," said Treola.

"How do you know?" said Del. "Have you ever met him? In person?"

"Now, Del, that's not fair," said Crimson, cutting in.

"I have met him, and Treola's right. He will always know better than we do. We must trust in him to protect and provide even when we cannot see how his plan is working."

"I just want to see him," said Del, now holding back tears. "At least some people see him when they sleep!"

She glared at Emma and then got up from the circle, unwilling to finish her meal, and stormed away.

*****

Del had stayed by herself for the rest of the evening and slept away from the rest of the group. It seemed the company knew she needed to be alone. As she awoke, Del's leg ached where the arrow had pierced it, and her head throbbed. She instantly regretted most of what she had said the night before, although it all had a grain of truth to it.

"Good sleep?" asked Sam, who sat on a nearby rock with Emma.

"Sorry," Del said.

"Probably not us you need to apologize to," said Emma.

"Where's everyone else?"

"Trying to figure out where to go next in all this fog," said Emma.

"It is starting to clear, though," said Sam.

Del stretched and got to her feet. She could make out a few different colored glows through a silver mist that covered the forest. She marched toward the red glow, and Crimson emerged before her.

"Del, you're awake," he said.

"Crimson, I'm really sorry about everything I said

last night," Del said.

"It's okay," he said tenderly. "You have a lot on your mind. Mr. Thicket *is* with us, you know. Not in the way we'd most like him to be, but he is with us all the same."

"I know," Del said quietly.

Crimson and Del walked back to where they had slept, and the other lumens emerged from the mist.

"Did anyone find anything?" Sam asked eagerly.

The lumens shook their heads.

"The forest is vast," said Treola. "The best we can do now is trust Cinder to lead us—at least she is from this province."

"I never went into the forest when I lived in 1875," said Cinder.

"We did, though," said Del. "Sam, you must have an idea."

"Not really," said Sam. "The forest is totally different now, and we were always following either Crimson or Mr.—I mean, the Heir."

"Sam's right," said Crimson. "We didn't really know where we were going."

"We should probably just stick close to the mountains," said Sam. "The Heir's lair is inside a mountain and underground."

"We will do as Samuel says," said Treola.

The company packed their things and set off.

*****

As the morning light grew, the fog got lighter. Every now and again, the company would stop picking their way through the maze of fallen trees, and Del, Sam, and Crimson would climb on top of a trunk. They would look out on the decimated forest for clues as to where an entry point to the Heir of Mordlum's lair might be. Even though climbing on top of the tree trunks put them out in the open, Crimson felt it was worth the risk. "Maybe Sam or Del will see something that reminds them of the last time they were here," he had said.

The overall mood matched the grayness of the forest. Suddenly, Emma stopped in her tracks. She had been walking in the middle of the pack. Sam, Treola, and Kita were directly behind her and were forced to come to a halt when Emma stopped.

"Everything okay?" Sam asked.

Del, Crimson, and Cinder, who had been leading, turned back toward the rest of the group. Emma had gone as white as a sheet.

"What is it, dear?" said Treola.

"I've been here before," said Emma. "I've dreamt this."

"What have you dreamt, exactly?" Crimson asked.

"The fallen trees," she said. "I didn't realized before. It was dark, then the fog, but I'm remembering now. We're going to be…"

Emma swayed and fell to the ground.

The group rushed around her, but Treola pushed everyone back. "Give her space to breathe, please. We're going to be what, Emma?"

Emma's eyes rolled back in her head as she whispered, "Attacked."

Then she lost consciousness.

Crimson, Verdi, and Cinder pulled out their swords and made a circle with their backs to Emma and Treola. Crimson chirped a few tones, and Kita pulled out her sword as well. Del got her sword ready and looked at Sam, who did the same.

Treola shook Emma slightly—no response. She dug into the earth and sifted through the dirt quickly with her hands as if searching for something. She found a small twig, which she promptly popped into her mouth and chewed. Treola swallowed, grabbed Emma's hand, and fell down next to her.

"Is she okay?" said Sam.

Crimson bent down to Treola and looked at her. "She's asleep," he said.

"Kind of a strange time to take a nap," said Del.

"I think she might be trying to help Emma," said Sam.

The group continued to stand in an outward facing circle, weapons at the ready. It became apparent, however, that there wouldn't be an imminent attack. They relaxed a little.

Emma, from her sleep, gasped and then sat up, breathing heavily. Treola sat up as well. Still holding Emma's hand, Treola looked at her and said, "You are indeed a special one, aren't you?"

Emma smiled shyly. Treola's words managed to put a shade of pink back into Emma's cheeks.

"What happened?" asked Del.

Treola spoke first. "We weren't here. We were beside the Old Oak. But we did see him."

"Who?" Sam asked.

Treola glanced at Del and then looked over at Crimson with a smile. "Mr. Thicket," she said.

Del's heart sank, jealous of Treola, but even more jealous of Emma. Why was she getting all the time with him? Why was she being chosen? She wanted to be happy for Emma, but she wasn't. Fortunately, Del wasn't anywhere near as tired as the night before, so instead of saying something else she might regret, she just kept quiet.

"Did Mr. Thicket say anything?" Crimson asked.

"He talked only to Emma," said Treola. "Told her to trust what she had seen, and to trust Del Ryder."

At this, Del perked up. Mr. Thicket told Emma to trust her.

"I said that of course I trusted Del," said Emma. "And he just said, 'Then tell her what you've seen.' And that was it."

"So what have you seen?" asked Del.

"Like I've said before, it's hard to remember the dreams," Emma said. "There are a lot of muddled up images."

"You've got to try," said Del.

"Wait a sec," said Emma. "In the dream, while I was talking with Mr. Thicket, I could see other things. It was like he was putting images in my head, like I was looking at an old photo album, but each picture in the album was moving."

"What was in the album?" Crimson whispered.

Emma closed her eyes tightly and started to speak. "Kita is standing next to me. She's holding something that I've given her—something she must protect. Ahead of us is a light that isn't a light—like glowing blackness, if that's possible. Then, just images: a wall, snow falling, a boat, and water as far as I can see."

"What else?" Crimson asked.

"I'm flying—we're all flying on birds," said Emma. "And I see an old woman, and Guy, and my brother. And tunnels."

"Maybe that's the Heir's lair," said Sam.

"Shh," Crimson cut in. "Anything else, Emma?"

"A door, hidden by vines," Emma continued. "Now we're being attacked by dark lumens. Not all of us—just me, Del, and Sam. No! We're captured."

"It's okay, Emma," said Crimson. "Do you see anything else?"

"Yes," said Emma shakily, opening her eyes. "I need to get on top of this tree trunk."

Sam gave Emma a boost, and the rest of the company quickly joined her on top of the trunk. The fog had lifted. Emma pointed into the distance where a lone tree stood standing.

"That tree," said Emma. "The door to the tunnels is next to that tree."

CHAPTER TWENTY-FOUR

The Box of Light

Phil could hear footfalls and chirping coming from the main passageway. The Heir of Mordlum had only just announced that Phil and Guy would never escape, and already his dark lumens were coming for them.

Phil crawled past the opening in the floor through which they had seen the priest's wife and the Heir and moved into the darkness of the narrow tunnel ahead. Phil and Guy could easily outrun lumens, but the tunnel they were in was too small to stand. The boys had to keep crawling. Phil guessed that the lumens could run if they just crouched a little bit. Surely, they would have only a few seconds before being caught.

Phil's head hit something hard. Their way was blocked. Was it a door? Phil's hands scanned the surface of the wooden barrier for a handle of some kind. Phil bit his lip as a sliver of wood pierced his left hand. He felt an edge next to the place where the wood barrier met the stone of the walls. There was just enough space to get his fingers behind it. He pulled with all his might, but it didn't budge.

The lumen chirping was getting louder. They were

definitely in the tunnel now.

Phil took Guy's hand and moved it to the edge of the wood, pulling back on his wrist.

"Together," Phil whispered.

The footfalls and chirping was getting louder. The lumens were almost upon them. Phil and Guy pulled together, hard. The wood creaked and then popped off and hit the ground with a loud clatter.

"One of them's got me!" Phil cried as he felt a hand grab onto his foot. He kicked, and then he and Guy crawled forward as quickly as they could. The floor sloped down slightly, then a little more, then even more. The momentum of their fast crawl took both boys headfirst into a slide like nothing they had ever been on before.

They hurtled through the darkness, sliding along polished smooth rock. Phil bounced off the walls as the slide turned several times. It was like being on a waterslide, except the tube was made of solid rock.

By the time they finally came to a stop, Phil felt like he'd been beaten up. The last blow was Guy's larger body crashing into him at the bottom of the slide. It was still pitch black. Before the boys could get to their feet, three other figures rolled into them—dark lumens. Phil stood up. His head didn't hit anything. He felt rock walls on either side of him. There seemed to be a tunnel ahead—at least he hoped there was.

"Guy, get up and run!" Phil ordered as he took off into the total blackness ahead of him. He ran and ran, feeling the tunnel walls the whole way.

"You with me, Guy?" Phil asked.

"Yeah," said Guy. "Do you think they're after us?"

"Just keep going," said Phil.

Phil didn't care if he was going to smack into a wall in the dark as long as they got away. He had seen the army, and he had seen what the Heir of Mordlum was capable of. They had to get away. Suddenly, he felt an opening with his right hand. He stopped, turned, and reached out for Guy.

"In here," Phil said.

They stood together silently in the dark.

"I don't hear anything," said Guy.

"You okay?" Phil asked.

"No," said Guy. "That was insane."

"But nothing broken?"

"No, I'm okay," said Guy.

"They might still be after us," said Phil. "We have to keep moving and hope we can find some light. This tunnel's wider. You take the left wall. I'll take the right. We're going to take any door we find."

They moved along the tunnel, feeling the walls.

"Here," said Guy. He pulled Phil over to his side and through an opening in the rock.

They followed the new tunnel that Guy had just found, moving swiftly in the dark, working together well. They found another tunnel, then another.

Finally, the adrenaline started to wear off, and Phil started getting really scared. They were lost in the total darkness below the Heir of Mordlum's mountain. Dark lumens could still be looking for them. As he held Guy's hand, he could tell by his squeezing that he was scared too.

"What are we going to do?" said Phil. "I think we might have lost the lumens, but now what? There's no light down here."

"I've still got the box," said Guy. "Sirah told me to

use it when all other light had faded. When we had no other option."

"I'd say we're there," said Phil.

Bright light shone as Guy opened the box. For a moment, Phil couldn't see a thing as the light blinded him. Then his eyes adjusted, and he looked around. There was nothing special about the tunnel they were in, but there was something very special about what Guy had just opened.

A small bug flew from the box. It was the source of the light. It was far brighter than any glow-bug Phil had ever seen, not that he had seen too many. It was tiny, but it let off enough light to light much of the tunnel.

It buzzed away from the box and along the tunnel, away from the boys. The light around them started to get dim.

"We better follow it," said Phil.

The boys jogged to catch up. Once they did, they were able to stay at a good walking pace as the glow-bug continued through the tunnel system. There were all kinds of twists and turns, doorways, and openings leading in all kinds of different directions. They were in some kind of underground maze, and their only possibility of finding their way out seemed to lie with a glowing insect.

"What if it's just flying around?" Phil asked.

"I don't think she would have given us a useless glow bug," said Guy. "It's got to help us somehow."

Sure enough, the glow bug did help them. It led them through the maze for what seemed like hours until they started to hear something—a faint trickle of water.

Upon hearing it, Guy said, "You don't think it's leading us back to the hidden village, do you?"

"I bet it is," said Phil. "We're going to be okay."

They ended up on the banks of an underground river. The village wasn't in sight, nor was the underground lake, but Phil felt sure that this was the same river where they had first met Tolstoy. Perhaps they just needed to follow it to find Tolstoy and Sirah and explain everything that they had learned.

The glow bug led them from the riverbank toward a small outcropping of rock. It didn't look like much, just something that blended in with the rest of the cavern. As they got close to the outcropping, the bug flew in behind the rocks through a small, well-hidden opening. Phil and Guy followed.

Behind the rocks was a cave. It had been so well hidden, that without the glow bug's lead, they never would have found it. There was no way out of the cave, however, other than the way they had entered.

"It's led us all the way here to a cave," said Guy. "How's that helpful?"

Guy had no sooner said these words than the glow bug flew into a tiny hole in the floor. The hole was only big enough for the glow bug, and as soon as it passed into it, the cave went completely dark.

"Great," said Phil. "We just followed a glow bug for hours for it to find a nice place to sleep."

"And I'm starving," said Guy.

"Well, we can't stay here," said Phil. "At least if we follow the river, it's probably going to lead to the secret village."

"I guess that's all we can do," said Guy. "Maybe that's all the box was for—to lead us back to the river."

Phil started feeling his way along the cave wall to find his way out. Then, the floor began to glow—not the whole floor, just a circle on the floor—a deep green circle. Then, the circle began to lift. Phil stared in wonder at a circular piece of rock glowing green and separating from the rest of the floor.

As the circle of rock rose above the level of the floor, blinding light shot out. Phil squinted and glanced over at Guy, whose face was full of disbelief. The rock was being lifted by hundreds of glow bugs. They glowed white, but at the heart of them was a green glow that seemed even more powerful than the bugs themselves.

The rock and the bugs hovered toward Phil and Guy, whose eyes had adjusted well enough to look more closely at the bugs. Phil stared intently.

"Is that what I think it is?" Phil asked Guy.

"We can go home," said Guy.

In the middle of the glow bugs, under the hovering circle of rock, was a Crystal Seed, glowing green.

Phil reached out toward the bugs. As his hand got close to them, they moved out of his way, as if encouraging him to take the seed. His fingers gripped the seed, which seemed attached to the circle of rock. He plucked it away as if picking an apple from an apple tree.

As Phil held the Crystal Seed in his hand, the bugs flew back down, replacing the circle of rock and disappearing below it. Phil and Guy were left with the gentle but persistent glow of the Crystal Seed.

"We have to figure out how to find Del, Sam, and Emma," said Guy.

"Then we'll all get out of here," said Phil, mesmerized by what he was holding in his hand. He had the power to take them all home. In the palm of his hand, he had the power to rescue all of them from

Azdia, never to return to this awful place again.

"Don't worry. You will see your friends soon enough." A voice echoed through the cave. But how could this be? How did they not see him before?

The Heir of Mordlum walked into the cave, flanked by four dark lumens.

"Yes, you will see all your friends soon enough," said the Heir. "But I'm afraid none of you will be going home. Now be a good boy, Phillip, and hand over the seed."

Phil, bewildered and exhausted, didn't know what to do. He simply stood speechless, looking helplessly at Guy. The Heir of Mordlum reached over, and as easy as anything, took the Crystal Seed from Phil.

Guy lunged for him and tried to throw a punch. Two of the lumens grabbed Guy and held him back.

"You still have a choice, Phillip," the Heir of Mordlum said. "You could be great, and you can still be on the winning side."

Phil stayed silent.

"I see you may need more time to think," the Heir continued. "I have a good place where each of you can be alone and think for a good long time."

The Heir of Mordlum turned to his lumens. "Take them," he said.

Phil felt the cold grip of dark lumen hands clasp around his arms. He almost passed out from exhaustion, confusion, and simply being beaten. In that moment, he realized that Guy was strong, and not just physically. He thought about how Guy was really the better man than he was. Phil wanted to be the leader. He wanted to be stronger but couldn't seem to be strong when it really counted. Guy could. Del could. He had even seen Sam do it. But not him.

Phil's head was spinning. He knew the truth about the Heir of Mordlum. He knew he wasn't really Mr. Thicket. He knew he wasn't good, but Phil wondered if any of that really mattered. It wasn't as if everything he said was a lie. No one seemed to question that he was actually bringing everlasting life to the lumens. That was a good thing, even if he wasn't using the best ways to do it.

The Heir of Mordlum offered Phil what no one else could offer. He could be a great man. He could command hundreds, maybe thousands, of lumens. Phil knew that his friends were better than him, and if they somehow managed to get home, that would always be the case. But what about if he stayed? What if they all stayed and he chose to be on the winning side? Then he'd be better than all of them.

The Heir of Mordlum could give Phil greatness, and even after everything that had happened, he still liked his Mr. Thicket. He liked him better than Del's Old Blythe. Who needs another grandpa to love you when you can have a man like the Heir of Mordlum giving you real power? Who wants games and stupid stories when you can have greatness?

As the lumens marched him along the dark passageways, Phil's head began to clear. He didn't need longer to think. He knew what he wanted. He had made his choice.

CHAPTER TWENTY-FIVE

Through the Door

"There are other trees still standing, Emma," said Crimson, pointing through the mist. "Are you sure that tree is from your dream?"

"Absolutely," said Emma. "Beside that tree, there is a door that gets into the tunnels. I know it. I've seen it, but…"

"What is it, Emma?" asked Del.

"We can't go there. We'll be captured—me, you, and Sam. They'll get us."

"No, no. Don't you see?" said Sam. "That's how we'll get in. The door is for sure going to be locked or something. But if we let ourselves get captured, and then all of you come and rescue us once they've opened the door, then we have our way in."

"They are probably only looking for human beings, not lumens," said Del.

"It could work," said Treola.

"But it's far too dangerous," said Crimson.

"We must try," said Treola.

"I can't allow the Malak to be captured by the enemy," said Crimson. "What if we are unable to rescue them? Then the Heir of Mordlum will have all the Malak, and we won't have the forces to fight back against him. All hope will be gone."

"We will always have Mr. Thicket," said Treola.

"I know," said Crimson. "I'm just saying that it is not worth the risk. We can find another way."

Emma had closed her eyes as they had been arguing. She opened them. "No, Crimson," she said. "Sam's right. I'd just blocked it out. This is how we get in in my dream. This is what we have to do."

Emma's declaration settled the argument, and the whole company began making preparations. Del, Sam, and Emma kept their packs but gave their weapons to Verdi, Crimson, and Cinder. The enemy would no doubt confiscate them upon their capture, and it didn't make much sense to hand them more swords. As the lumens were packing their supplies and checking their own weapons, Emma took Del aside.

"I don't remember this part of the dream," she said.

"What do you mean?" asked Del.

"What I told Crimson—it's not totally true," Emma explained.

"Which part?" asked Del.

"I know that the door is there," said Emma. "I know that we get captured and that there are tunnels. I just don't remember seeing any glowing lumens in this part of the dream. I don't remember any rescue."

"Why did you tell Crimson what you told him?" Del asked.

"Because Treola is right," said Emma. "This is our best chance. You're not going to tell him, are you?"

"Not yet," said Del. "But I want to ask Sam."

Del called Sam over.

"What do you think, Sam?" said Del after filling him in. "Should we tell Crimson?"

Sam turned to Emma. "You said that you didn't remember seeing any glowing lumens in this part of your dream?"

"Right," said Emma.

"Maybe that's because you couldn't see them," said Sam.

"What do you mean?" Emma asked.

"Maybe they were too small," said Sam.

"Sam, you're brilliant," said Del, as she raced over to where Crimson was packing his satchel, next to Treola. Sam and Emma followed.

"Crimson, where are you going to hide while we're getting caught?" Del asked.

"I'm not sure," said Crimson. "I figured we would transform into something close by—a rock or a bush, perhaps. We would try to blend in. We would change back once your captors opened the door."

"But you might be seen before you ever even get in place," said Del. "You should do what you did with us in the forest of the Old Oak. You should all make yourselves as small as you can. We'll carry you to the door. Then, when we're caught, we'll just take you in with us."

"That could work," said Crimson.

"It's inspired," said Treola.

"It was Sam's idea," said Del.

Sam was beaming.

*****

The lumens shrunk themselves, with Crimson

holding Kita's hand to do the transformation for her and Verdi shrinking Tabby. They turned out to be very small. When Crimson had singlehandedly shrunk himself and four children all in the same night, a feat that nearly killed him for the amount of energy it had used, he had shrunk them to about the size of a blade of grass. These lumens were even smaller. None of them were any bigger than one of Del's fingernails. She could barely see Tabby in Verdi's hands—she looked like a speck of dust.

Del, Sam, and Emma would need to be very careful with the tiny lumens. They would be easy to hide but equally easy to squish. Emma had a place on her necklace that had a small opening where two of the lumens could crouch inside and be completely concealed. Treola and Kita took that spot. Verdi, with Tabby, went into one of the pockets in Sam's sweatshirt. Crimson tucked himself into a turned-over fold in one of Del's socks.

Each of the tiny lumens also still had tiny packs and tiny weapons that they had shrunk, including extra swords for Del, Emma, and Sam.

*****

The tree was quite a bit farther than any of them had anticipated. Crimson kept tapping at Del's ankle, which tended to tickle. She kept having to kneel down to talk with him and each time explain that they were not there yet. It was like she and her sister used to be when they were younger and going on road trips with their mom.

Between the stops for Crimson, Del thought about home. The last time she had been in Azdia, she had wanted nothing more than to get back home. She had missed her mom and even her sister. When she had finally gotten home, it had been a disappointment. In Azdian time, she had been gone for weeks or maybe even months, but it had been only a few hours on Earth. Her family hadn't even noticed she'd been missing.

Now she knew this was how it worked. She missed her mom and sister this time, but she'd been through that before. She guessed that this was a lot like the first time you go to camp in the summer—something Del had never done. It's just easier to be away the second time. This time, she had been much more focused on rescuing Mrs. Manters, Phil, and Guy.

She wondered, as she got closer to finding them (at least she *thought* she was getting closer), why she was suddenly thinking about her family. She knew the Heir wasn't her father—at least, she thought she knew. But what if he was?

Is that why she had been chosen as the chief of the Malak? Was it because the Heir was her father, and the priest and his wife were her grandparents? Maybe that's why she felt so attached to Mrs. Manters and why she felt she needed to rescue her so much. Maybe it was more than the legend of Eleanor. Maybe this was all about family.

But if all of that was true, then why hadn't her mother told her, and why hadn't Mrs. Manters told her? None of it made sense. She wished she knew who the Heir of Mordlum really was, but more importantly, she wished she knew who *she* was or was supposed to be.

She thought about how her sister never seemed to care about things like who their real father was.

Suzanne was much more like their mom than Del was. She was all about boys, make-up, and making Del's life miserable. Del was never going to be like that. Maybe she was more like her father. Hadn't the Heir of Mordlum told her that she was a lot like him?

She was unable to keep her mind from going in circles until, without warning, the branches of the tree from Emma's dream were over their heads.

Emma broke the silence that they had kept since the last time they had stopped. "This way," she whispered.

Emma led them past the tree trunk and then stopped. She looked very pale, close to one of the trances that they had seen her have before when connecting to her dreams.

"Are we close?" asked Sam.

"We're here," said Emma. She bent down and moved some moss and vines out of the way. Underneath was the edge of a door.

Del bent down. They would have never seen it unless someone had pointed it out.

"What now?" Del whispered.

Her answer didn't come from Sam, Emma, or any of the tiny hidden lumens. Another voice gave the reply in halting, broken English. "He said you would come to us."

Del felt the point of a sword at her back. She looked at Sam and Emma, who both had swords pointed at their backs as well. Three dark lumens had them.

"Don't try to run," said one of the dark lumens.

"Or fight," said another.

A fourth, then a fifth, dark lumen emerged from behind a fallen tree trunk. One of the lumens checked each of the children's bags but found nothing. Another lumen banged on the door, which opened. Their captors led them through the door and down a flight of stairs to a tunnel. The plan was working. They were inside. Crimson and the rest of the company could easily overpower five dark lumens once they turned back to regular size.

"This was a mistake," said Emma. "I remember now."

"What do you mean?" said Del.

Del did not need to hear a response. They rounded a corner, and the tunnel widened as it sloped down. There must have been fifty dark lumens lining the hallway.

The lumen with his sword at Del's back raised his voice—"We have Del Ryder!"

The crowd of dark lumens cheered, and as one group they marched along the tunnel—fifty guards for three kids.

CHAPTER TWENTY-SIX

The Troops of Eighteen

Once Phil had told the Heir of Mordlum his decision to join his side, the Heir had taken Phil to a room that Phil assumed was his private library. Books lined the walls. There was a grand piano in one corner. There were three easy chairs and a desk with a large black chair at it. Lanterns hung at regular intervals along the bookcases. They were alone.

"I know you're not really Mr. Thicket," Phil said.

His mentor remained silent.

"I'm okay with it," Phil continued. "I'm with you no matter what. I just want to know who you really are."

The Heir walked along one of the walls, and pulled a book off the shelf. He flipped through it casually and then put it back. He sat down at the piano and began playing gently.

"Some of them can believe I am Mr. Thicket for now," the Heir began. "For many lumens, Mr. Thicket stands for salvation and protection, and that is exactly what I will bring them. Eventually, I want them to know that darkness means life for them. I want my enemies to be confused about who I am. I want them fighting amongst themselves. But when all who stand against me are eliminated, and all that is left is my Azdia, an Azdia of beautiful darkness, then I will banish the name of Mr. Thicket, and all will know my rightful name."

"Mordlum?" Phil offered.

"Mordlum was weak and foolish. He let his love for a woman cloud his vision. I made that mistake once as well. He did not learn from his mistake, but I did. I know what it is to lose, and I will never lose again. He chose a life of loss when he gave up his reign, when he submitted to her. He will know what true loss is now that I have her."

"Then she really is Eleanor?"

"She is. She was powerful once, but no more. She tried to change me—said I could be forgiven the way Mordlum was. Forgiveness! Ha! The thing about forgiveness is that it only applies when someone has done something wrong. They are the ones who are hurting this land—spreading the lie that light is good, when the light is the very thing that kills the lumens. I bring darkness, and I will do everything necessary to drive out the light that kills. I will not apologize for saving everyone who turns to the darkness. If anyone needs forgiveness, it is them, but I will never give it."

"But isn't that a little harsh?"

"My dear boy, no. It's loving. Forgiveness is too great of a risk. Suppose they said that they came to see things my way, that they would be on my side. Suppose they apologized for standing in my way. Suppose they sought forgiveness from me, and suppose I granted it. How would I know that they were not spies? You see, if they are as committed to their cause of light as I am to the cause of darkness, they would lie to me to stop me. I know you children did as much when I first met you, and you knew very little of the light."

Phil looked down, a little ashamed. He wanted the Heir of Mordlum to tell him the full truth, but here he was not having always been completely honest with him.

"Phillip, my boy, don't look so disheartened. This is the way of things. I wouldn't expect it any other way. You shouldn't trust me or anyone else, and I won't trust you either. It's too risky. You say you are with me, and you may be telling me the truth, but in the end, that doesn't matter, because I have something that will protect me."

"But I am with you," Phil declared. "I'll do anything for you."

"No, you won't," said the Heir. "There are things you are not yet ready to do. But that's all right, my boy. It's all right because I have your friend Guy."

"What are you talking about?"

"Phillip, I am so pleased that you are with me. There is great potential in you, but I trust no one, and this is the lesson I want you to learn today for your own good. You will learn the lesson of leverage. If you are truly with me, then wonderful—we will rule together; we will bring about a dark age of salvation for this world. But if you aren't with me—if you are treacherous or choose to leave me, then your friend will have to die."

Phil ran at the Heir of Mordlum with flailing fists. The Heir easily stopped him by grabbing Phil's left wrist in one hand and twisting it behind his back. The Heir's other arm wrapped itself around Phil's chest.

"This is good," he whispered in Phil's ear. "Remember this lesson. Remember your rage and use it. You will need it in our fight."

The Heir released Phil by throwing him to the ground.

Phil stood up and glared defiantly. "Tell me your real name."

"I will show you thousands who already know my name because they have shown their allegiance to me. Then you will know."

*****

Phil and the Heir of Mordlum flew on their birds high above the eighteenth province back to Tamavaros, the massive city that had once been known as the lumen town of 1875. Phil looked below, and there were thousands of dark lumens lining the streets. They had exchanged their building tools for weapons of war. Each lumen on the street had a sword, spear, or bow. Many were wearing armor.

They flew over a great gate at one end of the city. Beyond the eastern wall was a sight even more devastating and impressive than what was within. It was a massive camp that stretched farther than Phil could see—more lumens by the thousands, all equipped to fight against anything that stood in their way. At one end of the camp was an entire herd of feldroes. They were held in place by ropes and harnesses, and they roared ferociously, as if aching to get free from their restraints.

Phil's heart sank when he saw a familiar creature soaring high in the air. It was the same kind of winged creature that had attacked them in the Violet Wood on their first visit to Azdia. As his stomach churned, Phil thought about how, deep down, he had known that these horrible things must be on the Heir's side. Phil remembered how, when they had first met the Heir of Mordlum, he had killed one of the creatures and rescued them, earning their trust. This man had no problem killing in order to get what he wanted. Now he had even admitted that he would kill Guy if Phil stepped out of line. Somehow, Phil was following a murderer. How had it come to this?

They circled back around and over the city, flying low over the legions of troops. The lumens were not chirping in their usual language. They were chanting something over and over again. Phil listened carefully to try to pick it up, but he couldn't understand it.

They were chanting, "Dae-gan, Dae-gan."

The birds swept up and landed on the tower. The Heir and Phil got off their birds. The chanting got louder. "Dae-gan, Dae-gan, Dae-gan."

The Heir walked to the edge of the tower. He pulled his cloak back, and it billowed behind him in the breeze. Attached to his belt were the three Crystal Seeds. The Heir pulled two of them from his belt and held them high. Lightning shot from the Seed of Light high into the air. "We are ready!" he shouted.

A great cheer went up, and in the distance, Phil saw three winged creatures fly up into the clouds. Fire shot up and out of chimneys throughout the city. The great bellows of feldroes out in the camp could be heard even over the noise of the city.

Then the chant started again. "Dae-gan, Dae-gan, Dae-gan."

Phil approached the Heir. He was standing so close to the precipice that Phil could have easily pushed him over. He reached out a hand but got scared. He backed away and mumbled to himself. "There are so many of them."

The Heir chuckled and turned toward Phil. "This is only part of my full fighting force," he said. "They will join more in my other great city in the thirteenth province. From there, we will not be stopped."

"What are they chanting?" Phil asked.

"You wanted to know my real name," the Heir replied.

Daegan put the Crystal Seeds away, took Phil's hand, and moved him over to stand next to him. Their joined hands were held high for all to see.

Daegan called out loudly, "He is one of us now. Others will join us or be destroyed. Darkness is here, and we will all live forever!"

The crowd cheered again, and to Phil's shock, the chant changed. "Phillip! Phillip! Phillip!"

When Phil had stood on this tower before, he had thought this was what he wanted—crowds cheering his name. He was starting now, for the first time, to understand the cost.

Daegan put his arm around Phil and said, "That's right, they know you."

He leaned closer to Phil, his lips pressed up against his ear. "Now, do not let me down," he whispered. "You wouldn't want your friend to suffer."

"Sir," a voice called from behind them

Daegan and Phil turned around. A dark lumen stood in front of them, wearing all black. "What is it?" said Daegan.

"We have her," said the lumen in slow, broken English. "We have Del Ryder."

CHAPTER TWENTY-SEVEN

Dreamdust

The dark lumen guards marched Del, Sam, and Emma through the maze of tunnels that was the Heir of Mordlum's lair. Del knew there was no way they would be able to overpower fifty guards, so there was no point in any of the light lumens transforming back to their normal size. How were they going to get out of this?

The tunnels inclined down, and occasionally, there were flights of stairs. Del had hoped she might be able to keep track of the turns, thinking that they might be able to find their way back to the door, but she lost track. It was all too complicated.

The dark lumens chirped to each other continuously, and every now and again, broken English could be heard. Mostly it was the words "Del Ryder" that stuck out in their conversation. They always sneered her name with a combination of disgust and pride, as though Del was both garbage and trophy.

Del remembered the dark lumens as always smiling and happy, but these were not like that. They seemed angry. She wondered if perhaps the Heir kept the happy ones as servants to give him food and things like that but made the angry ones into soldiers.

As they marched, dark lumens took turns pushing Del, Sam, or Emma in the back. They passed by a series of wooden doors, each with a small opening.

"Del!" said a human voice from behind one of the doors.

"Guy, is that you?" Del tried to stop, looking at the opening. There were Guy's eyes.

A dark lumen pushed Del to keep her moving as she called, "You're really here. Are you okay?"

"We came to find you," said Guy. "But…"

With that, a dark lumen hit at the door hard, covering the opening with his hand.

"Quiet!" one of the guards said.

The guard directly in front of Del pulled out a set of keys, sorted through them, and inserted one of the keys into a lock in the door next to Guy's cell. The door swung open into the empty room, and a dark lumen pushed Sam inside. They locked him in.

Emma was placed in a second cell, and the guard with the keys opened a third for Del. As she went to walk past the guard, she felt a tickle on her leg. She glanced down to see Crimson crawl up her leg a little and then jump from her leg to the guard's hip.

The guard pushed Del into the cell and closed the door. Del immediately looked through the slot. The guard put his keys back on his belt, and Crimson crawled toward them. He ran his hands over every key on the ring. All the guards moved along the hallway out of Del's sight.

Judging by the silence, all of the guards had left this part of the hallway. They had completed their deed.

Del Ryder and her friends were prisoners. Of course, there must be a couple of guards somewhere, but surely all fifty wouldn't have stayed.

The guards had led them straight to Guy. All they had to do was get the doors open, which would in fact prove to be fairly easy.

Del saw a tiny glow moving along the floor. It was Crimson. He stopped in front of her door as he was joined by the other lumens. They must have slipped under the doors of the other cells.

Their glows increased as they began to transform. Cinder, Treola, Kita, and Verdi stood full-size in the hallway. Where was Crimson? She saw Treola bend down and pick up a red key. In a few seconds, Del's door swung open.

Crimson had transformed himself into a key that exactly matched the one needed for Del's cell door. The key glowed a little and changed shape ever so slightly. Treola tried it in the next door, but it wouldn't turn.

"Try a different key, Crimson," she said and then turned to Del. "I guess he knew which key was yours, but not the others."

Crimson and Treola tried three different shapes of key before getting Emma's door open. Sam's door was next. They opened a fourth door, and Guy came bounding into the hallway. Del and Sam almost tackled him to the ground with their hugs. They let go, and Guy and Emma stood face to face.

Guy didn't move, his face turning pink. Emma, however, threw her arms around him. "I'm so glad we found you," she whispered as she let him go.

"Del, you've been right all along," said Guy. "We came through the portal after you and figured we needed help to find you. We found Mr. Thicket, but he's not Mr. Thicket, is he? He saved us again, though. He saved me, but you're right—he's evil. But Phil's joined him anyway—Phil's on his side, and he knows that he's not good."

Del couldn't believe it. She knew that Phil liked the Heir of Mordlum more than the rest of them, and she could understand if he'd been tricked, but Phil knew he was evil and was still going along with him? Emma looked despondent as well.

"It will be okay," said Treola. "Is Eleanor here?"

Guy looked as if he was just noticing the lumens. He stood for a moment staring at Cinder, ignoring Treola's question. "Is that really—?" Guy began.

"Yes, it's Cinder," said Sam. "She's the one who helped us in 1875."

"I knew you looked familiar," said Guy. "No Crimson, though?"

"Crimson's right here," said Treola, holding out the red key.

"Cool!" Guy exclaimed.

"Eleanor?" said Treola.

"Right," said Guy. "She is here. You guys know Eleanor is the priest's wife?"

Del, Emma, and Sam nodded.

"Of course you do!" Guy exclaimed. "She should be through one of these doors."

The remaining doors in the hallway had no openings in them, and they seemed heavier than the first few that had held the children. They opened one door and found nothing.

The second door revealed an open room with a few bookshelves, a table and chairs, and several torches and lamps. In the center of the room was a large cage, and inside it was Mrs. Manters. She stood up as soon as the company entered.

"What are you doing here?" she asked.

"We're here to rescue you," said Del.

Treola raced over to the cage with the red key and began trying it in the lock. "My lady," she said as she nodded with her head.

"Treola," said Mrs. Manters. "How could you bring them here?"

"With all respect, my lady," said Treola. "Del Ryder is now the chief of the Malak. Your husband told me he had commissioned her to rescue you if he failed. We simply joined her in her mission."

"What!" Mrs. Manters was getting noticeably angry. "My husband did what?"

Del stepped forward. "When you were captured, he went in after you. He told us to rescue you if he didn't make it back. And he…"

Treola continued trying different shaped keys in the lock without any luck.

"This is terrible," said Mrs. Manters. "My husband is still out looking for me, or perhaps killed already, but even worse, you brought Emma straight to the enemy. She cannot be here—she is too important."

"What do you mean?" asked Del.

Mrs. Manters ignored the question and yelled instead, "Is that key doing anything?"

Verdi stepped forward. "Your hand, my lady."

"At least someone here has some sense," said Mrs. Manters as she held hands with Verdi through the cage. The two of them shrunk down through blinding light. Mrs. Manters became just small enough to pass between her bars. Still holding hands, Verdi brought Mrs. Manters and himself back to normal size.

"Thank you," she said.

While Verdi had been freeing Mrs. Manters from her cage, Crimson had become himself again.

"What's done is done," said Mrs. Manters, a little more calmly. "But we must act swiftly. I'm assuming that you are the famous Crimson. Much thanks is owed to you for your help and friendship to Del—thanks to all of you, really. And I don't know you three."

"This is Cinder, Verdi, and Kita," said Treola.

The three lumens bowed low.

"Emma, Del, and the other children must leave this place at once," said Mrs. Manters. "I will see you out, and then I'll take Verdi here, who seems quite industrious, with me to find Phillip. We won't leave him behind."

"How are we going to get out of here?" Del asked.

"You mean you don't have a plan?" asked Guy.

"We do indeed," said Treola. "Emma already told us how we will escape."

"I did?" said Emma.

"In your dream that you told us," said Treola, "we were flying. We need to find one of those winged creatures that attacked us—surely he has more hidden somewhere."

"No, there's something better," said Guy. "Birds— and I think I know the way."

*****

Turning the first corner out of the cellblock, they were met by two dark lumens. Crimson and Verdi, who were right next to Guy in the lead, had them knocked out in no time.

Guy led the Company of Light through the twisting tunnels. He stopped in front of a large wooden door. Del didn't recognize the tunnels or the door.

"I think I took a wrong turn," said Guy. "But if we go through this door, there should be a way through."

Guy opened the door, and the company passed through. They were in a vast cavern, which Del thought was easily as big as the football stadium back home. There were tree roots hanging from the ceiling. Three dark lumens were gathered around a large cauldron at one end of the cavern. They looked up at the company but ignored them and went back to mixing whatever potion they were cooking up.

"They don't seem to care we're here," Del whispered.

Still following Guy, the company began making their way across the cavern toward a door on the far side. They had covered about half of the distance when Del noticed that the room had become much brighter. Was it her eyes simply adjusting to the gloom? No, the room was definitely brighter.

"Are those roots supposed to do that?" Sam asked, pointing up.

The roots above their head were all glowing a light purple.

"That's Dreamroot," said Guy. "It's from the dead forest."

"I've never seen life return to a dead tree before," said Treola. "Those roots should not be glowing."

"We must move," said Eleanor. "Before someone notices we're gone."

The company ran across the cavern toward the door

on the far side. Before they reached it, however, it swung open, and the Heir of Mordlum strode through. Phil followed and half-hid behind him. The company stopped in their tracks.

The Heir surveyed the cavern as dark lumens poured into the cavern through all available doors. The company was surrounded by at least fifty dark lumens. The Heir looked up at the Dreamroot, all lit up.

"Where is it?" was all he said.

"You cannot have it," said Eleanor, stepping forward.

"I know it's here," the Heir continued. "You can give it to me willingly, or I will just take it by force—now step forward, Emma, my dear."

The rest of the company turned toward Emma. What did he want with Emma? As soon as Del looked at her, she figured it out. Emma's necklace was glowing. It was getting brighter and brighter, matching the glowing roots above their heads in intensity.

"What's happening?" Emma questioned.

"She doesn't know, then," said the Heir.

Eleanor shook her head.

"My dear Emma," the Heir continued. "There is a Crystal Seed inside your necklace. You possess the Seed of Dreams, and you will give it to me now."

The Heir pulled out a Crystal Seed from under his cloak. "Don't make me use this," he said.

"But—" was all Emma could get out. Suddenly, all eyes were drawn to the ceiling. Something was happening to the roots. They were glowing brightly, and a low rumble echoed through the cavern. The purple glow kept intensifying, and the roots began to shake as though an earthquake were rocking them this way and that.

"Are they supposed to do that?" asked Sam.

"I've never seen anything like it," said Treola.

The shaking roots rumbled louder and louder until suddenly, a popping sound took over. Pop after pop echoed from above as though someone were making a giant bag of popcorn. The roots were exploding, and all that was left of them was glowing purple dust, which floated gently down like fog on a cold autumn morning.

"Stop!" the Heir ordered as he raced toward the company. "You're destroying my Dreamroot!"

The Heir never did get to Emma, however, or anyone in the company. The purple dust cloud reached them all first. Treola grabbed Del and Emma and pulled them to the ground.

"Lay as flat as you can," said Treola.

Del, Emma, and Treola lay sprawled out on the floor. Nobody else seemed to have reacted like this. Del watched as the purple dust surrounded first of all Eleanor and the Heir; then Phil, Guy, and Sam; and then all the lumens. Suddenly, everyone in the room collapsed.

"What's going on?" Del whispered.

"That dust is from the trees of the Violet Wood," said Treola. "A forest which grew from the Seed of Dreams. It just put everyone to sleep."

Emma grabbed Del's hand.

"We're going to be okay," she said as purple dust settled on them.

CHAPTER TWENTY-EIGHT

Return to the Old Oak

Colors swirled above and around Del's head as she ran through a thick forest. A myriad of colors shone out from leaves that sprang in front of her, blocking her from making any fast headway. Branches shot up under her feet to trip her, and some tree limbs swung down, almost taking her head off. She ducked and jumped, avoiding each stray branch. Leaves larger than her flew past her, but she made each one miss her.

Though other-worldly, the forest was familiar. She didn't know where she was running, but she felt as though she needed to escape. Where had everyone else gone? How had she gotten out of the Heir of Mordlum's lair? Her legs felt as though they were going to fall off, and her lungs began to burn.

Then she tripped over something. She fell to the ground hard and felt something sting her side.

"Ouch!" she cried out.

It had happened again. Something had stung her. She looked up, and a large dark leaf was descending upon her. The last time this had happened, Phil had been there to pick her up. This time, she was alone.

The leaf covered her before she could react, cutting Del off from the colorful glow of the forest. She ran her hand over the bump on her side. It hurt, but it was somehow different than the bump from the sting that had happened to her before.

She felt the leaf on top of her, and it instantly transformed into a cozy blanket, and the forest floor changed into a bed. Del pushed the blanket back. Her eyes were met with a blinding brightness, but she knew immediately where she was.

The smell of fresh baking wafted over her. Del's eyes adjusted to the light of day beaming through the open window. The room was full of all kind of things: an old-style bicycle, Japanese or Chinese Pottery, beautiful paintings, and on the desk, an old-style blue and white see-through computer shaped like a teardrop. How had she gone from the forest to her room in Blythe Thicket's cottage?

Remarkably, Emma stood in one corner of the room, smiling at Del. Emma's necklace glowed with beautiful purple hues.

"How?" was all Del could manage to say.

"He told me to give you a message," said Emma, walking over to the bed. "He said you need to slow down and pay attention. Stop running, and you will meet him."

"I don't know what that means," said Del.

"Neither do I," said Emma.

"Why isn't he here?" Del asked.

"He was here," said Emma. "But he's gone now. He just told me to give you a message, and then he disappeared—that's all I know. He was really insistent about slowing down."

"I don't know how we got here or what's going on, but we can't stay here," said Del, pushing back her blankets.

Del slid her feet to the floor, and Emma grabbed her hand to help her out of the bed. Del's side pinched with pain, and she winced. She opened her eyes and was back in the forest. She wasn't holding Emma's hand. Instead, Phil hoisted Del to her feet from the forest floor.

"That was close," Phil said. "C'mon—we've got to move."

He pulled Del along through the trees, which continued to thrash about, making terrible and terrifying noises. Del was bewildered. Where had Emma gone? Where had the cottage gone?

Phil and Del ran through the forest just as they had long ago. Phil did the leading, never once letting go of Del's hand.

"We can make it out of here," he reassured her. "Don't worry, Del; we can get out of Azdia."

"Phil," Del said. "I need to slow down."

"We can't," Phil said. "We've got to keep going. We've got to get out. We can keep ahead of the trees."

"Phil, it'll be okay," said Del. "I promise."

"Are you sure?" The voice had changed, as had the grip on Del's hand. Phil had, in an instant, changed into Sam. Her best friend ran alongside her, puffing as he went.

"Are you sure?" Sam repeated. "Because if you're sure the trees won't get us, then we'll just stop right here —together. I'm always with you, Del, and I believe in you. You are the chief of the Malak."

Del slowed to a jog and stopped ducking and jumping

out of the way of the swinging branches. Nothing hit her or Sam.

"I'm sure," she said.

Del and Sam slowed to a walk. The entire forest calmed down. The glowing colors continued to dance across the branches and leaves overhead. Del remained calm, and the forest, as though it were a winx, matched her perfectly.

The two best friends didn't say anything to each other. They just walked together as though they didn't have a care in the world, and for a few moments, Del didn't. She was once again beginning to believe.

"Do you know where you're going?" Sam asked.

"I know where he is," said Del calmly. "I know where to look."

As they walked deeper into the forest, their path became blocked. Tall, thick hedges made a wall extending to the left and right, and a large boulder stood directly in front of them.

"This shouldn't be here," said Del. "I know where I'm supposed to go, but how are we supposed to get through?"

"With help," came a different voice from the friend by her side. Sam had changed into Guy. "We're all with you, Del."

Guy walked up to the stone, and although it towered over his head, he was somehow able to roll the stone away to open up a clear path forward. Guy stepped out of the way and made way for Del to pass through.

She looked past the stone into a familiar glade. She saw the stone steps that led up to the dais from which Eleanor had made her speeches long ago. Beyond that, at the center of the glade, rose a massive Oak Tree.

Leaning against its trunk was an old man, short and stocky. He wore a tweed jacket and a familiar peaked hat. He held a walking stick in one hand.

*****

Blythe Thicket winked at Del. She wanted to run to him, to hug him, but something about his face told her that she was still to take things slow. She kept walking toward him, and her hand instinctively went to her side. There was no bump and no pain.

"That only happened to remind you, little Del," said Blythe Thicket.

Del continued walking toward the Old Oak as they spoke.

"To remind me?" Del asked.

"To remind you of where all healing comes from," said Blythe Thicket. "To remind you of me."

"But I don't need reminding," said Del.

"Everyone needs reminding of love and goodness and beauty," said Blythe Thicket.

"Why do I have to be in pain for that?" asked Del.

"It's not the pain that I want to remind you of—it's the healing."

At these words, Del had completed her walk to the Old Oak. She stood under its branches, face to face with Blythe Thicket.

"Are you here to rescue us?" asked Del.

"I'm quite certain that rescue is why *you* are here, little Del," Mr. Thicket replied. "Do you remember my riddle?"

"Yes, but…"

"But you haven't been acting upon it," said Mr.

Thicket.

"No, but Mrs. Manters was captured and I'm sorry."

"Do not be sorry," said Mr. Thicket. "Your wisdom is one of the reasons I chose you as the chief of the Malak. When the Heir of Mordlum captured Eleanor you were right to go after her even though it meant postponing the mission I gave you in the riddle."

"We were just doing what Reverend Manters told us."

"You mean you had the wisdom to listen to him. As it turns out the adventure you are in is the very quest you have needed. You are now ready for a greater battle with the forces of darkness that is still to come."

"But why can't you just stop the darkness?" Del asked.

"That's not how it works, little Del," said Mr. Thicket.

"But why not? Why do I have to be here? Why am I the chief of the Malak?"

"It seems you've found your questions," Mr. Thicket replied. "No games or stories to distract us here in your dream, it seems."

"I'm dreaming?" asked Del.

"But of course you're dreaming, little Del," said Blythe Thicket. "You're actually all asleep in the Heir of Mordlum's lair."

"Why am I the only one here with you?" asked Del.

"I wanted to talk to just you," Blythe Thicket said. "The others are waiting for you."

"Waiting for me?" asked Del.

"To lead them," said Blythe Thicket.

"I don't know if I can lead anyone," said Del.

"You must," said Blythe Thicket. "You must defeat the darkness as much for you as for the inhabitants of

Azdia. You are the one, little Del. Nobody else can do it for you."

"I don't understand," said Del. "Can't you just explain it to me?"

"If you learn everything at once, it will overwhelm you. It must be this way for now, for your sake. But remember, you are not alone. I am on your side, and you have your friends, including a new friend—the one I asked you to find."

"Emma?" asked Del.

"Yes, that's the one," said Blythe Thicket. "A beautiful name—Emma. She must be protected at all costs. Promise me that you will take her across the sea and follow the riddle I gave you."

Del wanted to protest and ask more questions, but something about Mr. Thicket's tone told her that she needed to just do what he asked.

"I promise," she said. "And I'm sorry."

"Another apology," Mr. Thicket sighed. "Why are you sorry?"

"For all the questions—and for doubting you."

"Never apologize for questions—or doubts for that matter. It means you're human, and it means you're learning—and that is very good. Don't forget that in the middle of any doubt or questions you may have, I am with you—I am for you. I may not answer everything you want answered at the moment you want it answered, but that doesn't mean that the question is wrong or shouldn't be asked."

Del nodded.

Blythe Thicket continued: "You must wake up now before the forces of darkness do. Stay as quiet as you can as you wake the others."

"But I've only just gotten here," said Del. "Can't we have longer? I have so many other questions."

"We will see each other outside of your dreams, little Del—never fear."

Blythe Thicket smiled warmly. Del's heart pounded within her chest. She loved Blythe Thicket as though he were the perfect grandparent. She wished more than anything that she could spend longer with him.

He held out his arms to Del, and she fell into his embrace. She wasn't fully prepared for the emotions that flooded through her. She burst into tears as she was held the way she always wished a member of her family would hold her. In Blythe Thicket's arms, she felt an amazing combination of joy and sorrow: joy at being loved without condition and sorrow at never having received that love from her own family. How she wished for a better family than what she had!

She wept in his arms for what felt like hours even though it was probably less than a minute.

"You don't need to be perfectly strong," Blythe Thicket assured her. "Though you have a strength beyond what most people will ever possess. I will be your strength; I will be your shield and protector. I promise to uphold you, even in the darkest places. Now go, little Del, chief of the Malak."

Blythe Thicket squeezed Del hard. She closed her eyes for a second, and upon opening them, she was back on the cold stone floor next to Emma and Treola. She looked around her. Her friends, the Company of Light, perhaps a hundred dark lumens, and the Heir of Mordlum were all there. Every one of them was still asleep.

CHAPTER TWENTY-NINE

Getting Out

Del crawled away from Treola and Emma toward Sam. She wanted to wake him up first, as she knew he would understand what had just happened to her without her having to explain too much.

She knelt over Sam and looked at the eerie sight around her. It was creepy that everyone was asleep. Her gaze fell upon the Heir of Mordlum. Del reached down to her hip where there hung a sword. She got to her feet and walked over to the Heir.

He looked kind of peaceful as he slept. Why was he the way he was? Why was he so evil? Del pulled her sword from its place and held it above the Heir's body. It would be so easy to push the end of it straight through his chest. Would it be easy? Del had never pushed a sword through anything, let alone into a person. She couldn't believe she was contemplating killing someone in their sleep.

This is not my way, Del thought. *This will not be our way.*

She put the sword away, walked back over to Sam, and shook him awake. His eyes opened, and Del held a finger up to her mouth to indicate that he should stay quiet.

"Everyone's asleep," Del whispered. "We're going to sneak out of here, all of us, before the dark lumens wake up. Help me wake up everyone else, but keep them quiet."

Sam nodded. He and Del went around the room waking up the other members of the company. Everyone gathered near the exit they had been originally heading toward on the far side of the room—that is, everyone except Phil. He still lay asleep next to the Heir of Mordlum.

"I think we should just try to carry him," said Crimson. "He's with the Heir now, and if he wakes, he may shout out."

"No," said Del. "He's not really with the Heir. We can trust him."

"I hate to say it," said Guy. "But I think Crimson's right. I mean, Phil left me in a cell and went off with the Heir."

"We must save him," said Eleanor.

"I'm the chief of the Malak, and I'm waking him up," said Del.

She walked over to Phil and woke him up in the same way she had woken Sam and half of the company. Phil, however, reacted quite differently than the others. He didn't shout out or anything like that. Instead, tears started to form in his eyes and he hugged Del tightly.

"Am I ever glad to see you," he whispered.

"Really?" said Del.

"Yeah," Phil replied. "Now we're all together and we can go home."

"We've got to get out of here first," said Del as she got to her feet.

She helped Phil to his feet. They walked quietly over to the rest of the company. Phil made a beeline to his sister. "What are you doing with a Crystal Seed?"

"I didn't know anything about it," said Emma.

"It makes sense, though, doesn't it?" said Sam. "All the weird dreams you have."

"You told them about your dreams?" Phil asked.

"Well, they started coming true," said Emma. "Phil, all these years I've been dreaming about Azdia. Now we know why—it's because of my necklace."

"This is crazy," said Phil. "But we can talk about it when we get home. We can use the seed in your necklace to go home."

"I'm afraid you cannot," said Eleanor. "That necklace is protected by a powerful charm. Only Mr. Thicket knows how it opens to reveal the seed. We must leave this room. We must get away before any of them wake up."

"He has other seeds," Phil said, pointing to the Heir of Mordlum. "If we get one, we can go home."

"No," said Del. "It's too risky. We just need to go."

"How many seeds does he have?" asked Eleanor.

"Three," said Phil.

"It may be worth the risk," said Treola. "Keeping the seeds out of his hands is our highest priority."

"I just know we are supposed to get out of here as fast as we can," said Del.

Phil was already on his way, however. He looked back at the company and mouthed the words, "I know where they are—don't worry."

Del whispered, perhaps a little loudly, "Phil, don't."

Phil was already kneeling next to the Heir of Mordlum, moving his cloak out of the way in order to gain access to his belt, which held the three seeds. He unclipped one seed and held it up for everyone to see.

"Now, the others," Treola whispered.

But Phil didn't go back for the other seeds. He had a different mission in mind. He stood back up and walked toward the company. He knelt down in an open space of the floor where no dark lumens slept.

"Phillip, no!" Eleanor cried.

It was too late. Phil placed the seed on the ground and activated it. It vibrated on the ground, making a rattling sound that echoed throughout the chamber. A beam of light shot out from the seed, projecting an oval of light that hovered in midair ready for anyone to jump through back to the graveyard.

"Guys, we can go back home," said Phil triumphantly.

The noise of the seed accompanied by the brilliant light had been too much. Dark lumens started to rouse around them. Del knew that they needed to make a decision quickly: jump through the light-bridge back home or stay with Crimson and the Company of Light to fight for Azdia. She supposed they could always come back, but finding the company might be difficult. Del, as usual, was unable to make a quick decision.

It seemed, though, that everyone had hesitated, and in the moment of hesitation, the decision had been made for them.

The Heir of Mordlum jumped to his feet, and before anyone could react, he was next to Phil. He grabbed Phil by the wrist and cried out, "Traitor!"

Then he smiled at Phil. "I like that about you, Phillip, my boy," he said. "You were willing to turn on me, just as you were willing to turn on your friends before. It shows me that you understand the highest value of all: take care of yourself at all costs. You will indeed be great one day."

"I care about my friends," Phil said defiantly as he struggled against the Heir's grip on him.

"And we care about you," said Del. "We're not leaving without you."

"Then none of you will ever leave," said the Heir. "You cannot escape."

In a flash, Phil stomped hard on the Heir's foot. Phil broke free for an instant, but he wasn't going to get very far. He certainly wasn't going to get to the company before the Heir recovered or before a dark lumen grabbed him.

"Guys, run!" Phil yelled. "Get out of here!"

And with that final shout to his friends, Phil dove toward the oval of light. He made contact with the light, and it sucked him through.

His voice rang out from the oval: "It was the only way you could get out!"

"He's left without us!" cried Guy.

"So we don't get caught," said Crimson. "He took away our only reason to stay in this room."

"Run, everyone!" yelled Eleanor.

The Company of Light bolted out of the room before any dark lumens or the Heir could react.

*****

The company raced through the maze of hallways, pursued by the Heir's dark lumens. Guy was in the lead, followed by Emma, Del, Sam, and Eleanor. All of the lumens lagged behind a bit with their shorter legs. It was a good thing they lagged, too, because as dark lumens caught up to the company, Crimson, Verdi, and Cinder fended them off with their swords.

"Where was the seed when you left earth?" Eleanor puffed as they ran.

"What?" Del responded.

"The seed—where did you leave it?" Eleanor asked again.

"Right next to Blythe's stone, under the thicket," said Del. "Why?"

"Me must pray that Phillip does not move it," said Eleanor. "The Heir's smoke will not be able to come out of the seed while it is next to Blythe's stone. That place is enchanted with a very good and powerful magic."

"We're almost there!" Guy yelled.

Del recognized the hallway they were in. They ran by the room that she had slept in before. The company sprinted around a few more turns, and Guy led them straight toward the large double doors of the Great Hall. They burst through.

Their loud entry into the hall immediately set the birds off. The twelve bird squawked loudly and left their perches, circling the room.

The company ran to the far wall and stopped under the empty bird perches. Del looked around the room at the life-sized statues of lumens and human beings around the room. She looked closely and was sure that two of the people looked like younger versions of the priest and Eleanor. If only the priest were here now with that scepter that he had used to beat back the smoke in the church basement. If only they could somehow summon the statues to life to help them fight against the hordes of dark lumens that were pouring into the hall.

"We will have to fight," said Eleanor.

Kita chirped and handed her sword to Eleanor as if to defer to the better fighter.

"I think you'll be better with this than me," Emma said to Guy as she handed her sword over as well.

The dark lumens did not attack but made a large semi-circle several lumens thick. There were easily a hundred of them, perhaps more. The birds still circled overhead.

"What are they waiting for?" asked Sam.

"For him," said Del.

The Heir of Mordlum strode into the room, and the dark lumens began chanting, "Dae-gan, Dae-gan."

"What are they saying?" asked Del.

"That is the name he has chosen for himself," said Eleanor.

"It's not a very nice name, is it?" said Emma.

"I think that's kind of the point," said Guy.

"We will not be able to stand against them for very long," Verdi grumbled.

"My lumens are the least of your worries," the Heir called out. He held a Crystal Seed aloft, and green lightning shot out of it. The lightning struck over the Heir's head and danced across the ceiling of cavern in all directions.

"We have no chance against him," Cinder whispered.

"We may still be able to escape," Treola whispered back. "My lady, do you think you and Guy could throw me high enough to reach one of the birds flying overhead?"

"What?" said Del. "No!"

"I am reasonable," said the Heir. "I do not wish to kill

any of you. All I want is the necklace, Del Ryder, and Eleanor. The rest of you are free to go."

"We will never stop fighting!" Del yelled back.

"My dear Delaney, there will be no fight," said the Heir, coolly. "If I wished, I could destroy you all. Perhaps a demonstration is in order."

The Heir shot lightning across the room toward Crimson. Crimson was quick, however. He dove out of the way and rolled away from the company.

"Now!" yelled Treola.

The Heir shot a second blast of lightning toward Crimson, who dodged it again, just as Eleanor and Guy threw Treola into the air. The Heir aimed at Treola but let the bolt off too quickly and missed. Treola reached out with her hand to grab onto the talon of the cream-colored bird, but came up short. She glowed a beautiful silver glow, and her arm suddenly stretched longer. The edge of her fingers just brushed against the bird's wings.

Before the Heir could send of another lightning blast, Treola had changed into an incredible silver bird. Her wings stretched out, and she circled with the other birds above the crowd of lumens and the Company of Light. She shone beautifully, as if thousands of twinkling stars lined her feathers. She changed her flight path and swooped down to the Company of Light. Each lumen except for Kita reached out their hands and touched Treola's wings as she flew by. It was as if Treola had just scored the winning goal and was returning to high-five her teammates. In some ways, that is exactly what had happened, and it had all taken less than three seconds.

"Attack!" yelled the Heir, as he sent off more lightning, this time right toward Del. Emma pushed Del out of the way, and by the same magic that had saved them in Del's dream, the necklace around Emma's neck absorbed all of the lightning. Emma lay on the ground, clearly in shock but unharmed.

The dark lumens thrust forward, but they were too slow. Crimson, Verdi, and Cinder all changed into large, glowing birds as Treola landed amongst the company. Guy helped Emma up, and they jumped together onto Cinder. Sam and Del chose Crimson. Eleanor jumped onto Verdi, and Treola carried Kita. The four lumen-birds soared into the air.

The Heir continued shooting lightning at the company, but almost every bolt went toward Emma and was absorbed by the necklace.

Verdi and Eleanor were the first to reach the hole in the ceiling. They disappeared through it, followed by Treola and Kita. The others were almost there.

That was when the Heir pulled out one of the other Crystal Seeds and whistled in a high pitch. His twelve birds hovered in midair, aligning with one another, waiting for him. A thin beam of light shot from the other seed straight at his birds, covering them with a purple glow.

The birds immediately began convulsing, beating their wings faster and faster. A black skin started to wrap itself around each bird, concealing the bright colors of its feathers.

Cinder, Guy, and Emma disappeared through the hole in the ceiling, and Crimson, Sam, and Del were right behind them.

"Oh no," said Sam, who was sitting behind Del.

"What?" said Del, turning slightly.

Sam didn't answer but just moved to the side a little for Del to catch a last glimpse of what was below them in the Great Hall. Del's heart was racing, but then felt as if it stopped. She knew they wouldn't be safe at all when they got out. Instead, they would have twelve nightwings after them.

CHAPTER THIRTY

The Protector's Storm

Though Cinder and Crimson were both carrying two passengers each, they were still the fastest of the birds. They gained on Treola and Verdi as the whole company made their way above the mountains toward a massive storm cloud.

The twelve nightwings were in pursuit. The Heir of Mordlum was riding the one in the lead.

Streaks of lightning came from the Heir toward them. Crimson and Cinder were agile, narrowly dodging everything that he threw at them. The black cloud ahead loomed.

Del hung onto bird-Crimson with all her strength. Sam sat behind her, clinging tightly to her waist. Del loved flying, but this was different. They were being attacked by the worst creatures they had ever seen in Azdia. Del didn't know if every nightwing they had ever encountered had been under the Heir's control, but these were, and that frightened her all the more.

Cinder had passed Crimson, and they had both almost caught up to Treola and Verdi. Guy turned a bit, and Del could see he looked sick, as if he were going to throw up. He wasn't screaming, but he looked like he needed to. Emma looked scared as well, but something about her face told Del she was excited to have Guy holding her in place.

The wind picked up, and it began to rain, making it much harder to swerve quickly. In a flash of light, everything changed. The Heir sent two quick lightning bursts. Crimson and Cinder managed to dodge them, but at the moment the Heir had taken aim, all the birds had been aligned with one another. The first bolt struck Verdi, and the second bolt stabbed at Treola—both direct hits.

Immediately, Treola and Verdi changed into their lumen forms. Then it was as if everything stopped for a moment, bodies hanging in mid-air: Treola, Verdi, Kita, and Mrs. Manters.

They fell.

Cinder and Crimson went into a steep dive. Crimson flew past Mrs. Manters, leaving her for Cinder, who caught her easily in her talons and pulled up toward the storm cloud above. Crimson picked up speed and hurtled toward Verdi, who was dropping like a stone.

Treola and Kita clung to each other as they fell. Then, they were surrounded by a glowing light—but it wasn't Treola's silver light. The light was pink. It was Kita. Beautiful pink wings stretched out and began to flap. Treola's limp body was held gently in the bird's talons. Kita had done it. She had learned to metamorph completely—there and then. She had changed into the very thing that was needed at that moment—a bird. She flew up, following Cinder.

Crimson's speed was like nothing Del had ever experienced. He was already carrying Del and Sam, and still he flew to save Verdi. They got closer to him, but the rocks below were approaching fast.

Crimson pulled out of the dive with incredible velocity. It felt as if some great giant were pressing down on Del's back and shoulders as they flew back up toward the black cloud above. Del looked down at the bird's empty talons. Crimson had not been fast enough. Verdi was lost.

As all of this happened, the twelve nightwings circled above. The Company of Light flew closer to the black cloud. The Heir gave a great screeching cry, and his creatures called back to him. His own nightwing hovered in midair as he raised his arm and gave a signal to his birds of prey.

At his signal, they went into action, bellowing as they went. The sound of the screeching and roaring was terrifying. Sam clung to Del, and she clung to Crimson. Crimson, Cinder, and Kita flew with all their might toward the black cloud as the twelve nightwings flew in an attempt to cut them off.

The company reached the cloud first, and as they entered it, they began to be pelted with rain. Lighting flashed from the cloud, lighting up the blackness, which was the only time Del could see the other birds or the nightwings.

Everything was chaos. Del felt the rush of bat-like wings flying past them. When lightning flashed, she could see great black talons bearing down on them. She was sure that if the nightwings didn't get them, the storm would. She had seen this kind of storm destroy a ship and take the lives of two of Crimson's best friends.

Del was panicked, but all she could do was hold on. Her mind raced with thoughts of the end of her life.

She would never see her family again: her mother, her sister. She would never meet her father. She would never grow up and have a family of her own. She was scared, but then it was as if her heart turned within her. She remembered Blythe Thicket's words to her from her dream—"I promise to uphold you, even in the darkest places."

Crimson continued to pound his wet wings. Del was sure it wasn't Crimson in control anymore—the wind was pushing them further into the cloud.

Del stopped her mind from racing. That was what she was supposed to do—take in everything around her and really look and listen—look and listen for Mr. Thicket.

Lightning flashed around them.

"We're going to die in this storm!" Sam shouted.

For the first time in their flight, Crimson spoke. "Do not fear. It is often when things are darkest, that Mr. Thicket changes things."

"But what can he do?" asked Sam, sobbing. "He's just an old man in a cottage. He can't help us."

"Crimson's right, Sam," said Del. "Mr. Thicket will protect us."

"He's doing more than just protect us this time," Crimson half-laughed. "Mr. Thicket sent this storm to save us, and he is in the storm with us. Look carefully when the lightning flashes next."

"What are you talking about?" asked Sam.

"The lightning never hits us," said Crimson. "But it has already hit at least three of those terrible beasts."

"I didn't see anything," said Sam.

"Me neither," said Del.

"This storm is not like the storm on the sea that took the lives of Hollow and Egreck," said Crimson. "This is

Mr. Thicket's storm. Look again."

The cloud lit up with lightning again, and rather than turning away when she saw a black wing, Del looked directly at it. What she saw looked less like lightning and more like a jagged spear made of light piercing the chest of one of the creatures.

Del's heart skipped a beat. It was true. It was really him. Mr. Thicket had always been gentle and kind with her, but in the storm, he was powerful. If Del hadn't already known him, she would have been scared out of her skin.

The storm was their protection from the forces of darkness. The storm raged furiously as if it were a parent lashing out at someone who had severely hurt or offended its children. This was, of course, exactly what was happening.

Each time the thunder boomed and lightning flashed, Del would see Mr. Thicket holding his great jagged spear, throwing it and destroying the nightwings. She never did see the Heir of Mordlum in the storm and wondered if he had fled once he had realized to whom the storm belonged. Perhaps the Heir had never entered the storm.

Had Treola, who had been leading the way at first, known that the storm was their best hope—that it was from their protector? Had all the lumens known? Perhaps Del was beginning to see Azdia as they saw it.

The storm began to settle down. There was no more lightning. Del figured that if the storm was settling, it meant they were finally safe.

A sudden increase in the wind pushed them until they exited the storm cloud. There was no sign of any nightwings or the Heir of Mordum. Everyone in the company was accounted for—except for poor Verdi.

"Where is Mr. Thicket?" said Sam.

"I'm not sure he works like that, Sam," said Del. "He's with us, though—even if we can't see him."

"You're learning, Del," said Crimson. "You are indeed the chief of the Malak."

Below them, Del could see a small village with no more than about fifteen cottages. Lights flickered at the windows of each house, and smoke rose from the chimneys. Everything looked peaceful and quaint.

The birds descended, and they touched down quietly just behind one of the cottages. All the lumens changed back to their regular form. Kita immediately ran to Del and touched her. She chirped a few sounds and then looked down, disappointed.

"It will take her longer to learn languages," Crimson explained. He was checking Treola, who was lying nearby. "She's quite hurt, and we all need rest. We need to find his house."

"Whose house?" asked Sam.

"We have a friend here," said Crimson.

CHAPTER THIRTY-ONE

The House with the Green Door

"Where are we?" asked Del.

"We are in 1403," said Cinder. "At least, we think we are. We need to find a house with a green door."

With only about fifteen houses in the village, it didn't take them long to find Yah-yah's house. Cinder knocked on the green door, and Yah-yah himself opened it. His face beamed at the sight of the Company of Light. He chirped a few times. Del offered him her hand, which he shook.

"Come in," Yah-yah said in English. "There may be just enough room for all of you."

"Your brother?" asked Cinder when they had all pushed through the small door.

"I lost him," said Yah-yah. "I couldn't keep him from turning dark."

"Where is he now?" said Emma, looking around anxiously.

"Not here," said Yah-yah. "We have kept our village peaceful by taking the dark lumens to the edge of the eighteenth province and letting them join the dark ones there."

"So you're adding them to his army?" Guy accused.

Yah-yah looked down. "It was not what I wanted at first, but when it was my own brother… At least he's alive. But I see the company has grown, and I do not know everyone, and you don't all know me. I'm Yah-yah, and you must be the chief of the Malak, our savior."

Yah-yah bowed low.

"I'm Del," said Del. "But if you want to bow to anyone, it should be her."

Del nodded at Mrs. Manters.

"You aren't?" said Yah-yah.

"She is—the lady Eleanor," Cinder said.

"Amazing," said Yah-yah.

Cinder finished the introductions. "The others here are Sam, Guy, and Emma. That is Treola, and you know Kita." Kita was sitting next to Treola, whispering to her, doing what she could to help her recover.

"Who has Tabby?" asked Del suddenly.

"Don't worry," said Mrs. Manters. "I kept her throughout our flight."

Mrs. Manters brought Tabby out and handed her to Del. Tabby turned from pink to purple.

"You must all need something to eat and drink," said Yah-yah, striding toward the kitchen. "Where's Verdi?"

Del glanced over at Crimson, who hung his head.

"Verdi didn't make it," said Cinder.

Yah-yah wasn't in the kitchen long. He emerged with bread and cheese and a large jug. He began pulling out goblets from a sideboard near a large table at one end of the living space. When they all had their goblets, he raised his high.

"I'm sorry about Verdi," said Yah-yah. "I know he

was a brother to you, Crimson. You have all come here for rest, and you will get it. I don't know how you came to be on my doorstep, but no doubt you have some adventures to share, and no doubt you have been battling the darkness that has taken hold in our land. I stand with you, and I stand with Mr. Thicket."

The group lifted their glasses, and their voices rang out. "To Mr. Thicket."

Del noticed, however, that Crimson only half-heartedly said the toast. He took the smallest of sips and then sat down and remained quiet. He and Tabby were the only ones left of Hollow's crew: Hollow, Egreck, and Verdi were all gone now.

Del walked over to Crimson and handed him the winx. "I think you need her more than I do right now," she said.

Tabby started changing to blue and purred gently. Crimson managed a smile.

Emma cleared her throat. "Everyone, Guy has something to say."

"What?" said Guy.

"Tell them what you told me," Emma said.

"Well, before Phil and I found the Heir's place, we found a hidden town," Guy began.

The room fell silent as he continued: "It was on an underground lake. I think they were lumens from all over province thirteen."

"That's Kita and Treola's province," said Cinder. "Did you meet anyone?"

"We were helped by two lumens named Tolstoy and Sirah," Guy said.

At the mention of their names, Treola lifted her head and opened her mouth to speak, but no sound came out. Kita stroked Treola's head and whispered in her ear, laying her head back down on a cushion at the end of the couch where she lay.

"But the real problem," Guy continued, "is that the Heir of Mordlum knows where the town is, and we accidentally led him right to a Crystal Seed that was hidden nearby."

Treola struggled to lift her head again. She breathed in heavily. Kita tried to guide her back down, but Treola batted Kita's hands away.

"I must speak," Treola said faintly. Her voice was gravelly and low, barely audible. "Sirah is the keeper of the Seed of Transformation. I feared the worst when I saw the Heir had that seed. The hidden town, Sirah, Tolstoy—they are all in danger. They must be warned."

"Surely they will know they are in danger," said Cinder.

"None of the lumens in the town seemed to know anything about the Heir," said Guy. "They just talked like they were hiding in the mountains from the darkness, but they had no idea, really."

"We must take word to them," said Treola, now coughing. "I will go."

"No," said Cinder. "You're too weak."

"And you'll never find it," said Guy.

"You found it, did you not?" said Treola. "It is my province, and Sirah is a friend. I know how she thinks, the kinds of places she would hide. I must be the one to go."

Kita chirped a few words.

"You may indeed be the best to accompany Treola if she is going to go, Kita," said Crimson. "You can continue to speak words of healing to her."

It was clear that Treola would not be convinced otherwise, although she did in the end agree to rest until the sun rose again.

*****

The company continued talking into the night, catching Yah-yah up on everything that had happened. Throughout the stories, Treola rested, Crimson continued to brood even with Tabby close by, and Sam looked puzzled.

Del, sitting next to Sam, elbowed him gently in the ribs, "What is it? Spit it out."

"What happens if the Heir gets all the Crystal Seeds?" Sam asked.

"He would possess more power than any of us can imagine," said Eleanor. "He could do whatever he wanted."

"Then don't you think that is what he's really after?" said Sam.

"That *is* what he's after," said Del.

"Yes, but he can't get the one in your world," said Cinder.

"Don't be so sure," said Del. "I remember something Mr. Thicket said to me. Crimson, do you remember?"

Crimson stayed silent. Del continued: "He said that he feared that the Heir of Mordlum may have found a way to bring the seed from our world to Azdia."

"Is this true?" asked Eleanor.

Crimson nodded.

"Then Philip may still have a role to play," Eleanor said.

"I can't believe he just left us," said Emma. "He can

be such an idiot."

"Your brother desperately wanted to go home," said Eleanor. "He wanted that for all of you. In the end, he dove into the bridge so that we would escape. He knew if we had tried to fight to free him, we would not have succeeded. We would have all been captured or killed. He went home for all of you."

"Still, it doesn't feel very good," said Guy. "And it didn't feel very good to be locked up while he went off with the Heir."

"He came back to the good side, though," said Del. "I could see it in his eyes. He's on our side—I know it."

"We will have to hope that he realizes that the seed in the graveyard, the Seed of Connection, must be protected," said Eleanor. "We must protect all the seeds we can."

Emma held the charm of her necklace in her hands. "What about my necklace?" she asked.

"Only Mr. Thicket knows how to open your necklace," said Eleanor. "The seed inside is well-protected."

Del thought about the riddle and Blythe Thicket's insistence in her dream that she follow it with Emma by her side.

"I think Mr. Thicket gave Crimson and me clues to open the necklace," Del said. "Or maybe clues to keep it safer."

"What did he tell you?" Eleanor asked.

"That Emma and I need to go across the sea," Del said. She decided to leave it at just the first line of the riddle. When Blythe Thicket had first told her and Crimson the riddle, he had warned her about trusting absolutely no one. She had told Sam, but Blythe

Thicket had openly said that Sam was trustworthy, and Del agreed. Sam knew enough to follow Del's lead and keep quiet.

"No more splitting up," said Emma, who was sitting next to Guy. "We're all staying together this time."

"Treola is determined to go to the hidden village and warn them," said Eleanor. "Kita and Cinder will both accompany her. It will be dangerous, but we may still find some allies in the north. Yah-yah, are you willing to help us beyond giving us safe haven tonight?"

"There is nothing keeping me here now, my lady," said Yah-yah. "I am at your command."

"Then you and Crimson will travel with the four Malak to 1401 on the coast," said Eleanor. "Find a vessel and set across the sea as Del says. She is the chief of the Malak and will guide you all."

"What about you?" asked Del.

"I must search for my husband," said Eleanor. "I fear something terrible has happened to him. He may have been captured or hurt or…"

"I will go with you," said Del. "Going across the sea can wait. Or maybe the priest—I mean Mr. Manters—is on the other side of the sea."

"He is on this side, Delaney," said Eleanor. "And you must cross the sea if that is the direction Mr. Thicket has given. Your mission is for all of Azdia. Mine is simply one of the heart. My husband and I have been together almost 50 years, and I cannot let him go—not like this. I will gladly give myself for him, but I won't pull others away from the true mission—your mission, Delaney. You must go across the sea."

Del reluctantly agreed. She understood, but selfishly, she wanted Eleanor along with them. Del knew she couldn't lead the way Eleanor did.

"You must set off in the morning," said Eleanor, standing up and putting a sword in her belt. "You'll be safe here, at least for tonight."

"You're not going now?" asked Del.

"My goal was to get you to safety," said Eleanor. "That is done, and I will begin my search."

"But what if we need you?" Del pleaded.

As she said the words, she thought she saw the shape of a man pass by the window. She wasn't scared, though. She knew she wasn't seeing things but also knew that if she rushed outside, there would be no one there. It was just his way. Eleanor looked through the window and then turned to Del and smiled.

"Little Del, I think he calls you," said Eleanor. "You are seeing more and more clearly. You don't need me anymore. He will protect you. Perhaps one more toast, but not too loudly. We wouldn't want to wake Treola."

Yah-yah quickly made sure everyone's glass was full; then the entire company, except Treola, who was sound asleep in the other room, repeated softly, "To Mr. Thicket."

After the toast, Eleanor took Del by the hand, and they walked together toward the small green door.

"I can't thank you enough," said Eleanor. "When you first arrived to rescue me, I was upset that you had come for me and not been focused on the real mission of bringing back the light. I honestly wasn't sure that we would be able to get out, but we did."

"We did it together," said Del.

"It wouldn't have happened without you," said Eleanor. "You're their leader now. I thought you would need training, but I know now you are ready. This whole experience has made you ready."

Eleanor looked past Del toward the rest of the company. "Farewell, my friends," she said, as she opened the small green door. Del followed her outside.

"I need to know something before you go," said Del.

"Anything."

"Who is the Heir of Mordlum? I had a dream where he claimed to be my father, which I know isn't true. But if he's Mordlum's heir, then he must be—"

"He's evil," said Eleanor, cutting Del off. "I know what you're thinking, but the Heir is not our son as many of the lumens believe—Reverend Manters and I never had any children."

"Then who is he?" asked Del.

"All we really know is that he is responsible for the return of the darkness. The lumens gave him the title of 'Heir' because he took up the dark work that first began with Mordlum.

"We knew our efforts to fully restore the light would never succeed unless we stopped him. My husband tracked him across Azdia, all the while believing that the Heir could be reasoned with—that perhaps there was a glimmer of light deep within him. Sadly, Reverend Manters was wrong. When they finally faced each other, there was no light in the Heir—he was bent only on evil. All that remained was for the two men to fight, and that day the Heir was defeated, or so we thought. That is why I was so shocked when you said you'd met him.

"When my husband and I first sent you into Azdia, we thought you were going to be the one to complete our job of fully restoring the light. With the Heir gone, we thought you would simply be building upon what we were coming close to completing. I see now, that things are much darker than they ever have been, and you will be a greater force for light than either me or my husband. You are the one who will truly defeat the Heir."

"So, nobody knows who he is? Not even Mr. Thicket?"

"I don't presume to know what Mr. Thicket knows, but I do know that usually Mr. Thicket allows us to discover what we need to know at the very time we need to know it."

"That's not always helpful, is it?"

"Del, you must trust him—he will get you through."

"I do trust him; it's just hard when I have so many questions."

"Questions and doubt are human and normal—but don't forget to come back to him. He's with us, and I know you know that."

"You sound like him, you know."

Eleanor held out her arms to Del and gave her one last hug.

"Oh, Delaney—be brave," said Eleanor as she held Del close.

"Good luck," Del whispered.

"And you," she replied. And with that, Eleanor Manters slipped into the blackness of the night to begin the search for her husband.

Del went back inside the house.

"We've talked enough for tonight," said Crimson. "We have quite a quest ahead of us. Time for some much-needed rest."

Each member of the company found some space in the living room to stretch out on some blankets that

Yah-yah had provided. Del was squeezed between Emma and Sam. Her eyes were heavy. Normally, her mind would be racing as she lay down to sleep, but she was focused now, and surprisingly unafraid. She had Mr. Thicket, Sam, and the company by her side, and she had Emma to watch over her in her dreams.

"I feel bad," Sam whispered just as Del was drifting off. "The whole time we've been here, I never really thought much about Mr. Manters. I hope he's all right."

"We all do," said Del. "Now go to sleep."

"Goodnight, Del," said Sam.

"Goodnight, Sam," Del replied.

Epilogue

Phil dropped out of the darkness of the bridge and found himself under the thicket once again. It was a little disorienting when returning, going from the total darkness of the bridge to being enveloped in the light of the portal. For a second, Phil was blind from the light; then the oval disappeared.

Phil heard a groan. He was not alone. He blinked, trying to get his eyes to adjust to the dimness. It was still light out. Not much time had passed on Earth.

There was another groan. Phil could see the pant legs of a man inside the hedge. The other half of him was outside. He was clearly trying to pull himself out.

Phil squeezed past him and helped pull him out of the hedge into the open. The priest screamed in pain as Phil pulled.

"I'm sorry," Phil said. "What happened?"

The priest just moaned. His eyes wouldn't focus on Phil but were opening and shutting as if he had no control over them.

Phil took a good look at the priest. What had happened to him? He looked as if he had been badly beaten. Blood ran from his puffy nose, and he had scratches across his hands. His black cloak was soaked in blood on one side.

"How did this happen to you?" Phil demanded.

The priest groaned again and then mumbled to himself, "Joseph."

"It's me—it's Phil," Phil said.

"Hospital," the priest exhaled.

"Right," said Phil. "What was I thinking?"

Through all the adventures he had had in Azdia, Phil had still managed to hold onto his cell phone. He pulled it out and dialed 9-1-1.

What do I tell them? he thought to himself. The operator came on the line, and Phil told her that he had found someone dying in the graveyard. She told him to stay where he was, and they would find him.

"You've got to tell me something," Phil pleaded with the priest.

The priest shot an arm out and grabbed Phil's shirt. "Keep seed safe," he said, and then his eyes rolled back in his head as he continued, not making any sense. "Must tell Del... Eleanor... scepter... failed... Joseph..."

As he said each word, the priest got more agitated and tried to sit up. At the name Joseph, the priest lost all energy and fell back to the ground, unconscious.

"No," Phil cried. "Wake up! Wake up! I need you to tell me what's going on."

Phil tried to shake the priest awake.

"I left them all," Phil said to the unconscious priest. He began to cry. "I left them, and they needed me. I was such an idiot. I wish..."

Phil heard sirens in the distance. The ambulance would be there soon.

Phil dove back under the hedge. He grabbed the

Crystal Seed, put it in his pocket, and returned to the priest. "I'll keep it safe," Phil said.

Phil was terrified. He didn't know how exactly to keep the seed safe, but he wasn't about to leave it in the middle of what was about to become a crime scene. The sirens were getting louder. Phil had no idea what he would say to the paramedics—or worse, the police—when they got there.

"I'm sorry," said Phil to the priest.

The priest didn't open his eyes but mumbled from his sleep, "I'm so sorry, my Eleanor. I should have told you everything. This is all my fault."

Phil saw flashing lights coming along the lane. He jumped to his feet, turned, and sprinted in the other direction faster than he had ever run before.

Thanks for joining the Company of Light in Azdia!

Did you enjoy the story? Here are four things you can do now.

1) Leave a Review

It would mean a lot to me if you left a reader review and rating wherever you bought this eBook. Most readers never leave reviews, but they make a massive difference. Every review matters. Reviews help other readers find good books, and can make books more visible in the bookstore.

2) Recommend this series to someone

Has anyone ever recommended a book to you? I bet they have. Think about who might love the Del Ryder Series and tell them about it.

3) Sign up for my newsletter

Here is some of what you can expect from my newsletter:

- Preview chapters of books before they are out.
- FREE short stories and other writing not available anywhere else, including episodes of the Adventures of Crimson and Hollow, the prequel to the Del Ryder Series.
- Be the first to see new book covers.
- Notifications the moment new books are available.

Sign up at mattbrough.com

4) Let me know what you think

I love hearing from readers. I really do!

Follow me on Twitter: twitter.com/mbrough

Or on Facebook: facebook.com/mbrough

Email me at matt@mattbrough.com

Thanks again for reading *Del Ryder and the Rescue of Eleanor,*

Matthew

AUTHOR'S NOTE

Some parents are great at telling stories off the top of their heads to their children. I am not. I need much longer to think and revise. Fortunately for me, when I do try and "tell a story," my creative daughter can help me figure out what comes next.

My dad is a master at telling stories. He tells great jokes as well. He knows how to engage people. I'm guessing he would never call himself a storyteller, but he is. This book is dedicated to him and to two characters that he made up when my sisters and I were young. As the youngest in the family, I can barely remember his "Ruth and Joanne" stories, but I know they helped shape me as an author.

When I tell the story of what influenced the writing of Del Ryder, it almost always starts with my mum reading C.S. Lewis to me. Perhaps it is because I can more readily trace the impact of those books on my current writing simply by re-reading them. I can't do that with my dad's stories, but the impact of them, and him, is there nonetheless.

If you are a parent and are reading this, I want to encourage you to both read and tell stories to your children. Both activities engage the imagination and this may be one of the most precious gifts and best ways to prepare your children for their future. I want to thank both of my parents for sharing stories with me and training my imagination.

ACKNOWLEDGMENTS

The list of people to thank continues to grow, making it much more difficult to include everyone here. I have a very supportive family, some great friends, and even some people that I barely know who have read this book and given feedback. Thank you to all.

I do wish to single out my wife, Cheryl. She deserves a collaboration credit for this volume and likely for all subsequent books in the series. Besides being supportive throughout the writing process, Cheryl acted as story consultant and content editor. Almost every plot point in this novel went through her critique, and, in more than a few cases, she provided the key to moving the story forward. Without her work, this novel would not be what it is. Thank you, my love.

ABOUT THE AUTHOR

On a road trip across western Canada, a boy and his two older sisters listened as their mother read them The Lion, the Witch and the Wardrobe. Although he knew he loved the story, and as a teenager went on to fall even more in love with The Lord of the Rings, it wasn't until the year he was turning 40 that Matthew David Brough felt the full force of these books. That was when he sat down to write a story and out came *Del Ryder and the Crystal Seed*, the first book in a fast-paced fantasy adventure series for ages eight and up.

Matthew is the devoted husband of Cheryl, loving father of Juliet, and pastor of a small Presbyterian Church in Winnipeg, Canada. In both his reading and writing, he avoids books that moralize or "preach," but loves stories of hope.

CPSIA information can be obtained
at www.ICGtesting.com
Printed in the USA
LVOW03s1225160717
541557LV00001B/20/P